# For the Duke's Eyes Only

## LENORA BELL

piatkus

PIATKUS

First published in the US in 2018 by Avon Books,
An imprint of HarperCollins Publishers, New York
First published in Great Britain in 2018 by Piatkus
by arrangement with Avon Books

1 3 5 7 9 10 8 6 4 2

Copyright © 2018 by Lenora Bell

A CIP catalogue record for this book
is available from the British Library.

ISBN 978-0-349-41766-0

Printed and bound in Great Britain by
Clays Ltd, Elcograf S.p.A.

Papers used by Piatkus are from well-managed forests
and other responsible sources.

MIX
Paper from
responsible sources
FSC® C104740

Piatkus
An imprint of
Little, Brown Book Group
Carmelite House
50 Victoria Embankment
London EC4Y 0DZ

An Hachette UK Company
www.hachette.co.uk

www.littlebrown.co.uk

For Maisie, my British surrogate grandmother.
Thank you for all the perfect scones,
BBC dramas, and for your wedding band.
I wear it with great pride.

# For the Duke's Eyes Only

# Prologue

ROUND. ROUGH. NOT-DIRT. NOT-ROCK.

India's fingers recognized the hard curve of metal before her brain caught on. "Coin!" she shouted to Daniel. "I think I found a coin!"

She pulled a handful of dirt out of the shallow hole she'd dug.

Daniel loped over on his long legs, a wide grin on his face. He'd finally outgrown her this summer, a fact he exploited mercilessly by holding things out of her reach or outrunning her across the woodland fields surrounding Bracket Hall, her family estate.

"Let me see." He held out one of the delicate bowls they'd stolen from a china cabinet.

She released her handful of soil into the bowl. There was a metallic clinking sound.

A glint of copper.

The most beautiful thing she'd ever seen, except for Daniel's copper-brown eyes, shining with excitement as he knelt beside her in the dirt.

They'd been excavating the woodland fields around Bracket Hall every summer for years and hadn't found anything more interesting than grubs and the occasional rusted farm tool.

"We did it, Indy. We found buried treasure," he said in an awed voice.

The pet name made her heart glow. No one else shortened her name. Her elder brother, Edgar, was away at school and her mother wasn't given to endearments. Father was more likely to call her a noisome pestilence, if she was unlucky enough to catch his notice.

Daniel's fingers shook as he brushed dirt off the coin. He polished the small disc with his shirt hem and held it up to the sun. "I think it's Roman."

She stretched out her palm. "Let me have a look."

The coin was warm from his touch and from the sun. She traced the rough, embossed surface with her fingernail. "An emperor wearing a pearl diadem. Honorius? We'll consult a coinage guide."

"There can't be just one." Daniel held her gaze, anticipation lighting his eyes. "You know there's always a hoard of coins."

Most of the time they fought about almost everything. Who could jump their horse higher, or eat the most apples, or whose elbows and knees had the most bruises and scrapes.

Bruises were a badge of honor in their summertime world. A day with Daniel meant dares and danger, but today they labored as a team, dirty and happy, grinning wider with each new discovery.

They dug until their arms ached and until the sun had nearly abandoned them.

The coins piled higher. They were mostly

copper, corroded by age and speckled with pale green, but there were several silver coins as well.

The person who had buried these coins had thought they would come back for them later. What had happened to prevent their return? War. Disease. A life interrupted.

A living connection with history—not an etching in a book but tangible and real.

Not just two children digging in the dirt. Historians. Adventurers.

"Must be fifty coins by now," crowed Daniel. "We're rich!"

"We're already rich, you dolt."

Both of their fathers were dukes, their estates in the town of Hartfield separated by a two-hour walk. Bracket Hall was on the eastern side, while Daniel's home, Hartfield House, was on the northern end.

Somewhere in France, Daniel's father, the Duke of Ravenwood, a diplomat and army commander, was bravely battling Napoleon.

India's father, the Duke of Banksford, was . . . probably drunk by now. He'd been in one of his mean-red tempers when she'd escaped the house. Stomping around, shouting at the servants and haranguing her mother over an imaginary mistake in the housekeeping.

But she wouldn't think about that. Not now. Not on this a perfect day.

"Stop a moment," said Daniel, flopping onto the ground. "I'm thirsty."

She sat down beside him. He wiped the back of his hand across his cheek and left a streak of dirt. She knew her face was similarly filthy but she didn't care. She never had to care what she looked like with Daniel.

She'd tried to explain as much to her mother but the duchess hadn't understood.

*You're his betrothed. Do you want him to remember his bride as a young harridan with soil under her nails and scrapes on her knees? Now do sit up properly, fold your hands, and kindly refrain from using the vulgar tongue. We are not Bow-bell cockneys.*

India knew her future groom couldn't care less if she sat properly and used correct speech. His knees had matching scrapes and he was the one who'd taught her the naughty words. He was twelve, which made him only one year older, but he liked to think he was far more experienced and worldly.

He handed her the water flask and she gulped the cool stream water.

"This is only the beginning, Indy," Daniel said dreamily. He rolled onto his side to face her. "After I return from my schooling we'll be married and then we will travel the world and become famous archaeologists."

She nodded enthusiastically. "Where will we travel to first?"

"Athens, to see the Parthenon!"

"And then we'll journey to Egypt and search for the long-lost tomb of Antony and Cleopatra."

They lay back in the grass, the crowns of their heads nearly touching, staring up at the sky. There were so many possibilities written in those purple-tinged clouds.

"We'll make astounding discoveries," Daniel said, with great confidence and conviction. He flipped one of the Roman coins across his knuckles so it appeared to walk across the back of his hand.

He was far more dedicated to learning coin and card tricks than Latin verbs. Sometimes he pulled cards from the bodices of her gowns and coins from her ears. She pretended to be annoyed but secretly she loved it.

Secretly, she loved *him*. Even when he was annoying. Even when he made fun of her studiousness and called her a stick-in-the-mud.

She wasn't one of those girls who cried when he tugged on her plaits, or screamed if he opened his cupped palms to reveal a wriggling centipede.

He'd never told her in words but she could tell that he loved her. More than anyone else in the world loved her. And loved her for *her*. He liked her adventurousness and the way she could best him at just about anything. Well, maybe he didn't love that part. But he never belittled her for wanting to become an archaeologist.

And she was hopelessly devoted to him.

Not that she'd ever tell him as much.

His head was swollen to grandiose proportions already. Everyone doted on him, especially his beautiful, sweet-tempered mother. India's mother was beautiful as well, but she was cold through and through, like a coin buried too deep to reach.

Daniel stacked the coins into a tower. "Let's keep these just between us," he said casually, but she heard a hint of hesitation in his voice.

"What do you mean? We must give them to the British Museum. We'll have our names in the papers."

"Must we give them to the museum? We could . . . keep them . . . only for a little while."

He cupped her hand with his and poured several coins into her palm. "Feel that, Indy. Copper and silver. Doesn't it feel right? It's an omen from the Roman gods. It means that all of our dreams will come true."

Did he dream of their future together as he lay in bed at night, just as India did?

He closed her fingers around the coins. "This is our treasure. If anything happened to our families or our fortunes, we could sell these and it would be enough to finance our first adventure."

She pulled her hand from his grasp and tumbled the stack of coins into a messy pile. "Don't be silly. We can't own these. They're a piece of history. They have stories to tell."

"We found them."

"We can't own history. The coins belong in a museum for everyone to admire and study."

Her earnestness was met with a mischievous smile. "Let's keep them just for a few days. What's the harm? It will be our little secret."

*Our little secret.*

Her heart beat faster. It would be nice to share a secret with Daniel.

"If we keep them it can only be for a few days," she said firmly. "You will sketch the coins and I'll write detailed descriptions and then we'll present our findings to the museum."

"Who's to know if we keep just a few as tribute for our hard work?" Daniel rifled through the coins. "What about this one? Look." He held it up between his thumb and forefinger. "It's you, Indy."

"What do you mean?" She looked closer at the coin he held. Minerva, goddess of wisdom and warfare, standing tall with a spear in one hand, an owl perched on her other hand, and a shield at her feet. "Are you saying that I remind you of a goddess?" she asked teasingly, punching his arm lightly.

"Ha." He poked her arm with the edge of the coin. "I'm saying you always have your nose in a dusty old book if you're not fighting with me."

Very true. Reading was her favorite escape from her father's unpredictable rages. She liked reading Mr. Shakespeare's dramas most of all. She imagined herself as an actress portraying Juliet to Daniel's Romeo, or Cleopatra to his Antony.

She rifled through the slender circles of temptation.

There was victory in the lopsided curve of Daniel's smile. He knew he had her. She'd never been able to resist his grin.

"This one should be yours," she said a little shyly, dropping a coin into his palm.

He examined the coin. "I thought you would choose Hercules," he teased.

She rolled her eyes. "You wish." She'd chosen a silver coin showing two clasped hands. "It probably symbolizes a military treaty, or something like that, but I thought . . . well it reminded me of our . . . friendship."

"It's perfect, Indy." His gaze locked with hers and there was a new softness in his eyes. He closed his fingers over the two coins.

Her heart warmed as though it hadn't seen the sun in thousands of years. Happiness clasped her mind . . . until a strident voice ruined the moment.

"Lady India, you're covered in filth! Come away this instant."

"Mother?" India leapt to her feet. "What are you doing here?" Her mother rarely ventured from the house, and she always sent a servant if she needed to fetch her daughter.

*Something was wrong.*

Daniel jumped up as well. "Your Grace, we were just play—" he began, but the duchess cut him off.

"Not another word. Follow me, both of you." She caught Daniel's eye. "Your mother is here to collect you."

India and Daniel exchanged a look. Something was afoot. He always rode his horse to India's house. Why had his mother come searching for him?

"What on earth are those?" asked the duchess, gesturing at their treasure trove.

India moved in front of the coins to block her mother's view. "Just some old counterfeit coins. Probably worthless."

"Leave them, then." Her mother made an impatient tsking sound. "Hurry now."

Daniel knelt and scooped the coins into his handkerchief. India tied the ends of the handkerchief into a knot and thrust the small bundle into the inside pocket of her cloak.

They followed the duchess out of the woods and back toward the house, tracing the long avenue that branched in two around a circular rose garden with a gray marble fountain at its center. Two crows were bathing in the fountain, splashing the water with blue-black wings, but they cawed hoarsely and flew away when the duchess marched past, her blue gown fluttering behind her in the wind that had suddenly arisen.

"Who's that man?" India asked Daniel in a low whisper. His mother was standing next to an unfamiliar man beside a carriage whose crest she didn't recognize.

"Father's friend Sir Malcolm Penny. But I thought he was in France with Father . . ."

India could tell by the uneven set of Daniel's shoulders that he was worried.

Sir Malcolm had his arm about the duchess's shoulders, helping to support her. Daniel's mother, usually so cheerful and smiling, looked faded and sad.

"Daniel." She held out her hand. "My dear, dear son." His mother's voice caught, and for an awful moment India thought the duchess might burst into tears.

Sir Malcolm gripped her shoulders tighter. "Daniel, come with us now."

"What's happened?" asked Daniel, a rising tide of panic in his voice.

"I'll explain in the carriage," answered Sir Malcolm.

"But I rode Jupiter here," said Daniel. "Can't I ride him home?"

"We'll have a groom return him," said India's mother.

"Come," said his mother softly.

Daniel gave India a wobbly smile and joined his mother and Sir Malcolm without another word of protest.

After their carriage departed, India's mother turned to her. "Your father wishes to speak with you."

"What's happened, Mother?" asked India, truly anxious now.

"The duke will explain."

"Tell me now, please." Forewarned was forearmed. "Did I do something wrong?"

She searched her mind for a transgression. Had she left a book out of place in his library? She was so careful, so very careful to leave everything exactly as she'd found it.

"It's nothing about you. It's about the Duke of Ravenwood."

She hurried to keep up with her mother as she marched up the front steps. "What has happened? Tell me, please."

"Scandal."

Her mother set her lips and would say no more, no matter how India pleaded.

One word only: scandal.

How could scandal touch Daniel's perfect family? He had a noble, even-tempered father, a doting mother, and a younger brother who worshipped him. India had always wished they could be her family.

The Duke of Ravenwood was a little absentminded at times, but he'd encouraged her interest in antiquities and had promised to bring her back a pile of books from France.

"Compose yourself, my girl. You look a hoyden," her mother said with a disapproving frown, stopping outside of the duke's study.

India wiped her cheeks with her sleeves and smoothed her plaits as best she could.

Her mother laid a hand on her shoulder and steered her into the study.

Her father was slumped in a chair near the hearth.

She'd learned to swiftly gauge his moods. The bottle of brandy on the table next to him was only half gone. Good. He might still be in the jocular and expansive frame of mind. Singing bawdy songs and recounting hunting stories while the stag's head mounted on the wall stared down with blank, unseeing eyes.

In this mood he might raise a glass to her and toast her betrothal to Ravenwood's heir.

It was to be a financially advantageous match for her father.

She'd overheard the servants whispering about gambling debts and she'd noticed that when her father returned from his trips to London he drank even more.

She approached his chair warily, poised to run if she'd miscalculated his mood. She glanced back at her mother, who stood watching from the doorway, her pale violet eyes as blank as the eyes of the dead stag.

"Do you know what this is?" the duke snarled, holding up a piece of faded parchment.

Fear bloomed like graveyard roses in her mind, dark and filled with the scent of decaying things. She made herself as small as possible, imagining that she was a small woodland creature, too small for a mighty hunter to notice.

"No, Father. I don't." She kept her voice soft, her words brief. Anything could spark his rage.

The wrong word. The wrong gesture.

"This is your marriage contract." He ripped the document from top to bottom and threw it in the fire.

She ran to the hearth but the flames were already consuming the paper. "Why did you do that?" The words escaped from her lips before she could bring them to heel.

"I forced Ravenwood to agree to the match by uncovering his secrets. Now his secrets have ruined him, and I'll have no part of it."

"I don't understand." She'd always thought their fathers had arranged the match because they wanted to ally their families and fortunes. She hadn't raised any objection because she wanted to marry Daniel. And he wanted to marry her.

The duke poured more brandy and swallowed it in one gulp. "Ravenwood is dead. There are rumors he's being charged with High Treason.

Sir Malcolm said nothing was certain, but I know the truth. Ravenwood's a filthy traitor who's been aiding our sovereign's enemies."

"It's not true." She backed away from the hearth. "Rumors can be proven false."

"Or they can be proven true. He may be dead, but if he's found guilty of treason, his lands and estates could be forfeit and his son won't inherit a penny. Though there hasn't been such a bill of attainder in more than a decade, I'm not taking any chances. You must marry into a wealthy and powerful family."

"I don't care if he's penniless and has no property." They might argue, and fight from time to time, but Daniel was her best friend in the world.

Her only friend.

And now his good, kind father was dead. Oh poor Daniel. She must go to him. Comfort him.

"I care," said her father with a smirk. "You'll marry a rich lord and soon. Shouldn't be difficult to find an elderly lord who will pay a high price to reinvigorate himself with a child bride." His short bark of laughter was mirthless and hollow.

Her body felt brittle, as though it were made of glass, and her mouth was so dry she couldn't swallow. All she could think of was that she needed to run away.

Run to Daniel.

She wasn't a prize calf to be sold to the highest bidder.

Her father lurched out of his chair and she took a step backward.

"Best to marry you off early before you give it away to a stable hand." His gaze traveled to his wife. "You have your mother's wanton eyes."

"I'm going to marry Daniel," she blurted, even though she knew she shouldn't cross her father.

He stalked toward her.

She stood her ground.

"You'll marry whom I say you'll marry," he said coldly. "You were born for my profit. I gave you that name to bring me luck and I've had nothing but ill fortune ever since. Now apologize for your insolence."

She'd heard it all too many times. Forced to stand at attendance while he railed against the fates. He'd named her India to bring him luck on an overseas investment scheme, which had all gone to hell, and it would have been better if she'd never been born, and she was a rude, ill-tempered child and . . .

"I told you to apologize," he said, his eyes narrowing.

He slapped her across the cheek. Not a forceful blow, just a warning volley, but tears sprang to her eyes and red dots danced in front of her vision.

Not waiting for permission to leave, she ran out of the study, avoiding her mother's startled protests. She didn't stop running until she burst out of the house and sprinted across the courtyard to the mews. Daniel's horse, Jupiter, was still in the stables but he was already saddled and ready to leave.

"I'm to ride Jupiter to Hartfield House," she announced to Old Gregory, the stable master. "And don't change the saddle. I'll ride astride." She was never sitting sidesaddle again.

She didn't want to be a lady. A pawn in her father's schemes.

She never wanted to see him again.

From this day forward she'd strike out on her own. Not Lady India, but Daniel's Indy, his partner on life's grand adventure. She would go anywhere with him. She could face anything with him at her side.

Old Gregory opened his mouth to protest but then he stared at her face. His expression darkened. "He's hitting you too now, is he, my little lady?"

She nodded, battling back fresh tears.

Muttering curses under his breath, Old Gregory helped her up into Daniel's saddle. She had to bunch up her skirts, and strain to reach the stirrups, but she'd manage.

She allowed Jupiter plenty of slack as she rode across the fields and roads. Darkness fell but Jupiter knew the way home because Daniel visited her nearly every day.

When she reached Hartfield House, Sir Malcolm's carriage was waiting by the front steps. The horses were restless and stamping their hooves, the coachman and grooms already mounted.

A shocked groom helped her dismount from her saddle.

The door of the carriage opened and Daniel climbed down. "What are you doing here, Indy?"

"I brought Jupiter back. What are *you* doing?"

Her lip trembled. "Leaving without saying good-bye?"

"We're going to stay with Sir Malcolm for a time," explained the duchess, leaning out of the carriage door. "At his estate near London."

"Father's dead," said Daniel, his face expressionless and striped with shadows from the light of the lanterns mounted on the carriage.

Colin, his younger brother, whimpered softly from inside the carriage, and his mother placed her arm around his shoulders.

"I know. I'm so sorry." She wanted to fling her arms around Daniel but everyone was watching them. "Please take me with you. I can't stay here. My father forbade us to wed but I told him we would marry with or without his consent."

"Of course we'll marry, you dolt," said Daniel.

"Then take me with you," she whispered.

"I'm sorry, my dear," said the duchess. "I wish we could take you. I know your home is not a happy one."

"We'll be back soon," said Daniel, conviction filling his eyes. "It's not true what they're saying about Father. It can't be true."

"Of course it's not true." Indy reached into her pocket and drew out the handkerchief filled with coins. "My father said something about your fortune being forfeit," she whispered. "You take the coins. Perhaps you'll need them."

Nothing would help when his father was gone but she wanted to give him something.

Daniel gently pushed the coins away. "Give them to the museum, as we agreed."

"We must go now. Say your farewells, Daniel." His mother turned to Sir Malcolm. "H-he's not Daniel anymore, is he? He's Ravenwood now."

"That's right. He's the duke now," said Sir Malcolm.

Daniel shifted his shoulders into a solid line. "I'm the duke." He said it as though it had just occurred to him, as though it was a heavy burden to bear.

He bent forward and for a moment she thought he meant to kiss her, but instead he plucked a coin from the air near her ear and held it out. "Goodbye, Indy."

"Where did that come from?"

"Had it up my sleeve." One side of his lip quirked, a glimmer of her carefree friend resurfacing.

She took the Minerva coin, struggling not to cry. "G-good-bye."

He climbed back into the carriage and a groom closed the door.

She ran after the carriage, lungs aching and legs on fire, until it became a black speck in the distance, until she was sure they weren't going to turn around and come back for her.

She slumped against a sturdy tree trunk by the side of the road. The tears came then, sliding down her cheeks like warm rain.

Her fingers still clutched the coin Daniel had given her.

Minerva with her spear and owl imprinted on her palm.

*An omen from the Roman gods, he'd said.*

What good was treasure if it meant losing everything she loved? What if she never saw his teasing grin again?

Tomorrow she'd take the coins back to the field and bury them.

Maybe if she buried them deeply enough everything would go back to the way it had been this morning.

Daniel's father would still be alive.

Summer would begin over again.

The birds would sing and the sun would shine and they would have so many treasures to find.

"You can't keep us apart," she yelled, hoping the gods might hear.

No one answered.

She was all alone.

# Chapter 1

❧

THE TROUBLE WITH fake moustaches, Lady India Rochester was discovering, was that they had an alarming propensity to come unstuck.

Especially when the lady wearing the clever disguise happened to be perspiring.

And most definitely when the lady was perspiring because she was currently committing at least four crimes in a daring attempt to infiltrate the all-male Society of Antiquaries.

The porter scrutinized her card, his ponderous jowls drooping as he frowned. "Mr. Pomeroy?"

"That's right." Indy cleared her throat, dropping her voice a half octave for good measure. She smoothed down her moustache, praying that the adhesive paste held. "My uncle, Lord Pomeroy, is excavating near Rome and sent me in his stead."

"Highly irregular."

"Is it really?" Indy shrugged, feigning a nonchalance she was far from feeling. "Well *I* don't want to attend the meeting—bound to be a yawning bore, what?—But I did promise the old boy I'd send him notes. Do let me in, there's a good fellow, and I'll promise not to snore too loudly from the back bench."

The man wasn't budging. Apparently he'd been hired by the Antiquaries because of an abundance of caution and an utter lack of humor.

Frustration pulsed through her mind. She must pass through this door.

They'd left her no choice but subterfuge.

She had as much right as any to study the Rosetta Stone at close quarters before it was moved back to the British Museum for public display, always to be surrounded by onlookers and guards.

The stone was the key to unlocking the mysteries and secrets of hieroglyphics—the difficult-to-decipher written language of the ancient Egyptians. It bore three columns of the same inscription, each in a different language: Greek, Egyptian script, and hieroglyphics.

She'd spent much of the last two years on archaeological expeditions and needed to view the script on the stone to corroborate her translation of a text that she believed could lead her to one of archaeology's greatest prizes—the burial place of Cleopatra and Mark Antony.

Even thinking about it quickened her pulse.

If she located Cleopatra's tomb, the men couldn't laugh at her anymore, they couldn't exclude her from their societies and dismiss her work. Even the famous antiquarian the Duke of Ravenwood—her former best friend and current enemy—wouldn't be able to ignore her achievements.

Indy had made it her life's work to study the powerful, influential women who had helped shape history.

Her shoulders tensed thinking of the way Ravenwood had publicly challenged her theories on the female gender of the ancient Pharaoh Hatshepsut.

*Shrug it off. Don't let thoughts of Ravenwood destroy your dilettante disguise.*

The scandal sheets called her Lady Danger. She'd survived multiple knife attacks, venomous snakebites—and the lady patronesses of Almack's.

One overzealous porter was child's play.

"Now see here, I don't like this delay one bit." She infused her voice with aristocratic disdain. "Sir Malcolm will surely hear of your insolence. Uncle sent word that I was coming."

A letter she'd forged—yet another punishable offence.

Her own father was dead and her brother was now the powerful Duke of Banksford, but even he might not be able to save her if she were arrested today.

Men tended to take their rules very seriously, especially the ones that kept women submissive, subservient, and on the wrong side of doors.

"Wait here, sir." The porter disappeared into the arched doorway of Somerset House, leaving Indy standing on the Strand. Carriages rattled past. A man attempted to herd sheep across the avenue. A rattrap vendor demonstrated his wares by shaking cages filled with live rats in the startled faces of passersby.

Had the porter noticed something odd about her appearance?

A quick check of her makeshift whiskers assured her the paste was holding . . . for now.

Blue-tinted spectacles covered her telltale grayish-purple eyes, and a short brown wig hid her long dark hair.

She'd bound her bosom with linen to achieve the illusion of a young buck dressed in the first stare of fashion: blue greatcoat over a frock coat of black superfine, gold-embroidered waistcoat, buff-colored trousers, and polished black boots.

She looked quite dashing, if she did say so herself.

Indy's mother loved to remind her that she displayed none of the pleasing traits of femininity. She never simpered or flirted, abhorred frills and furbelows, carried a dagger at her hip and knew how to use it, and had once been told that her gait resembled that of a swaggering tomcat.

Her one feminine indulgence was a bold, sensual French perfume, but today she'd remembered to douse herself with a masculine scent.

*Every detail's in place. There's nothing to worry about.*

Soon she'd cross the threshold of the most exclusive antiquities society in the world. And none would be the wiser.

Not even Ravenwood. Even her rival wouldn't notice her because she planned on being entirely unexceptional. For once in her life she'd stay silent, suppress her flair for the dramatic, speak only when spoken to, and attract absolutely no undue attention.

Wouldn't her mother be proud? Her etiquette lessons put to use at last.

*What was taking the blasted porter so long?*

Indy leaned on her ebony-knobbed walking stick and whistled a popular air, her breath visible in the cold October air.

A mother and her pretty marriage-aged daughter passed by and Indy tipped the brim of her beaver top hat with the knob of her walking stick. The daughter giggled and cast a flirtatious glance over her shoulder.

The poor thing looked as though her arms were lost in little hot-air balloons and she might lift off and float away at any moment, airborne by her sleeves. Women's sleeves had widened to outrageous proportions of late. And the millinery. Don't get Indy started on the hats. Monstrous straw bonnets the width of Viking shields, bristling with plumage and stiff satin bows.

They were weapons, those hats. Men had to move out of their path for fear of being blindsided, she'd found out today.

Indy flexed her shoulders, enjoying the comfortable fit of her custom-made coat.

Strutting the streets of London in male garb had been astonishingly freeing. Why hadn't she done it before? The city had spread itself before her boots, whispering of untasted pleasures.

Smoky pubs where she could order a haunch of beef and a brandy without causing an uproar or being forced to deflect boorish advances.

Boxing establishments, clubs, and gaming houses . . . every door thrown wide.

The door of Somerset House opened again. "Apologies for the delay. Right this way, Mr. Pomeroy," said the porter with an obsequious bow.

"Well it's about time, my good fellow," muttered Indy, striding through the arched doorway into the vestibule as if she owned the place.

They passed under an archway crowned by a bust of Newton, signaling that the Royal Society of scientists and philosophers shared this wing of Somerset House with the antiquaries.

No females except for serving maids ever passed through this doorway.

Did it give the gentlemen a feeling of superiority every time they entered their hallowed halls, free from feminine interference?

*Nob-headed nonsense!*

Hoarding knowledge for the consumption of only one sex was the greatest folly, and she was going to prove it to Ravenwood, and the other pompous lords, all puffed up with pride and prejudice.

She wasn't just going to sneak through their precious door . . . she was going to blast the entire thing off its hinges.

She would prove that females were not inherently inferior to males. That women of vision and power had shaped history and would continue to do so.

Realizing her gait had taken on a militant cadence, she slowed her steps to an indolent amble befitting Mr. Pomeroy, bored dandy and rake-about-Town.

After climbing a semi-circular staircase, the

porter led her to the meeting room and seated her in the backmost row of benches that lined the walls. The meeting hadn't yet begun and a loud hum of conversation reverberated in the spacious room.

She noticed Ravenwood immediately—he was sprawled in a chair at the foot of the central table that must be reserved for titled members.

She had a habit of looking for him in every room she entered as her frame of reference.

If he was in the room it meant a public showdown—hackles raised and witty retorts and barbs at the ready.

Daniel, her fun-loving childhood friend, had become a rogue known for hunting beautiful women in England, and treasures abroad, amassing both amours and antiquities as nothing more than trophies.

Once upon a long-lost summer they'd dreamt of traveling the world together and making important archaeological discoveries.

*What a cartload of steaming shite.*

He'd betrayed her. And now his methods for hunting antiquities were as wildly unscrupulous as hers were rigidly ethical. She studied ancient cultures, she never stole their accomplishments. She surrendered any artifacts she discovered to the government of the country where she made the discovery for further study and display.

When she brought a small token back to England with her, she purchased it for a fair price through the proper channels and donated it to the British Museum for public display.

As far as she could tell, Ravenwood spent most of his time drowning in drink and lounging about instead of practicing any actual archaeology. He simply purchased whatever treasure he desired from the underworld. And then he kept the priceless antiquities locked away in his private collection. For his eyes only.

Anger swelled, nearly propelling her toward him. Their constant rivalry kept the scandal sheets in business.

*Lady Danger versus the Rogue Duke.*

A public war of the sexes that usually devolved into cynical laughter on his side and shouted epithets and smashed porcelain on hers.

She did like giving him a sharp and biting piece of her mind every time she saw him.

But not today.

There would be no warfare today.

*Stay seated. Keep your blade holstered. Don't call attention to yourself. Look anywhere else in the room but at Ravenwood.*

Study the oil lamps and candles spilling warm light over the books and artifacts arranged along the central table. Peruse the bust of George the Third presiding over the mantel.

Pretend to admire the Tudor tapestry woven in vibrant reds and blues hanging on the wall.

Don't notice *him*.

Don't notice that his eyes were the same color as the candle flames reflecting in polished oak. Pay no attention to the way the snowfall of his cravat served as a contrast to his tanned skin and the angular lines of his handsome face.

Perish the thought that his athletic frame seemed to have grown even more athletic about the shoulders and arms since she'd seen him last.

What did the infuriating man do, row the length of the Thames every day? His powerfully sculpted physique didn't fit with his indolent reputation.

The problem with Ravenwood was that he was nearly impossible to ignore.

Take today, for example. All eyes in the room were on him and every ear tuned to his resonant voice because he was holding forth on the asinine topic of nipples.

Yes, *nipples.*

Indy heaved an inward sigh. Of course he was. Should she expect any less? And he wasn't just holding forth.

He had visual aids.

"See here, chaps," he said, gesturing at the marble bust of Aphrodite on the table in front of him. "This one is slightly larger than the other, which lends a wonderful air of veracity to the sculpture, wouldn't you say?"

"Let me have a closer look." The Earl of Montrose brought his monocle to his eye and peered at the statue's rounded charms. "Ah yes, very life-like indeed."

Ravenwood skimmed his finger along the underside of a marble breast.

Which shouldn't make her heart beat faster or do damnably fluttery things to her belly.

"Most females, I've observed," Ravenwood continued, "tend to possess one breast that is slightly larger than the other. It's like their charming bosoms are giving me a cheeky, lopsided grin."

*Oh ha ha*, thought Indy. *Very amusing.*

"You're the expert in these matters," said the Duke of Westbury, who was sitting next to Ravenwood.

"I am, rather." Ravenwood extracted a small silver flask from a pocket somewhere and took a long swallow.

Who brought a flask to an antiquities meeting?

And another thing—why didn't women's clothing possess enough pockets for stashing flasks and other important items? She'd have to ask her dressmaker to add more pockets to her traveling gowns.

"Care for a nip?" Ravenwood asked Westbury, who accepted the flask.

Indy had no idea why Westbury was here. She'd never known her brother's friend to have any interest in antiquities. He was a notorious rake and inebriate, though she didn't think he was the mean kind of drunk, as her father had been.

Westbury had the countenance of a fallen angel, aglow with wicked beauty, but who could pay attention to him when Ravenwood was in the room?

Every single time she saw him she momentarily abandoned her intellect. And it wasn't just her—she'd seen it happen to countless other ladies.

Sensible, strong-minded, stouthearted ladies reduced to breathless, blushing, eyelash-flapping ninnies.

When he was in the room, she had a nearly uncontrollable desire to cause herself pain. Like that winter when they were children and he'd dared her to stick her tongue on a frosty iron gate.

She'd known she shouldn't do it, but she never backed down from one of Daniel's dares.

She'd had a raw patch on the tip of her tongue for days.

She hated that every time their paths crossed she couldn't take her eyes off him.

Her hand rose to her cravat. The starched male neck cloth hid more than her lack of a prominent Adam's apple. It hid the necklace she wore; a thin gold chain supporting the weight of a copper coin nestled within a pronged setting. The Minerva coin Ravenwood had chosen for her on that long-ago summer day, before everything went so wrong.

She didn't wear the coin around her neck because she harbored a sentimental attachment to their lost connection.

Not in the least.

She wore it as a constant reminder that she must never trust her heart to anyone ever again.

She was completely on her own in life's grand adventure.

*Lady Danger versus the World.*

She harbored no hope or illusions that Ravenwood might cease being the most infuriating numbskull known to man, and go back to being her devoted childhood companion.

The one with the devilish grin. The one who loved her for *her.*

The warrior goddess on the copper coin that

lay against her breastbone was a talisman protecting her from further heartache.

*He's not Daniel, the boy who stole your heart.*
*He's Ravenwood, the man who broke it.*

Her sworn rival. A cold iron gate on a wintry day that could only end in torment.

And that was why she wouldn't even glance at him the rest of the afternoon.

She must stay intent on her mission.

As soon as the meeting began, she'd find a pretext to slip out of the room and go to the ground-floor library where she could examine the stone undisturbed. It should only take a short time to compare the hieroglyphics on the map in her pocket with the script on the stone.

"You know what they say about antiquarians, don't you?" Ravenwood's rich tones ended her reverie. "We like it dirty," he said with a throaty chuckle.

Upending the flask over his lips he drained the last drops. "Have you gents heard the one about the archaeologist and the bone—" he began, but Sir Malcolm Penny, president of the Society, arrived before Ravenwood could regale his adoring public with more bawdy archaeological humor.

Seeing the two men together reminded Indy of the terrible day when Sir Malcolm had arrived to relay the news of the Duke of Ravenwood's death.

"Gentlemen, order please," said Sir Malcolm, taking his seat of honor at the raised table in the front of the room. The secretary seated behind him readied his paper and pens.

Indy shivered, and not because of Ravenwood's

proximity this time. She was about to become the very first female to attend an antiquarian meeting. A historic first, and no one even knew.

How she wished she could lord it over Ravenwood.

She glanced at him.

*Hellfire.* He was staring directly at her.

She ducked her head behind the back of the bench in front of her.

Oh *that* wasn't obvious.

Willing herself to appear casual and disinterested, she relaxed in her seat, fixing her gaze forward.

Sir Malcolm, with the aid of his secretary, began detailing a list of architectural etchings that had recently been bequeathed to the Society.

After what seemed like hours, Indy risked a sideways glance at Ravenwood.

He wasn't looking at her anymore. His eyes were unfocused, and his chiseled jaw kept sliding closer and closer to his chest. When it made contact, his head jolted upright, and then the downward journey began all over again.

Was he . . . *snoring*?

Indy snorted under her breath.

She needn't have worried about Ravenwood recognizing her.

The duke was obviously three sheets to the wind.

Or thirty.

EVEN FROM HIS slumped position Raven could tell that the stranger with the narrow shoulders and tinted spectacles was furtively watching him.

The pretend-to-be-drunk-and-make-an-arse-of-yourself routine definitely had its uses.

It made people less wary, made them underestimate you. Under the cover of inane jokes and patter, he'd assessed each man present and either added or discarded them from his list of suspects.

He wasn't here as a Fellow of the Society of Antiquaries.

He was here to expose a traitor.

Tinted Spectacles had arrived just before the meeting began. There was something familiar about him, though Raven couldn't place his finger on where he'd seen him before.

He almost looked like a Frenchman, with that slim moustache and his brown hair combed fashionably forward. His delicate, elongated fingers gripped the back of the bench in front of him with such force that his knuckles were white—a sure sign of mental turmoil.

Raven's job was to notice the small, overlooked details.

Fingernails too polished. Cuffs slightly too long.

Details could be exploited.

He was watching for anomalous behavior. Laughter where there should be solemnity.

A gaze that darted here and there instead of holding steady.

He didn't want to believe that one of his countrymen was behind the recent spate of security breaches within the Foreign Office's covert operations, but he couldn't trust anyone, not after what had happened in Athens.

He had to keep the smile on his face, keep the jokes flowing from his lips and the brandy pouring down his throat.

He had to pretend to be carefree when his entire life was crashing down around him.

*Don't dwell on it*, Sir Malcolm had said during Raven's briefing, after Raven had returned to London, battered, bruised, and shaken. *It happens to the best of men*, Malcolm had said.

*It doesn't happen to me. And it will never happen again*, Raven had replied through gritted teeth. *I'll find the traitor. I'll make him pay.*

Malcolm had given him a hearty clap on the back that had made Raven wince from the sharp pain in his ribs.

*Perhaps you should take a holiday first.*

That's what they said to agents they were ready to put out to pasture, Raven thought bitterly.

He'd been careful, he'd hidden his movements, coded his communications, but a fellow British operative, known to Raven only as Jones, had died in Athens during what should have been a clandestine rendezvous.

Raven had nearly died as well.

Staring up at a stained-glass window the color of blood and bruised flesh . . . the color people were on the inside.

The soft insides . . . the vulnerable places.

Jab a finger into a kidney and watch a man crumple.

There was nothing soft about Raven. Nothing vulnerable. He'd rid himself of all weakness and emotion long ago.

He'd given everything up for a higher purpose, and for the chance to clear his father's name.

When he became an agent for the Crown he'd been forced to alienate Indy. His best friend, his future life companion.

He'd left her behind, choosing instead this dangerous, solitary path.

Closing himself off from his emotions and severing all connections with those he loved. He hadn't seen his mother, or his younger brother Colin, in years.

He'd chosen this life. And he did *not* need a holiday. He needed to prove his fitness for duty.

Jones had been about to tell Raven something urgent about the Rosetta Stone when the surprise attack occurred.

Which had led Raven here.

Which had led him to Tinted Spectacles.

He knew the private details of the lives of every man at this meeting except for his.

"Who's the slender fellow sitting on the back bench?" he asked Montrose in a low whisper.

"Dammed if I know," the earl whispered back, shrugging his shoulders. "Never saw him before. Don't like his appearance, I must say. Loathe those dainty dandies."

Montrose was the model of an English lord with ruddy cheeks, an expansive waistline, and a very high opinion of himself. Raven had already crossed him off his list.

Too sluggish for espionage.

"Are you acquainted with the man in the tinted

spectacles?" Raven whispered to his friend West-bury, who was seated on his other side.

"Never seen him before in my life." West sighed. "Tell me, are the meetings always this skull-crushingly dull?"

"Always. Why are you here, anyway? I didn't know you were interested in antiquities."

"I'm thinking of selling a few pieces from my ancestral collection. Wanted to have an opinion on what prices I might expect. Never thought it would come to this," West whispered morosely. "But I've made several bad investments, and have too many sisters to bring out and it's damned expensive with their music instructors, and dancing masters, and new gloves and bonnets every time they leave the house. May have to bring *myself* out and find an heiress to marry."

Raven had kept a close eye on West of late. He hadn't made bad investments—he had a bad gambling habit.

Debts exposed a man to the threat of blackmail, but West wasn't on his list of suspects. He didn't speak multiple languages, and, even though he had vices, murder certainly wasn't one of them.

"Next we have a very handsome bequest of a Viking hoard found on the properties of the late Sir Stanhope," said Sir Malcolm. "If you will direct your attention to the crucible steel sword displayed at the center of the table . . ."

Sir Malcolm's job was to keep droning until Raven signaled that he'd finished his observations.

Malcolm was the closest thing Raven had to a father.

They'd gone to stay with him that summer Raven's father had died. Malcolm was a spymaster who had revealed that Raven's father had been an agent of the Crown.

He'd given Raven his father's private journal, a thin volume bound with cracked brown leather and tied with a silk cord. The last pages spattered in blood.

*His father's blood.*

The last entry scrawled in a shaking hand. A directive to Malcolm to give the diary to Raven and then a few lines for Raven, the words wavering, nearly illegible: *My son. I was going to tell you when you turned fifteen. That's the age I was when I became . . . what I am . . .*

Raven locked away the memory.

Something was happening on the periphery of his vision.

Tinted Spectacles whispered something to the man sitting next to him, slid out of his bench seat and crept from the room.

*Anomalous, indeed.*

Raven waited exactly three seconds before hiccupping loudly.

Sir Malcolm paused but kept reading from his ledger.

Several hiccups later, Malcolm finally stopped reading. "Your Grace, if you please," he remonstrated.

"Apologies, I'll just go and walk these off."

Raven bumbled out of the room but when he was out of sight he dropped the inebriated ruse and sped toward the central stairs. The attic held only the apartments for the resident secretary, which meant Tinted Spectacles must have gone below.

At the foot of the staircase he caught sight of a flash of blue and brown entering the library.

His hand moved reflexively to the pistol tucked into the back waistband of his breeches.

*Not necessary.* The man was too slender to pose a threat.

"Did that man say anything to you?" he asked the porter.

"Mr. Pomeroy? He said Sir Malcolm asked him to retrieve a volume on Viking mythology."

"Did he now."

"Is there a problem, Your Grace?"

"Not at all. I was sent on a similar errand. Back to your post."

"Very good, Your Grace."

Raven entered the large library noiselessly. Lamps burned on the tables, casting half-moons of light over broken columns, statuary, and piles of books and scrolls.

Pomeroy was examining a large shadowy object, mounted on a wooden frame, with a magnifying glass. He held a scrap of paper in one hand and was comparing it to the markings on the . . .

*Rosetta Stone.*

"Looking for something, Mr. Pomeroy?" Raven asked. "If that's truly your name."

The man spun around and his spectacles slipped down his nose, revealing eyes of a peculiar light purple color.

A color Raven would know anywhere.

He should. He dreamed of those eyes every night.

"Indy?" he exploded on an exhale, as though someone had punched him in the gut. "What in the name of Aphrodite's perfect tits are you doing here?"

# Chapter 2

❧

"**I** THOUGHT YOU WERE drunk," said Indy, because it was the first thought that leapt to mind. The thoughts she managed to keep to herself went something like this: *Shite. Balls! Damn his topaz eyes. Why, why, why?*

She removed her spectacles and slipped them into her pocket.

"Your moustache is crooked," Ravenwood observed.

Her hand flew to her moustache. Blast, he was right. She held the sorry thing in place with one finger, keeping the map behind her back with her other hand.

*There's hope yet that he won't report you. Keep him talking. Treat it as a lark. Above all, don't let him goad you into losing your temper. Don't let him under your skin.*

"Why aren't you drunk anymore?" she asked.

"Because the sight of you wearing whiskers is immediately and irreparably sobering. It's not a good look."

"It's a very good look. Girls were flirting with me on the street I'll have you know."

He quirked one eyebrow at her.

How did he even do that? She'd tried it in the mirror before setting out today with no luck. It would have, as he'd put it earlier, lent an air of veracity to her disguise. All rogues seemed to know how to raise one sardonic eyebrow.

"Those trousers, though," he said in a low growl. "They leave little to the imagination. I approve."

The fabric of her trousers became a second skin as his smoldering gaze caressed her thighs. His nearness hit her where it always did—below the navel, in the most erogenous of areas—and higher, speeding her heart and dimming her mind.

She eyed the taut stretch of his breeches over his muscular thighs. "That makes two of us, then. Did your valet have to help you wriggle into those breeches? They appear to be painted on. Borders on the indecent, really."

"Ha. You're in no position to lecture me on decency, as far as I can see. I could have you arrested on so many counts it addles the mind: impersonating the opposite gender, false representation for the purpose of breaking and entering, all manner of moral turpitude. They might have to create a new reform society exclusively for you."

"Poor Ravenwood," she cooed. "Do you need me to be locked away so I won't offend your maidenly sensibilities?"

He didn't take the bait. He'd always been better at remaining calm and keeping that mocking smile on his lips during their frequent altercations.

He almost never lost his temper, while she inevitably ended up foaming at the mouth with fury.

Wiping that smug smile from his lips was a goal she rarely accomplished. Life was one big joke to him. He always had a flask in hand and a laconic quip at the ready that invariably told her nothing she truly wanted to know.

"I need you to tell me what you're doing here," he said.

"Having a lark." She tossed her head, which didn't have nearly the same effect it did when she had long hair to toss about. "A friend and I placed a wager about infiltrating all-male societies."

That much was true. Her musical friend Miss Beaton was attempting to win a symphonic composition contest sponsored by the Royal Society of Musicians by using a male pseudonym.

Ravenwood hooked a thumb into his waistcoat pocket. "No, why are you *here*? In the library examining the Rosetta Stone?"

She shrugged. "Decided to take a tour because the meeting was so dull. You call this an exclusive society? Sadly lacking in secretive rites, I must say. Where are the intricate handshakes and the funny hats? I haven't even heard any talk of mythical Rosy Crosses or plots to take over the world."

"Wait a few hours." His smile became a smirk. "There's a doorway concealed behind the tapestry and we all go down to a secret chamber in the cellar and drink blood and debauch virgins in ominous rituals."

He would have to bring up debauching.

And she would have to picture him by candlelight as he bound her wrists, preparing to have his diabolical way with her . . . she applied a mental dash of cold water to her overactive imagination.

"All I saw," she said tartly, "was you fondling a marble statue. What's the matter, can't find a real woman to show you her bosom?"

The side of his lip lifted higher. "Speaking of bosoms . . ." He walked closer and she suppressed the instinctual urge to retreat. His gaze traveled over her cravat and waistcoat. "What the devil's happened to yours?"

"Women have been binding their chests and passing as men since time immemorial."

"Shameful waste of a damned fine bosom, if you ask me."

"I'd like to stop discussing bosoms now."

"You're the one who introduced the topic, and since you don't appear to be willing to answer my initial question I'll play along, until you grow weary of our battle of wits and innuendo and decide to tell me the truth."

"I thought you lived for our battles of wit and innuendo," she said with as glib a tone as she could manage.

"They do make life more interesting," he drawled. "But I'm after answers. Admit it, Indy." He walked closer. "You're trapped between a stone and a hard place."

The hard place being him.

All of him.

From the glint in his eyes, to those cheekbones like cutlass blades, to the impressive framework of muscles bulging beneath his coat.

She certainly wasn't going to think about any other parts of him that might have cause to bulge and harden.

Certainly *not*.

"Have you been brawling?" she asked. "That's quite the bruise you have over your eye."

"Don't attempt to distract me. It won't work."

"Raise the alarm then, have me arrested. You can crow about this until the blessed day you die." She shifted her stance, preparing to make a run for it if he called her bluff.

"I wouldn't sound the alarm."

"I've no idea the depths of depravity you sink to these days."

"I know you, Indy," he said evenly, ignoring her dig. "You wouldn't have risked everything to sneak into this meeting if it wasn't important. What are you up to?"

"Do you think I would tell you and risk having you take all the credit?"

"You know I wouldn't do that, either."

"I know nothing of the sort. I'm talking to the man who keeps the Wish Diamond in his private collection so that he can drape the necklace over his courtesans, when everyone knows that a diamond of such historical significance, formerly owned by Alexander the Great, should have been surrendered to a museum. You're nothing better than a . . ." *Stay calm, Indy. Don't lose your temper.* "An antiquities pirate." It was the tamest insult she could think of on short notice.

He struck a swashbuckling pose. "Care to walk the plank, my pretty?"

Indy glared at him. "So you admit that your practices are unethical."

"Can we please not rehash the tired subject of our ethical differences? What I'm more interested in is the improbable idea that you honestly thought I wouldn't recognize you."

"You *didn't* recognize me."

"I would have in a few more minutes."

"Keep telling yourself that."

"What are you hiding behind your back?"

*Blazing blue bollocks.* She'd noticed that he often directed conversations along one line and then suddenly, out of nowhere, introduced a new topic with the intent of tricking her into admitting something.

"Nothing." She tightened her grip on the paper she held, the map that she believed could identify Cleopatra's burial place in the region of the ancient city of Alexandria beneath a temple dedicated to . . . well, that's why she needed to read the Rosetta Stone.

Was it a temple to the goddess Isis, or the god Osiris? The hieroglyphs on the map were faded by age and frustratingly faint. She must do a careful comparison with the hieroglyphs and scripts on the stone.

"Then move your hands where I can see them," he said.

Flipping up the tails of her coat, she stuffed the paper down the back of her trousers. Another advantage to male attire she'd just discovered.

"See? Nothing." She held out her empty hands.

He snorted. "I know you just stuffed a paper down the back of your trousers."

She slowed her voice to treacle. "You're welcome to try and find it, Your Grace."

He approached her slowly, holding her gaze, stopping dangerously near.

There was no way she was going to retreat. There was nowhere to go. The stone was behind her, and Raven was in front, all copper eyes and sensual lips.

Broad, broad chest and flat, narrow abdomen.
*Brain softening to the consistency of pea soup.*
*Body taking control.*

All she wanted to do was rip off the itchy moustache, shake her hair loose from the confines of the wig, and unbind her bosom so that she could breathe more freely. Her bosom wasn't heaving. Not in the slightest.

"Don't think I won't put you over my knee and pull those trousers down, Indy," he said roughly.

"Don't think you won't encounter the point of my dagger if you try anything of the sort," she retorted.

"Why are you here?" he repeated. "Tell me or I'll put you over my knee and give you my own brand of punishment for breaking and entering."

*Don't. Don't even picture being bent over his knee. His hand moving to the edge of her trousers and tugging them over her hips. His palm covering the bare flesh of her bottom . . . blast her lurid imagination!*

As much as she hated to admit it, the best way

to convince him to leave might be to tell him the truth, at least the partial truth.

"I'm here because I've no other way to view the Rosetta Stone in person," she said carefully. "I've been working from an imperfect ink lithograph and I need to consult the primary source."

"You're translating something important?"

She would never tell him about the map. She didn't trust him even the width of a coin. She couldn't trust anyone. Male colleagues had sought to discredit her work too many times. "I need to consult the stone to verify something."

"Well then, by all means, please continue with whatever it was you were doing. Don't mind me. I'll just stand here while you work and then escort you out before anyone realizes there's an overly ambitious female in their midst."

*Don't mind him.*

When he stood there with his formidable arms crossed over his chest, looking like every filthy, forbidden fantasy she'd ever imagined in her lonely bed at night.

*Don't mind him.*

When she'd never been able to concentrate on anything else when he was nearby.

"I'd prefer it if you left the ambitious lady to her work," she said, crossing her arms over her (currently squashed flat) chest.

"Wouldn't the newspaper writers love to see us right now?" he asked with a sardonic grin. "I can imagine the headline: *The Rogue Duke Ruins Lady Danger's Daring Deception.*"

"Humph. I was thinking more along the lines

of: *Lady Danger Penetrates Male Sanctum, Pronounces it 'Right Dull and Dreary.'"*

"Pardon?" he sputtered. "Penetrates male *what*?"

"Sanctum." She tried not to laugh and lost the battle, the sound emerging from her lips halfway between a giggle and a snort.

The gleam of humor in his eyes told her that he enjoyed their verbal sparring just as much as she did, fight it as she might.

They faced each other in the lamplight, adversaries who used to be compatriots.

He knew how to make her laugh. He knew how to wound her.

He was her one and only weakness.

He always had been.


RAVEN KICKED HIMSELF for not recognizing her instantly. How could he have been so careless?

She was pure, unadulterated temptation.

Hell in Hessian boots.

Even with all her heavy black hair tucked under a wig. Even with that ridiculous moustache pasted haphazardly above her full lips.

Especially wearing tight trousers that hugged her shapely bum.

It was easy to maintain a steady stream of suggestive jests around her because that's where his mind always went when she was in the room.

All this talk of putting her over his knee had achieved a truly impressive result, which she would no doubt be able to discern the shape of should her gaze travel . . . damn it!

Her gaze traveled.

Even worse, her pink tongue appeared and she licked her lips. Did she even know what that did to him?

Staring at the outline of his prick and licking her lips.

Raven went weak at the knees. Literally. He longed to sink to the floor. Kneel in front of her. He wouldn't put her over his knee. He'd back her up against that basalt chunk of history and pleasure her with his tongue until she moaned obscenities.

She'd always been his weakness.

The one woman who made the hard choices even more difficult.

Whenever he saw her, all of the sacrifices he'd made seemed to make so much less sense.

"Tell me why you're here and maybe I can help," he said hastily, because his thoughts were going in too many forbidden directions at once.

"You think I trust you enough to ask for your help?" The look of contempt on her face nearly stopped his heart from beating.

Of course she didn't trust him. Not after what he'd done to her.

Hellfire, he wouldn't trust himself if they met on the street. He'd think: *That man's an overly confident jackass. What's he hiding?*

The cover he'd constructed to hide his clandestine activities had become all too believable.

*Mercenary fortune hunter. Notorious adventurer-rogue. Drunkard.*

The more despicable he acted, the more his celebrity grew. There were those who even wanted him to become the next president of the Society of Antiquaries.

And someone as brilliant as Indy had to resort to impersonating a man to attend a meeting.

It was so wrong.

"You're like a bad case of indigestion, Ravenwood. Always ruining my fun."

"And you're a pain in my arse, Indy. You know you could be thrown in prison for . . . this." He waved at her costume. "I'd prefer that your slender neck stayed free of a noose."

"You could have fooled me."

"Our professional rivalry doesn't mean I want to see you arrested."

"Admit it." Her gaze sharpened. "You enjoy our rivalry."

He would never admit it, but it was true. He anticipated their next meeting with a nameless emotion halfway between pain and pleasure.

He could no more ignore her then he could cut off his hand. Cut out his heart.

He couldn't have her for a friend, or a lover, so he took what he could get. If enmity were all he could have of her, he'd battle to the bitter end.

She was the most brilliant, complicated, vexing, and gorgeous woman in the world.

He craved her as a drunkard craved wine. As a stray cur craved a bone.

He rationed out his glimpses of her. Kept count of them in a journal. He even had a code name for her, as though she were another secret agent.

Minerva *attended my lecture on Roman mythology*

*at the Museum today. I was saying how they borrowed*
*an entire pantheon from the Greeks and she interrupted*
*and pointed out that the Romans had Janus, the god of*
*beginnings and endings, the god with two faces. When*
*she spoke about two faces she gave me the most cutting*
*look. The lady is a weapon.*

"I'd better go back to the meeting and you'd
better leave," he said in a rush, to stem his
thoughts. His mind had taken another wrong
turn. *Refocus. Regain control.*

"You go back to the meeting," she said. "Let me
stay a few minutes and I promise I'll leave quietly."

"Can't do that. I'm sworn to protect these premises."

She heaved a sigh. "You had to choose this particular time to return to London. Where have you
been these past months?"

"Greece. It's lovely there this time of year."

"Typical Ravenwood. Lounging on the beach
while your agents negotiate for stolen antiquities."

"What can I say? I live for leisure."

His mission had been to help negotiate a treaty
behind the scenes between Russia and the Otto-
man Empire, halting Russian expansion into
Greece. His specialty was conflict resolution.
Stopping wars before they started . . . or hasten-
ing their demise.

"I suppose that's where you found the bust of
Aphrodite," said Indy.

He nodded. "I'm donating her to the museum."

She raised her eyebrows. "Has the raven changed
his feathers?"

"Don't hold your breath."

"As much as I enjoy our little chats I have work to do, so go back to your flask and your bawdy jokes."

"Don't let me stop you. I'll even hold the lamp."

She eyed him warily. "So you can steal my ideas."

"So I can enjoy the view as you bend over."

She rolled her eyes. "Very well, stay if you insist. It's nothing to me."

The paper was still down the back of her trousers. She wouldn't take it out unless he left.

He lifted a lamp and held it over the dark expanse of the stone with its columns of engraved lettering.

"Wait a moment. Hold that lamp closer." She lifted her magnifying glass and studied the top rows of hieroglyphics.

She traced a line with her fingertip. "What on earth?"

"What's wrong?" Raven didn't see anything out of the ordinary. He'd viewed the stone before.

She stared at him with consternation in her eyes. "This isn't the Rosetta Stone."

"Of course it is," he scoffed.

"No, it's really not." She traced the hieroglyphics for the name of King Ptolemy with her fingertip, looping around the lasso symbol and over the back of the crouching lion. "This is a forgery. A clever one, but a forgery. Is this even basalt?" She rapped on the stone with her knuckle. "I'd say it's something much lighter."

"That's completely absurd. Why wouldn't this be the Rosetta Stone?"

"You tell me. All I know is that these," she traced the hieroglyphics again, "were not carved in ancient Egypt. Some of the hieroglyphics are illegible, as if they were carved by looking at a degraded copy of the markings. Also, the French made many lithographs before they surrendered it to General Hutchinson during the Capitulation of Alexandria. There were more traces of black ink on the real stone."

"It must be the dim lighting, or—"

"I'm afraid it's true," said a man's voice.

Sir Malcolm.

He walked into the room and Indy hastily replaced her tinted spectacles.

"It can't be true," Raven said.

"It's true," said Malcolm. "The stone has been stolen."

# Chapter 3

&

"WHAT DO YOU mean, stolen?" asked Raven, perplexed. It wasn't like Sir Malcolm to withhold such cataclysmic information.

"How can such a heavy slab of basalt disappear?" asked Indy.

"Good evening, Lady India," said Malcolm.

Indy gaped at him. "You know it's me?"

"I knew the second I saw you enter Somerset House," Malcolm replied.

"Then why did you allow me to enter?" asked Indy.

"I'm an admirer of your theories on the Pharaoh Hatshepsut—I think you're right about her gender. But that's beside the point, since you've just made yet another startling discovery. Very impressive, my lady." Malcolm made a short bow.

"Ravenwood had no idea it was a forgery," said Indy with a smug smile.

"You have a magnifying glass," muttered Raven.

"I have eyes," she replied.

Malcolm approached Indy. "I do think perhaps you're one of only three or four of my colleagues who could have discerned the deception so swiftly, my lady."

"Thank you." Indy inclined her head, smiling at Malcolm, clearly pleased to be acknowledged as a greater expert than Raven. "His Grace didn't even recognize that it was me earlier."

Perfect. Raven was trying to prove that he was fit for service and she was calling him unobservant.

"I was only pretending not to recognize you," he asserted.

"No you weren't. I had you completely flummoxed," she crowed.

"Is the meeting over already?" Raven asked Malcolm.

"Montrose is giving a lecture on Stonehenge and he's bound to blather on for at least an hour." Malcolm turned to Indy. "And as for your question on how the stone was stolen, we had a shipment of Greek sculptures with a great many crates involved, and workers with winches and carts milling about. They must have made the switch during the chaos, stealing the stone and replacing it with this forgery."

"It's a very clever forgery," said Indy, "except that the depth of the carving is slightly off in some places. If you look closely with a magnifying glass, it becomes even more apparent."

"I actually hadn't noticed the lack of ink from the lithographic processing," said Malcolm. "Again, I'm very impressed."

*Wonderful, just bloody wonderful.* What was Malcolm doing with all this flattery? Attempting to recruit Indy, as he'd recruited Raven?

*Over his dead body.*

"I'll find the workers and interrog—interview them," he said.

"Already attempted. Unsurprisingly, they've all disappeared," said Malcolm. "It was an operation of considerable forethought, skillfully and professionally executed. We've tracked a likely crate to Paris, but then the trail goes cold."

"So it was the French," said Raven.

"We don't know that for certain," said Malcolm.

Raven knew precisely who'd stolen the stone: Le Triton.

He'd spent years infiltrating the French criminal underworld and stalking the man who ruled its shadowy reaches. Le Triton wasn't his real name, but it was appropriate since he had only three fingers left on one hand—resembling Triton's trident in the Greek myth. His influence and control encompassed gambling, stolen antiquities, prostitution, arms, and nearly every other nefarious dealing.

Le Triton's calling card, the mark he left, was a clever forgery in place of the antiquities he stole.

Once an ancient treasure disappeared into his heavily fortified estate on the outskirts of Paris, it was never seen again. The private collectors who purchased his stolen antiquities were sworn to secrecy on threat of death.

Raven knew, because he'd found one of them who had been less than discreet. The fellow had been dead as a doornail.

"Why would the French do this?" asked Indy, her brow wrinkling.

"I can think of several reasons," said Raven.

"The stone is one of our most famous archaeological treasures and only on loan to the antiquarian society for further study. It would be hugely embarrassing to the antiquaries, and to England, if news of its theft were made public."

"And all of the secrets of Egyptian hieroglyphics have not yet been unlocked. Whoever has the stone holds the key," said Indy.

"Precisely," said Malcolm. "It could have been stolen by the French because they are on the hunt for a new archaeological treasure. Or, perhaps they've found the missing pieces of the stone and want to make a whole."

"Wouldn't that be incredible?" Indy's spectacles practically fogged over with academic fervor. "To see the stone made whole. To read the final lines of the texts."

Raven nodded tersely. "I'll leave for Paris immediately." This would take precedence over finding the traitor, for the moment.

"There's another possibility," said Indy, her moustache wobbling precariously as she spoke. "The stone could have been stolen by Russia and made to look as though France was the culprit. It would be to Russia's benefit to sow discord. The truce between England and France seems tentative at best."

"An interesting supposition." Malcolm met Raven's gaze above her head, as if to say, *isn't she a clever one?*

Yes, yes, she was too clever by a long sight. Raven wished she'd stop displaying her extreme cleverness to Britain's top spymaster.

While he admired Malcolm and respected him, he also knew the man placed his duty to crown and country above all else. He wouldn't be above using Indy for his own purposes.

"Lady India doesn't want the thieves to be French because she's so friendly with that pompous Beauchamp fellow at the Louvre Museum in Paris," Raven explained to Malcolm.

"You're just jealous," Indy retorted. "Monsieur Beauchamp has accomplished more for the field of antiquities study in the last year alone than you'll achieve in your self-indulgent lifetime."

The Frenchman may have been one of the first to crack the secrets of hieroglyphics, but that didn't make him a worthy partner for Indy. The thought of her with another man made Raven want to slam his fist into a slab of basalt, but how could he begrudge her any happiness that might come her way?

She deserved love, happiness—all of the things he could never give her.

Just not with Beauchamp.

Raven realized he was still holding the lamp and set it down. "His antiquities studies make Beauchamp a perfect suspect."

"Why would he steal the stone?" asked Indy. "He'd never be able to display it in the Louvre's new department of Egyptian antiquities without causing an international scandal."

"Indeed. Wars have been waged for lesser insults," said Malcolm. "For the moment, no one knows the stone is missing except the thieves and we three. We can't risk anyone else finding out.

The stone was to be moved to the British Museum in a fortnight's time for permanent display."

"I'll retrieve the stone within the fortnight," Raven assured him.

Indy rounded on him. "You didn't even know it wasn't the real stone. How are you supposed to tell the real one from another replica?"

"She has a point," agreed Malcolm. "I can't go with you. I have to stay here and make sure no one else discovers it's missing."

"I'm the only one who can find the true stone," declared Indy. "Send me, Sir Malcolm. You won't regret it."

"Out of the question," said Raven. "Nip that idea in the bud. It would be a dangerous and highly sensitive mission."

He could barely see her eyes behind the spectacles, but he was sure they had narrowed.

"What are you saying, Ravenwood, that I'm not capable? That I'm not discreet?" Indy asked.

He must tread carefully. Don't raise her hackles. "I'm saying that stolen antiquities are my sordid area of expertise, not yours, my lady."

"And hieroglyphics are my area of expertise, not yours."

"I'll go to Paris," said Raven. "Alone."

"You can't keep me in London," Indy retorted. "I've as much right as you to search for the stone."

"And I'm telling you it's too dangerous." He rose to his full height, glowering down at her. "I forbid you to search for the stone."

She had the gall to laugh in his face. "You don't tell me what to do."

*Fool. You know better than that.* Tell Indy to do something and she did the exact opposite.

She threw her shoulders back and crossed her arms over her chest. "I'm going to Paris. Don't try to stop me." She smiled at Sir Malcolm. "A secret mission on behalf of the Crown—how thrilling!"

"Don't be silly," Raven said, beginning to panic a little now. The foolhardy woman would get herself murdered. "It's not a lark. There will be real danger involved."

"Then you'd best hire extra guards to protect you." She lifted the front of her coat to reveal the dagger she always carried at her side. "I've nothing to fear."

She tapped the heels of her boots together. "Sir Malcolm, I leave you now. I'll breathe not a word of this to anyone. You have my word that I'll recover the stone within the fortnight."

Nothing stopped Indy when she set her mind on something. She must be the most stubborn, fearless female the world had ever known.

She marched away.

"Pomeroy," Raven called.

She halted and turned around. "Yes, what is it?" she asked impatiently.

"You might need this." He held out his palm. Her moustache had lost the battle and fallen to the floor during their conversation.

She walked back, plucked the wispy moustache from his hand, and stuck it above her lip. "Thank you," she said with great dignity.

Her exit was half swagger, half flounce, and all Indy.

Their meetings never ended well, and this one had ended even worse than usual.

"I like that lady," said Malcolm with a chuckle. "Is she always so biddable?"

"This mission is too perilous for Lady India. You know as well as I do that Le Triton is the most likely culprit."

"You'll just have to find the stone before she does, eh?"

"Why didn't you tell me that it was missing?" he asked Malcolm.

Malcolm's gaze moved to the counterfeit stone. "I was going to tell you."

Something was wrong. Malcolm never avoided his eyes. Understanding began to dawn.

"You weren't going to tell me," Raven said. "You were having me evaluate the men at the meeting for potential involvement in the disappearance of the stone. You were going to take the intelligence I gathered and send someone else to Paris."

Sir Malcolm sighed. "You're right. And we already know who was behind the attack in Athens. It was Le Triton."

Raven let that absorb. "Jones was about to tell me something about the Rosetta Stone when we were attacked. So that makes Jones the traitor. Le Triton killed him to silence him before he confessed to me." He'd been feeding information to a double agent.

"It's the most likely scenario. Though Jones might not be the only informant in Le Triton's pocket."

"I can't believe you were withholding this information."

"I've been worried about you."

"Athens was an aberration. I'm fully recovered and sharper than ever." Raven should have been able to defend himself against the attack. He'd defeated twice as many men before.

He'd been sluggish. He hadn't been sleeping well.

"You look fatigued." Malcolm laid a hand lightly on Raven's shoulder. "No shame in it. You suffered a grave injury."

Raven shrugged his hand away. "Don't do this, Malcolm. I'm fit and ready for duty."

Malcolm met his gaze for several moments. Raven didn't dare blink.

"Come by Sutton Hall tomorrow morning," said Malcolm. "If you pass your field examination, I'll grant you the mission."

Raven relaxed his tense shoulders. "I'll pass with flying colors."

"I'll have your passport readied in anticipation of such a result."

"You won't regret it."

Sir Malcolm smiled. "You sound like Lady India. You know . . ." He looked thoughtful. "We could use a dose of confidence and determination. We're one man down with Jones terminated. I've never recruited a female. She seems quite formidable."

Raven's mind recoiled at the idea. All he could see was Indy facedown on a street, blood pooling in the cracks of the cobblestones.

He would never let any harm befall her.

"Out of the question," Raven said coldly. "Don't even think about it."

"Why? Do you have an attachment to her still?" The way Malcolm said the words put Raven on high alert. Malcolm had witnessed the friendship between Raven and Indy that terrible day when he'd delivered the devastating news of his father's death.

Malcolm was testing him now.

*An agent must never let personal connections interfere with his duty.*

"There's no attachment. No feelings." Raven kept his voice steady. "I'm a brick wall. Brick walls don't have feelings."

"When I entered the room I sensed sparks between you."

More like a raging fire. "There's nothing between us. She hates me." And he'd do whatever it took to keep it that way.

"Really? Because I did some research at one point and discovered that your marriage contract with Lady India is extant. I'd call that an attachment, wouldn't you?"

Damn. There was no fooling a spymaster. "Her father never legally terminated our betrothal before his sordid demise. He must have been waiting to find out whether my father was exonerated."

"I thought she jilted you. That's what you told me. That's what the broadsheets reported."

"She did. She told me she wouldn't marry me if I were the last rogue on earth. In the eyes of the world, she jilted me."

"But on paper you're still betrothed and neither of you are free to marry another."

"It's only a technicality. I'll never marry, you know that."

"But what of Lady India? She's had other suitors. What if she finally decides to marry?"

The suggestion made his hands ball into fists. "Then I'll be happy to sign any papers her lawyer sends me," he said.

And that was a cursed lie. He wouldn't be happy about it because . . . no one would ever be good enough for Indy.

She could have had anyone. And practically everyone had courted her once they believed that he had been removed from the picture.

He'd kept count of her suitors, listing their shortcomings and unsuitability in great detail in his journal. She was simply too much woman for the lazy lords of London.

She intimidated the poor sods with her opinions, her intelligence, her ambition, and her beauty. She lived outside of society, pursuing her own dreams instead of becoming someone's wife. She was unpredictable and powerful and she was . . . standing in the way of his mission.

He must convince her not to go to Paris. Too much was at stake. His future with the Foreign Office and the chance to finally bring Le Triton to justice.

"Lady India's not cut out for our work, Malcolm. She's far too dramatic. There's nothing she loves better than creating a spectacle of herself. She's about as secretive as a hurricane. I don't want her careening through Paris making inquiries and whipping up trouble."

"Then you'll have to find a way to stop her."

"I'll find a way to keep her in London," Raven vowed grimly. "I'll have her kidnapped and trussed up in a cellar if that's what it takes to keep her safe."

Malcolm chuckled. "Or she'll have *you* tied up and stuffed away somewhere. She doesn't seem the sort to back down from a challenge."

"She stays, I go," said Raven vehemently.

He'd vowed to shield her from any association with his dangerous life. He'd find a way to protect her from harm.

Protect her from him.

# Chapter 4

꿍

INDY PACED THE length of her brother's library the next morning. "You should have heard him, Edgar. 'I forbid you,' he barked, as if that would stop me somehow."

"As if anyone could stop you," said Edgar, exchanging an amused glance with his wife, Mari.

Indy performed a smart about-face and began pacing in the opposite direction. "I can assure you that his arrogant directives only added fuel to the fire of my resolve."

"Naturally," said Mari, with a shake of her auburn ringlets.

"I *will* go to Paris and I *will* find the sto . . . stolen artifact before he does," Indy proclaimed. "Or die trying."

Mari smiled. "That's rather dramatic, don't you think? Surely a treasure hunt across Paris between sworn rivals will be more thrilling than dangerous."

"He seems to think there could be peril involved." Indy's hand moved to the hilt of the dagger in a holster by her side. "I've never shied away from difficulty."

"You can't tell us what's missing?" asked Edgar.

Indy shook her head. "I was sworn to secrecy."

A line formed between Edgar's brows. "But you've been planning this expedition to Egypt for months now. Your ship is ready to depart. You've hired archaeological assistants and guards . . . everything's in place."

"The journey must be delayed. Would you mind terribly contacting the ship's crew and arranging for paid vacation until my return? I don't anticipate it will take more than a fortnight."

The search for Cleopatra's tomb without the Rosetta Stone's clues would be pointless.

She'd arrived at her theory in a roundabout way that most antiquities experts might call naïve. She'd tried to put herself in Cleopatra's slippers.

She must have read Shakespeare's *Antony and Cleopatra* dozens of times. There was a line about Cleopatra garbing herself in the habiliments of the Egyptian goddess Isis.

And the Greek biographer Plutarch wrote that Cleopatra wished to be known as "the New Isis." Indy hypothesized that Cleopatra had thought of herself as the reincarnation of Isis, and Antony as the reincarnation of Osiris.

If her theory was correct, Cleopatra, believing herself to be a goddess, would have insisted on being buried beneath a temple, instead of inside a pyramid.

Indy had amassed a compendium of texts as well as steles, cartouches, and papyri, always searching for the names *Cleopatra*, *Isis*, and *Osiris*. And that's when she'd found the map tucked between the pages of a lesser-known work by a Roman historian.

The person who had drawn the map had thought they'd discovered Cleopatra's burial site. And the location and name of the temple fit with Indy's theory—at least she was nearly certain they did.

She couldn't risk asking anyone to help her verify her translation of the name of the temple. She needed to keep her suppositions secret for now. She must examine the hieroglyphs on the Rosetta Stone in person.

"Must be an important artifact if you're giving up Egypt," said Edgar.

"Perhaps it's not about the prize, Edgar dear," said Mari. "It could be about besting Ravenwood."

Edgar stroked his wife's hand. "Isn't there a proverb about that, my love? Pride goeth before a fall, I do believe."

"While I admit beating him to the prize will be satisfying," said Indy, "it's not the primary reason. I require the . . . artifact . . . for my research. If a private collector purchases it, it could be lost forever. I'll never let that happen."

She resumed her pacing, her mind unspooling the possibilities.

Whoever had taken the stone was highly organized and efficient. They must have a vast network of trusted hirelings at their command. They'd either stolen it for profit or for political gain.

She didn't care a straw whether the stone ended up being displayed at the British Museum, at the Louvre, or back in Egypt. Some might say that was a nearly treasonous thought. While she was a loyal British subject, she was on the side of history above all else.

When monarchs and military commanders and madmen altered the course of history, when they stole relics and moved them willy-nilly, with no regard for provenance or future study for the benefit of all mankind, it was so wrong. The present translations of the stone were incomplete. The world needed the stone to unlock the remaining mysteries of Egyptian hieroglyphics.

She couldn't trust Ravenwood to find the stone. She must find it herself.

She glanced up to find Edgar and Mari watching her with matching furrows between their brows.

Indy drew a calming breath. She knew they cared for her, and that's why they worried.

She forced a smile to her lips. "Please don't concern yourselves unduly. I can defend myself. Ravenwood leads a dissipated life of luxury and hires servants to do the real work. He's never had to face an attack in a dark alleyway, as I have, and lived to tell the tale."

"No one's impugning your bravery, Lady Danger, we're only concerned because we love you. And we were rather hoping the children's favorite auntie might have a long, if not peaceful, life," said Edgar.

"Where are the twins?" Indy asked. She always loved spending time with the irrepressible and precocious Adele and Michel.

"They're with my father at the toy shop," said Mari. "They'll be sorry they missed your visit. Won't you stay for tea?"

"Can't I'm afraid. I have several arrangements to conclude before I depart for Paris this evening."

Robertson, her brother's butler, entered the room. "Mr. Peabody from the *Observer* is here for your interview, Your Grace. I placed him in the Gold Parlor."

Edgar rose. "I won't be but a few moments."

"Why the newspaperman?" asked Indy.

"He's interviewing me about the steam engine I'll be racing in the speed trials in Lancashire next month." He kissed Mari on the cheek and they exchanged another heated glance that spoke of rumpled bedsheets and other such intimate things.

Indy had been instrumental in making their match, and she was very happy for them, but sometimes all the tenderness and moonstruck gazing made her feel uncomfortable.

When love went wrong it festered like an infected wound, threatening the body with gangrene. She would never expose her heart to the dangerous condition again.

"I wonder," said Mari, after Edgar left the room. "There's so much emotion in your voice when you speak of Ravenwood. I observed your argument at the antiquities exhibition before Edgar and I were married. It seems to me that since you and the duke have so many shared interests a partnership might be more productive than a rivalry."

"We may have shared aims but we have opposite methods of achieving them. He does no actual archaeological excavating—he simply purchases stolen antiquities."

"Shameful," murmured Mari.

"Reprehensible in the extreme."

"Edgar won't tell me what happened between you two—only that you're sworn enemies. Were you ever thus? Or was there a time when you were friends?"

"I should be going," said Indy hastily. "I must make arrangements to leave my household early."

Mari smiled. "You're more similar to your brother than you know. Both of you are stubborn as mules. Sometimes talking about something painful gives it less power over you."

"Who said it was painful?"

"I can see it in your eyes when you speak of Ravenwood. Such a degree of anger can only be born from pain. Won't you sit down and tell me all about it?" Mari patted the chair next to her.

"I'll stand, thank you," said Indy. "I must be going soon." She turned toward her brother's large desk that dominated one side of the library. "I only came to ask Edgar to oversee the change of travel plans. And to say farewell."

"I see," said Mari.

She saw too much.

*You must learn to hide your feelings better.*

"Ravenwood and I were childhood companions," Indy finally said, avoiding Mari's eyes. "Betrothed since birth by our parents. My father threatened to end the engagement once but he never legally did."

"Edgar never told me any of this. Do you mean that you're still betrothed? How extraordinary."

Mari sat up straighter. There was a strange glint in her eyes.

"Don't make too much of it," said Indy. "In the eyes of the world I jilted him. Only our close families know the truth about the existing contract. It's quite a complicated and difficult contract to dissolve and neither one of us intend to marry and so . . . it means nothing."

"Oh I completely understand. Why bother with legal proceedings unnecessarily?"

"Quite."

Mari's eyes danced with laughter. Apparently she thought there must be some other reason that Indy hadn't been eager to legally dissolve the betrothal.

There was no other reason.

She wore the Minerva coin around her neck as a reminder to never love, never trust, again.

And the marriage contract served as enforcement. She couldn't fall in love and marry, even if she wanted to.

And neither could Ravenwood. Which, for some unknown reason, gave her a feeling of great satisfaction.

"How did you jilt him, and why?" asked Mari.

"It was at my coming-out ball," said Indy, the memory bleeding into her mind. "I hadn't seen him in years."

Standing on the edge of the candlelit ballroom, wearing a ridiculous frothy white gown, waiting breathlessly for Daniel to ask her to dance.

"We wrote to each other faithfully while he

was at a private boarding school in Scotland. But then his letters grew few and far between. Eventually he stopped writing to me altogether."

"How strange. If you used to be friends then why did he stop writing?" asked Mari.

"I don't know why."

"Haven't you asked him?"

"Never," said Indy, her voice coming out too loudly. She clenched her fists. "I'll never ask him. I'll never give him that power over me. I don't need to know why he did what he did. Nothing will change with the knowledge."

"Indy." Mari's blue eyes filled with emotion. "You sound so like your brother. I hate to think you're so filled with hurt and pride that you won't clear up what might be a simple misunderstanding."

"A simple misunderstanding?" Indy didn't even attempt to modulate her voice now. "He bloody well kissed another blasted woman at my blighted coming-out ball!"

"Oh." Mari started. "I . . . well that does rather change things."

"It changed everything." Indy's life had been torn asunder. She didn't even like thinking about that night. It was still such a tormented memory.

He'd looked so handsome in his formal attire. He'd grown so tall and broad shouldered. Black coat and white linen and those amber eyes she hadn't seen in so long. He'd avoided her gaze.

*Why?* She'd wondered. *Why won't he ask me to dance?*

"I was a pathetic, stupid little partridge, standing there, waiting for the fox to ask me to dance when he was out in the gardens devouring a very merry widow," said Indy. "Kissing her for all the world to see."

His gaze meeting hers, almost as if he'd been watching for her.

She'd never been able to shake the feeling that he had planned the whole thing.

To be rid of her.

"The bloody fool," exploded Mari, her expression severe. "No wonder you don't trust the man. No wonder he's your enemy."

"Mother had planned a grand affair, she was hoping our storybook engagement might distract society from . . . the other scandals plaguing our family. Edgar wasn't in London at the time."

"Yes," Mari said softly. "I heard about what happened between Edgar and your father."

"When I caught Daniel—Ravenwood—kissing Mrs. Cavinder in the gardens I exploded with rage. I called off the engagement then and there."

Her mother had branded her a fool. Her father had descended too far into ruin and drink to have any opinion on the matter.

The sight of Daniel kissing another woman had ripped her heart from her body and from that day forward she'd become a rebel against society's dictates.

Love was for fools. Marriage was only a way for a man to claim ownership of a woman's person and property.

He'd betrayed her, and that was that.

When next she saw him, they'd both worn well-practiced masks. He was London's favorite rogue. She'd become a scandalously unconventional adventuress who was barely tolerated in society, and that only because her brother was a duke.

Ravenwood had shaped her life before, but now she was the one in control of her destiny. He'd been her best friend, and then he'd humiliated her and shut himself off from her. If she couldn't have the life they'd planned together, she'd be a success on her own terms.

She'd become a successful archaeologist and a world-renowned antiquities expert, and she'd done it alone. She didn't need anyone at her side. She could trust no one.

She used to love him; she didn't love him now, and that was that.

Life went on. She achieved things. She dug through layers and layers of sand, or dirt, baking in the hot sun for months at a time without finding anything, and then . . . the rapturous moment when a relic of history, long buried, emerged.

Another puzzle piece to fit into the story of another powerful woman from history.

She felt more connected to history than to her own life sometimes.

There was far less risk in studying the lives of people long buried. They offered up their secrets and they never hurt her.

She couldn't speak any of this aloud.

As Mari had said, words held power, and admitting how much she used to care about Ravenwood might give him more sway over her than he already possessed.

There was a knock at the library door. Indy was relieved. She could leave now and stop reliving these bitter memories.

Robertson appeared, an apologetic expression on his normally impassive face. "Your Grace, Lady India," he nodded at them in turn. "I have the honor of announcing His Grace, the Duke of Ravenwood, who would not be so kind as to wait downstairs and instead insisted on being shown to you directly."

Relief took flight and was replaced by the nearly unbearable mélange of dread and excitement Ravenwood's presence always provoked.

He entered the library with his signature stride, the one she'd tried to copy when she infiltrated Somerset House yesterday.

*Hear ye, hear ye, I command this room and everything in it,* his entrance blared, as if he were a medieval king preceded by a ceremonial trumpeter.

There was no way to stop her physical response. Her heart always beat faster when he walked into a room.

He bowed over Mari's hand, brushing his lips over her knuckles. "You're looking blooming as always, Duchess. Marriage agrees with you, I do believe."

Despite what Indy had just told her about Ravenwood's character, Mari had the temerity to blush fetchingly, color washing across her freckled cheeks.

*Ravenwood,* thought Indy. *Transforming otherwise sensible females into blithering ninnies since . . . forever.*

"Were your ears burning, Your Grace?" asked Mari. "We were just speaking of you."

"All bad, I trust?" That devilish grin, the one that used to make Indy's heart melt.

*Heart,* she reminded it sternly, *you are under my command, not his.*

"Yes, actually," said Mari, seeming to recall finally that she was angry with him for hurting Indy. "Very bad indeed." She frowned at him sternly.

"Ravenwood." Indy inclined her head, unwilling to give more than an inch of acknowledgement. "You must be here to see my brother."

"Actually I came to see you. I visited your house and a maidservant informed me that you were here."

Taken aback, Indy's mind floundered between potential retorts. "You know where I live?" was all that emerged.

She knew where he lived. Her daily constitutional walks often took her past one of his residences.

He kept several homes in London but favored the one in Mayfair. When he kept a mistress, he installed her in the house in Covent Garden, the better to display her at the nearby Royal Opera House. He had no mistress at the moment. She knew because the gossips would have delighted in informing her if he did.

Which was neither here nor there. Whether he had a mistress was none of her concern.

"Of course I do. Why wouldn't I?" He smiled blandly, as if this were a polite social call instead of what she knew it must be—he was here to convince her not to go to Paris.

"Would you care for some tea, Your Grace?" asked Mari, always one to iron over awkward situations.

"Thank you, no," he replied. "I'm only here for a brief conversation with Lady Indy and then I shall trouble you no further."

"If you're here to order me to be a good girl and stay home, you can save your breath," said Indy.

"We're not in a competition, not on this matter," he replied, his tone pitched low and even. "You mustn't make a rash decision. Allow me to elaborate upon the particulars of the situation more fully."

Robertson appeared in the doorway again. "The children have returned, Your Grace," he intoned.

Mari rose from her chair. "Would you like me to stay, Indy?"

"No need. This will be the briefest of conversations."

"Should I have the servants remove the breakables?" asked Mari. "I hear vases and such have a tendency to be broken when you two share a room."

"I'll behave if the lady will," said Ravenwood. "We won't have to argue if she'll listen to reason."

Indy pointed at the library door. "We won't have to argue if you turn around and walk back the way you came."

"I'll just be in the nursery if you need me,"

Mari said with a smile, leaving the door wedged open as she departed.

Ravenwood stalked toward her. "Don't be so stubborn, Indy, we want the same thing."

"Yes, to find the stone before it's either lost forever to a private collection or becomes an international incident. You have your methods and I have mine. We'll see which one is more effective. You can search the demimonde and the underworld and I'll use more orthodox methods."

"Will you please just listen for a moment?" He began pacing up and down the library, much as she'd been doing earlier. "I can't seem to make you understand that I've no interest in besting you in this matter. It's strictly concern for your safety motivating my advice for you to remain in London."

"Hogwash!" Indy declared. "Do you expect me to believe such a preposterous notion? You haven't cared for my welfare since we were children."

"Whether you choose to believe it, or not, your welfare is important to me. That's why I'm here. Will you set aside that prickly pride of yours for one moment?"

"You're lecturing me on pride?" Indy laughed sharply. That was the second time she'd been accused of being prideful today. "That's rich indeed." She lifted a brass paperweight shaped like a globe from her brother's desk and hefted it between her hands.

"Are you going to throw that at me?" asked Ravenwood with a wary glance.

Indy regarded the brass globe. "I'm going to tell you precisely how this conversation will go, to spare us both the pain of having to carry it out. Now listen carefully. You're going to tell me this mission is too dangerous for a lady, and then I'll tell you to go straight to the devil, and then—"

"I'll threaten to have you kidnapped and bodily restrained from traveling to Paris."

"And I'll say try it and you'll face a sharp blade."

"And then I'll say that sometimes I swear I want to . . ." His voice trailed away but his gloved fists clenched.

"What, Ravenwood? What?" She relinquished the paperweight and stalked toward him. "You want to kill me? My, what touching concern for my welfare that displays."

She was tall for a woman but he was tall for a man. He glared ferociously, his eyes heating with molten copper.

"I want to . . ." He jerked off one of his gloves and then the other.

"Strangle me?" she asked, her mouth suddenly gone dry.

He balled the gloves inside his fist. "I swear I want to . . ."

# Chapter 5

❧

*I WANT TO KISS you, you maddening, mule-headed woman.*

Maybe Raven could kiss her into agreeing to stay in London.

He rejected the idea. That's not why he wanted to kiss her.

He wanted to kiss her because that's what he always wanted.

He'd been denying his obsession for so long that when he finally allowed himself to think the thought, it refused to leave, sinking its teeth into his mind like a mastiff snaring a hare.

Gods, he wanted to kiss her so badly. He wanted to press his lips to hers when he glimpsed her statuesque curves across a crowded avenue. He'd wanted to kiss her last night when she'd cleverly detected that the stone was a forgery.

Most of all, he wanted to claim her lips right now, as she provoked him with her stubbornness; as she lashed out and accused him of being the worst kind of scoundrel.

He was the worst kind of scoundrel.

And that's why he could almost taste the heaven that would be her tart tongue. The bliss that would be the softness of her lips.

That's why his thoughts spiraled far beyond a kiss to Indy laid across that convenient mahogany desk with her drab cotton skirts hiked to her waist, panting as he pleasured her.

These were the times when it was the most difficult to remember why they couldn't be lovers instead of enemies. When she was out of his dreams and standing in front of him, warm and real, her chest rising and falling with emotion, the skin of her throat flushed, her eyes sparkling like the rare purple Wish Diamond, the centerpiece of the priceless necklace he'd discovered.

She'd accused him of keeping the necklace for his mistresses to model.

He'd kept the Wish Diamond because it was the exact same shade as Indy's eyes. It flashed with the same pale fire.

And he'd always pictured her wearing it.

No one else would do.

He slapped his gloves against his thigh. "Damn it all, Indy. Stolen antiquities are *my* specialty."

"Here we go, having the very conversation I predicted," said Indy with a mocking smile that reminded him of the one he always tried to maintain when he talked to her. "I explained to you last night that hieroglyphics are *my* specialty. You only want the glory and the fame of being a hero for England. I actually require the stone for my research."

"I understand that you require the . . ." he lowered his voice and whispered the next word, "stone." He transferred his gloves to his coat pocket and placed his hand over his heart. "I swear to you, Indy, that I will bring it back to you and you may research it to your heart's content."

Instead of mollifying her, his gallant proclamation only made her eyes narrow. "You'll bring me the stolen antiquity and lay it at my feet like some knight slaying a dragon for a princess, is that it?"

"If you want to view it like that." What was wrong with noble impulses? He'd fight the entire Paris underworld single-handedly if it meant keeping her safe.

"I'll slay my own dragons, thank you very much." She was standing so near he could see the gray and blue flecks in her irises that blended to produce that startling shade of purple.

There were faint lines at the corners of her generous lips. They were both growing older.

The lines only made her more beautiful.

He couldn't let Indy know that he already had a strong suspicion about who had stolen the stone. If he told her, she'd probably rush right to Le Triton's door.

He had to outsmart her, outmaneuver her, use every means at his disposal to frighten her away from going to Paris.

*Good luck with trying to outsmart her, you fool.*

*Careful now. She's already jittery and on edge.* "I know you're fearless and capable," he said. "But some of the French antiquities thieves who could be behind this theft are ruthless and cruel."

"Are you talking about Le Triton? I thought he was your friend. Aren't you cut from the same cloth?"

It took all of Raven's years of conditioning and training not to launch a stream of expletives.

"He's not my friend," Raven said in outrage. "Le Triton is evil and he's extremely dangerous. He runs a criminal organization from his impenetrable stronghold in Paris and he doesn't only deal in stolen antiquities but every nefarious enterprise you could imagine."

"Well I'm not scared of him. And besides, I think it far more likely that the Russians are behind the theft."

That was giving the Russians entirely too much credit, to his way of thinking.

"And another thing," Indy continued, her eyes flashing. "I don't need you, or any other man, telling me to stay home, to be quiet, to do my embroidery and let the menfolk risk their lives. You're talking to a woman who has fought off knife attacks and survived venomous snakebites."

"Indy, I know we haven't exactly been allies in the past few years, but I'm here to ask for a temporary truce."

"Don't call me Indy. I'm not your Indy anymore, and there'll be no truce."

He pinched the bridge of his nose and sighed heavily. "There's nothing I can say that will dissuade you from going to Paris, is there?"

"Absolutely nothing."

"What happens if we meet in Paris?"

"I'll cross the street."

"I mean at an event. The British society in Paris is quite insular. How are you going to make inquiries without arousing suspicions about what you're searching for?"

"A ha." She jabbed his chest with her finger. When had they drifted so close to each other? "Now I understand what you're truly worried about. You think I'll bungle the mission. Let the cat out of the bag."

"You're not exactly known for your tact and discretion."

She sniffed. "And you're not exactly known for your sobriety."

It was difficult to fight with her when she made him want to laugh. "There are things you don't know, *can't* know, about the circumstances of the theft."

"Things which Sir Malcolm shared with you simply because you're a man and you happened to be in the room when *I* discovered the stone was missing."

"Well . . . yes." And because he was a secret agent in Sir Malcolm's employ, a fact that Indy could never, ever know.

"You . . . you . . ." she sputtered, her eyes sharp as the facets on a diamond. She was rarely at a loss for words.

He decided to press forward. "Why don't you just go on your next archaeological expedition as planned? I'll send you a very clear ink lithograph of the entire script when I recover the relic. I'll personally supervise the printing."

"Men!" She shook her head vehemently and dark tendrils of hair fell across her cheek. "You're always underestimating me. You and every other man I meet. You may think me indiscreet but I would never jeopardize this mission."

"All well and good, but I know you too well. If there's trouble, you'll be in the thick of it."

She had a contentious nature and a flair for the dramatic, which would make his mission all the more complicated. He'd have to find the stone and protect Indy in the extremely likely event that she stuck her nose where it wasn't wanted.

She turned her head away, obviously fighting for control over her emotions. She had the noble profile of a Roman goddess. Minerva hoisting her shield and spear and heading into battle.

She took several deep breaths, exhaling audibly.

The scent of her perfume teased his senses. She couldn't wear something easily identifiable like other ladies. No roses or orange blossoms for her. She'd chosen something complicated that smelled like it must be extracted from strange flowers that only bloomed at night.

It was so much easier to combat this elemental attraction when there were literal oceans between them.

So much simpler to fight the power she held over him when her lips weren't so very close to his.

"We've reached an impasse." She brushed strands of dark hair away from her cheek with an impatient gesture. "As I predicted."

"We're like oil and water, you and I." He drew a shaky breath. "Never the twain shall mingle."

"Fire and ice."

"The North Pole and the South."

"I hate you," she said. "Quite thoroughly."

"So you've told me."

"'If I be waspish, best beware my sting.'" Now she was quoting from a Shakespeare play. Dirty fellow, that Mr. Shakespeare.

"'My remedy is then to pluck it out,'" he rejoined, surprising himself by recalling the next line.

"'Ay, if the fool could find it where it lies.'"

"As I recall," said Raven, "*The Taming of the Shrew* becomes rather bawdy at this point. Isn't there talk of tongues in tails?"

"Yes, and men being three-legged stools to sit on," she said, with the hint of a smile on her lips. "You know I'll never be tamed, or ordered about, right?"

"I'm well aware. I don't want to tame you. I want to protect you from being hurt," he said, his voice jagged with emotion.

And he wasn't only speaking of what could be, in Paris, but of what he'd done.

He'd wanted to make her hate him. And it had worked. Gods, how it had worked.

She inhaled, her full breasts brushing against his chest. Her softness made his body feel more solid. All of him solidifying . . . hardening like lava meeting the air, hardening to stone, but his heart kept glowing.

*His Indy.*

The fiercest person he knew . . . yet she was all extravagant curves, and they would fit together so beautifully. Two halves of a whole.

Forbidden thought.

She lifted her hand. The briefest touch along his jaw.

Forbidden touch.

"You haven't shaved since last night." The words spoken in a throaty whisper. Her finger tracing the line of his jaw.

"I haven't slept since last night," he said roughly.

"You honestly think this will be a perilous undertaking?"

"I know it will be."

He stood perfectly still as her finger continued its exploration. Over his chin, down his throat to his Adam's apple.

*Touch me. Caress me. Slap me.*

*I'll never respond.*

Never pull her close and lose himself in her scent, her lips, her Indy-ness. If he did he'd never come back up for air. He'd drown.

His chosen path would disappear. The oaths he'd sworn.

King and Country.

*To prevent and defeat treasonable or other dangerous conspiracies against the state . . .* or die trying.

No vulnerabilities. No attachments. Nothing his enemies could use against him, as Sir Malcolm's enemies had done. The spymaster's wife and young daughter had been poisoned to death one year before Raven had come to live with him.

*We prefer our operatives never to marry. If you were compromised, a family would be a liability. And if you were killed in the field, as your father was . . . well you know what agony that causes for a family.*

Her fingers moved to his lips and her gaze followed.

She was staring at his lips. Her thumb exploring, claiming territory.

He stayed completely still, not daring to breathe.

Stretched taut like a rope, fraying beneath the weight of his desire.

If he allowed himself to breathe, he would take her lips, as he'd dreamed of doing so many times, with fierceness and certainty.

Learn their lush contours by heart. Delve inside to taste her sweet, tart tongue. Swallow the *I hate you* and tease his name from her lips.

*Say my name. Say you want me.*

*Raven. I want you.*

He should say harmful, hurtful things. Push her away.

A new idea insinuated its siren song into his Indy-addled mind. What if he'd been going about this business all wrong? What if the best way to frighten her into staying in London wasn't to push her away . . . but to pull her close?

It could work. He had to try *something*.

He wrapped his arm around her slender waist. Dragged her against him.

And kissed her.

INDY'S STOMACH FLIP-FLOPPED and her heart danced in her chest.

She'd goaded him into losing control. Iron-willed Ravenwood. The impassive, mocking, infuriating man who always made her lose her patience, who always reduced her to a quivering mess of nerves and rage.

He was kissing her.

She'd won this round.

She'd won . . . his mouth pressed lightly against hers while his gold-brown eyes stayed hard and argumentative.

Half of a victory, then. She'd take it.

She'd take everything he gave and demand even more.

Victory tasted . . . incredible.

His lips moved against her softly, coaxing her lips apart, the sensation like nothing she'd ever known. She gasped into his mouth, betraying her wildly shifting emotions.

*His tongue inside her mouth.*

Like diving into an icy lake on a hot day in only your shift, nipples instantly tightening, blood pumping faster because of the instinctual threat of the cold stopping your heart.

The shock of sun-saturated heat meeting the freezing water . . . like tiny pins stuck under your skin.

The exhilaration.

*I'm alive. I live. There's never been anyone else like me. There's never been another kiss like this.*

His tongue showed hers what to do: *stroke and glide, find the buoyancy. Keep pressing deeper until the earth tilts and his eyes are the ground and your toes are hooked in the clouds.*

*You don't float away because his strong hands*

*clamp around your waist. Hands like heavy wooden
stocks closing around you, immobilizing you. You're
being punished for having so many dreams about him,
for fantasizing about this moment so many times.*

A softening in his eyes now, almost a smile
hidden in their depths. She smiled against his
lips and he nipped at her lower lip with his teeth.

Did lovers do that? Nip each other? She tried
it, nibbling on his lip. He tasted like brandy and
smoke and forbidden pleasures.

She pressed her body against him and his
hands tightened around her waist, pulling her
against his hips. His hands shaped the small of
her back and her hands wandered to his sculp-
tural buttocks.

Learning his shape, the muscles like marble, the
deep fissure down the center of his back, hillocks
of muscle on either side.

For some reason the feel of all that solid male-
ness drove her nearly mad. He was a cliff wall
and she must find handholds and footholds to
climb him, scale his heights.

His lips never left hers. They kissed and kissed,
needing nothing so prosaic as air.

They would live on kisses for the rest of their
lives.

They might kiss for an eternity. They might
turn to stone and be delivered to the British
Museum: *The Rivals' Embrace*, a study in marble.

He cupped her bum with his hands, squeezing
gently, and she moaned, just like in her dreams;
she moaned out loud, unable to stop herself.

They kissed and he took the lead, pressing

into her mouth, opening her wider with his lips, diving into her and then she, not wanting to be outdone, took control. Raising her hands to the nape of his neck, playing across the corded tendons, and dragging him deeper into the kiss.

She'd wanted this for so long.

No thought for what this meant or what would happen afterward, only: *yes, there, fill me and I'll fill you.*

She was a historian, an archaeologist, it was her job to hypothesize about long-dead passions and court intrigues.

*Let's write some history of our own. Inscribe this kiss in the record books.*

"Ahem."

The throat clearing noise came from somewhere far away. A cold, cruel world where kissing Ravenwood was the absolute worst possible thing she could do, and where being *caught* kissing him meant certain annihilation.

"Ravenwood. India." An irritated voice. A gruff voice.

*Edgar.*

Indy wrenched away from Ravenwood. The look on his face nearly made her erupt into hysterical laughter. His eyes were frozen wide in the quintessential I've-been-caught-kissing-your-sister expression of sheer and utter panic.

This was a disaster.

Indy took a deep, steadying breath and turned toward the door.

*Great mounds of steaming shite.*

Had she thought this was a disaster? It was far

worse than that. It was the blasted Apocalypse. The Four Horsemen would come galloping into the room any moment now, signaling the end of days.

Because it wasn't just Edgar gaping at them from the doorway. The odious Mr. Peabody, of the *Observer*, bobbed beside her brother with barely contained glee, no doubt already composing tomorrow's lurid headlines.

*Victory Declared for Mankind: Lady Danger Tamed at Last by Rogue Duke's Kiss.*

*Bollocks!*

What had it looked like to Edgar and Mr. Peabody?

*What do you think it looked like, you flibbering ninny? You were mauling each other like wild beasts.*

His hands gripping her bum, her arms tangled around his neck, lips locked.

Everyone remained frozen in the tableau as if no one wanted to be the first person to speak, as if time might spin backward and the scene could be avoided if everyone remained silent.

"What exactly is happening here?" Edgar finally asked, a perplexed expression on his face.

"Lady India had a fainting spell," said Ravenwood smoothly. "I was attempting to resuscitate her." He placed an arm around her waist. "Are you quite recovered, my lady?" he asked solicitously. "Perhaps we should fetch some smelling salts?"

That's when Indy's already frayed temper completely ripped apart at the seams like a bodice in a bawdy book.

She was angry with herself for touching his lips like a moonstruck young girl.

She was angry with him for kissing her so passionately that she completely forgot she hated him.

And she was furious most of all that they'd been caught in their moment of madness.

Only their intimate family knew that their marriage contract was still in existence. Everyone would say she was just another one of Ravenwood's doxies after Peabody published his titillating tale.

She was no man's doxy. Especially not Ravenwood's.

And so she lashed out in the first way her kiss-scrambled brain supplied. How did one go about wounding a rogue?

Hit him where it would hurt the most: his freedom.

"Why, you great dolt of a duke," she cooed, touching the tip of his nose. "You know I've never fainted once in my life." She removed his arm from her waist. "I think it's time for our little secret to be revealed." She whirled toward their audience with her most theatrical whirl.

"Indy," Ravenwood whispered warningly, only adding fuel to the fire.

"Dear Mr. Peabody," Indy trilled. "What you have just witnessed has a very logical and legitimate explanation." She paused for dramatic effect.

All three men leaned in closer to hear her next words.

She was almost beginning to enjoy herself now. She'd always loved a captivated audience.

"You see the truth is that His Grace has just made me the happiest lady on earth." She lifted his hand to her lips and air-kissed his huge knuckles. "By finally agreeing to set a date for our wedding."

# Chapter 6

⤙🕊⤚

RAVEN SWALLOWED THE wrong way and began choking.

Indy thumped him on the back. "Are you quite all right, darling duke? Shall I fetch you some smelling salts?"

She had a sadistic spark in her eyes.

"We've been betrothed since birth, you'll recall," Indy said in a confiding voice to Peabody, who looked as bewildered as Raven felt.

"But I thought you had, that is to say, I was under the impression, that your ladyship and His Grace were no longer betrothed," said Peabody.

Banksford laughed uneasily. "Ha ha." He clapped his hand onto Peabody's shoulder. "Nothing like a dram of drama in the morning. My sister's always had a theatrical streak. It's true that they've been betrothed since birth. The agreement was never formally ended. I'm very pleased to hear the wedding's back on." He laughed heartily. "Now do let me show you the small-scale model I've built of my new steam engine." He tried to lead Peabody away but the man wasn't having it.

Peabody stared at Indy, then at Raven, obviously trying to figure out just what was happening here.

Raven was occupied with doing the same.

How did the Byzantine maze of Indy's mind work? This was clearly some sort of gauntlet she'd thrown down.

A challenge.

He could call her bluff and put her to the lie in front of her brother and the newspaperman, or go along with the improbable story . . .

"Your Grace," said Peabody to Raven. "Is this . . . that is to say, did you, er, agree to a wedding?"

Now everyone was waiting for him to speak. Here's where he said something like, *there's no chance in Hades I'll ever marry and this is just one of our public stunts and we were kissing because . . .*

*They'd been kissing.*

In a flash, he understood why Indy was doing this. Partly to punish him, but also partly because if the story leaked out she would be shamed.

Men never had to face the consequences of indiscretions. It was always the women who bore the brunt of society's censure. She was already regarded with mistrust by London society but she would be utterly ruined if word of this impropriety spread.

She'd be a pariah and he'd still be everyone's favorite rogue.

This was her way of taking control of the situation. Writing her own story.

*Damn it all.*

He never wanted to be the cause of her shame. He couldn't believe he was about to do this, but what else could he do? She'd bested him yet again.

Raven lifted Indy's hand and kissed her knuckles, mirroring her earlier gesture. "Indeed, it is true. We shall be married as soon as conveniently possible."

"The sooner the better," said Indy. She smiled a glorious smile. A sunlit smile.

*A wicked smile.*

"I am she born to tame a wild rogue to one as conformable as other household husbands," she pronounced.

At this bastardization of the Bard's words, Mr. Peabody gasped.

She was determined to give them a show, was she? He'd play along. May as well give her a taste of her own medicine.

"We're planning a grand wedding." Raven stared at his faux intended with a besotted expression. "The grandest. Lady India's days of sensible frocks are over. She's professed a desire to be wed in a gown composed entirely of frills. Frill upon froth upon frill." He brought his hands to her neck. "Layers and layers of frills that start at her neck and cascade down to her daintily clad toes. The color will be . . . bright canary yellow. She'll look edible. Like a big, beautiful frilly pineapple."

Indy glared at him.

"Sounds as though we won't see much of the lady herself," said her brother skeptically. He wasn't buying their act, though Peabody was lapping up every word.

"Oh yes, my pineapple gown," said India with a truly impressive sigh of joy. "Of course, you may outshine me yet, my darling duke."

She smiled at the nonplussed Mr. Peabody. "Ravenwood showed me a portrait of his great-great-grandfather and expressed a desire to have a wedding costume that mimicked the splendid sartorial enthusiasms of his ancestor. He wants to wear a doublet of pink silk, with silver velvet insets, and he will wear shoes tied with satin bows, with silver spurs at the heels."

Raven cleared his throat. "I'm not sure that I said *pink* silk, dear heart."

"I'm quite certain that you did. I wouldn't forget something like that." Her laughter tinkled in a high voice she'd probably never used before in her life. "And there will be the . . . swans. Twenty swan couples, swimming in a pool with little golden crowns upon their heads. Swans mate for life, don't you know? And there will also be the . . . what was it you asked for, lamb chop?

*Lamb chop? Swans?*

The woman had lost her mind.

"Oh, I recall," she said. "You wanted there to be twelve ladies dancing. I demurred and said what would society think, you can't bring dancing ladies into a house of God, but you insisted so I said you could have the dancing ladies if I was allowed to have my . . ." she paused for a moment, "my champagne fountain," she concluded triumphantly.

Banksford coughed loudly. "Champagne fountain?"

"As tall as a street lamp, and filled with French champagne. The dancing ladies will emerge from it, all the bubbles will make them quite giddy, and then the guests can dip their glasses into the champagne and have a drink. Are you memorizing all of these details, Mr. Peabody?" Indy asked, whirling on the poor man.

"Ah . . ." Mr. Peabody nodded. "Swans . . . dancing ladies . . . champagne."

"And the zebra," prompted Indy.

"The . . . zebra?" asked the hapless Mr. Peabody.

"The one Ravenwood will ride to the church."

"Is this a menagerie or a wedding?" asked Banksford.

This was spiraling out of control. Raven had best put a stop to it.

"My own darling tropical fruit," he said in a syrupy voice to match hers. "Are you quite certain that you want all of these details in the paper? I thought we were saving some as a surprise."

She patted his arm. "Isn't that just like a nervous groom, worrying about things being printed before they're finalized—don't worry, ducky, everything will come off beautifully. It will be the most talked about wedding of the decade. You have my full permission to regale your readership with all of the scintillating details, Mr. Peabody."

"Much obliged, my lady. I will, I most certainly will," Peabody said, nodding until his chin disappeared into the folds of his collar.

"We're off to Paris tomorrow to have our matrimonial costumes designed," said Indy.

*Oh here we go.* She'd find a way to go to Paris come hell or high water. Now she'd go as his fiancée.

"Come along, my scheming pineapple," Raven clamped an arm around her waist. "Peabody wants to view your brother's steam-engine model."

Banksford gave Raven a brief nod, his eyes telling Raven to take Indy away before they dug their hole any deeper.

Raven and Indy descended the stairs in silence, received their outer garments from a footman, and exited the house.

"Have you gone mad?" Raven asked her when they were a safe distance away.

"No madder than you, grabbing me like that. What was that?"

"That was a kiss."

"No, that wasn't a kiss." She spun toward him. "That was a declaration of war, and you know it. You were trying to shock me. Manipulate me. Don't try to deny it."

She walked faster, putting distance between them. Raven caught himself admiring both the lightning speed of her deductions and the way her bum bounced beneath her skirts as she marched along.

"Indy, slow down for a moment. Where are you going? Didn't you arrive in your carriage?"

"I walked. I like a constitutional walk in the mornings, it clears my head."

"My head certainly needs clearing. Or maybe I require an entirely new head because I think we just announced our intention to marry."

"Oh don't worry about a thing, my irredeemable rogue. After our trip to Paris you'll do something unforgivable and I'll call off the wedding again. Problem solved."

Her words were light but he heard the underlying accusation. He'd done something unforgivable. She was still angry and hurt, as well she should be.

It had been wrong to kiss her today. This was her way of seeking revenge.

"So you don't intend to go through with it?" he asked, just to be clear.

She stopped walking and gave him a horrified look. "You don't think for one second that I'd marry you over a mere kiss? That's patently ridiculous. I would never marry you. Not in a million years."

"So you've told me."

A mere kiss? That had been the best kiss of his life.

There'd been nothing *mere* about it. And what's more, seeing her so upset about the possibility of marrying him triggered all manner of emotions that he wasn't equipped to identify at the moment.

The thought of marrying him wasn't the *most* painful thing in the world.

He'd like to think it ranked slightly higher than having one's fingernails ripped off by pincers, a torture method favored by the inventive Monsieur Le Triton.

"I know why you did this, Indy."

"Do please explain everything to me," she said with a sarcastic smile.

"You want to hurt me. I understand that. But it was also a very clever way of turning the tables and shaping Peabody's narrative. Instead of printing a prurient account of our embrace, he'll announce our wedding plans and focus on all the outrageous details you fed him."

"Precisely. I believe it's called an evasion tactic."

Not for the first time he had the thought that Indy could probably teach his fellow agents a thing or two.

"Then we travel to Paris together. Unless you've decided to stay in London?" At her incredulous glance he said, "I didn't think so."

How was he going to explain this to Sir Malcolm? Not only had he failed to convince Indy not to go to Paris . . . they would be traveling together.

For the space of a few steps he panicked, until he realized that this might actually be for the best. Short of having her kidnapped, there'd been no way he could have kept her away from Paris. This way, he'd be able to keep an eye on her, to make sure she stayed safe.

During the day they could go on innocuous excursions such as interviewing Beauchamp at the Louvre, or paying a visit to Boris Petrov, the Russian ambassador to France.

But by night, Raven would do the real work. He'd discover where Le Triton was keeping the stone and conclude the mission swiftly and with cold-blooded precision.

The only problem would be finding a way inside Le Triton's fortress.

No one had ever been able to penetrate his lair before. It was too heavily guarded. Details of the interior were scarce. The precise location of Le Triton's vast antiquities collection within his stronghold was a closely guarded secret.

A young couple walked past them on the footpath, gazing into each other's eyes, the man laughing heartily at something his clever wife had said.

"This happened because we were fighting," Raven said. "Fighting passionately. Sometimes an argument becomes a conflagration."

"'Where two raging fires meet together, they do consume the thing that feeds their fury,' is that it?"

More Shakespeare. "It was entirely my fault. I'm the one to blame."

An emotion he couldn't interpret chased across her face. "I think I had something to do with it."

"We must never kiss again, Indy."

His thoughts sang a rebellious counterpoint to his words.

*Don't make any promises. What if the wheel falls off the coach on the way to Dover and you're stranded at a coaching inn?*

*What if she climbs into your bed in the middle of the night? Do you honestly think you'd be able to withstand such an onslaught?*

He'd damn well find the fortitude to withstand it.

*Even if she crawled into your bed naked? Even if she . . .*

Never. Again.

"You have my word of honor as a gentle-woman." Indy placed her hand over her heart. "No more kisses. You'll be quite safe with me as your escort."

Excellent. Keep everything light and funny. No real emotions or revealing of secrets.

Everything had to return to the way it had been before the kiss.

They were embarking on a perilous mission. His duty was to see the stone home to England, and to keep Indy safe in the process.

INDY'S THOUGHTS RICOCHETED between self-castigation and a bizarre sense that what had happened had been somehow inevitable, as though all of their past arguments and confrontations had been escalating to this moment of reckoning.

Ravenwood walked beside her, shortening his long strides to match her gait, a concerned expression tugging at the corners of his mouth.

"I've already made arrangements for a private coach to Dover." He was all business now. Stern set to his lips and confident walk. "From there we will go by steamship to Calais."

"I've journeyed to Paris before. I'm an experienced traveler. What I want to know is this: What skills do you bring to this mission other than the fact that you happen to have been born male?"

"Are you serious?" He raked his hand through his hair, leaving a few brown strands sticking straight up, which somehow only served to make him more devastatingly attractive.

"Deadly serious," she said.

"Well, for one thing, I'm a duke."

"That's not a skill."

"It's an entrée into Parisian society, both the high and the low."

"Is that all? You're a duke?"

"You know my skills. I'm a famous hunter and collector of antiquities."

"Infamous."

"Precisely. I'm infamous for my single-minded pursuit of pleasure and treasure."

"Not really the skills I'm looking for in a business partner. Will you be any use in a surprise ambush?"

He made a fist that looked as though it could smash through a brick wall. "Does this answer your question?"

"What if your opponent has a blade?"

"This is all the weapon I've ever needed. These . . ." He flexed the enormous muscles in his arms. "And this." Copper-brown eyes beneath thick dark brows lit with a wicked promise. His smoldering gaze nearly incinerated the gown from her body.

Indy drew a shaky breath. "Be serious. Bedchamber eyes aren't going to defend you from a cutpurse in a dark alleyway. You do entirely too much lolling about in houses of ill repute. Your arms may be . . . solid muscle . . . but it's practice that builds the reflexes necessary to defend against surprise attacks."

He shrugged. "You'll have to save me then, Lady Danger. We're a team now. At least for the next fortnight."

"We're not a team." She shook her head vehemently. "We're a provisional partnership. A distrustful duo. Temporarily entangled and soon to be separated again."

"I'll swagger around and carry a big knife. No one will challenge me," said Ravenwood.

"If you carry a knife and don't know how to use it, you could be the one facing its blade," she said. "I've trained with fencing and knife-fighting instructors to become combat-ready should the day come again when I must defend myself against another attack."

"I prefer pistols, myself. Much more straightforward. Point and shoot."

"Too cumbersome. Too much time to load. What you want in close combat is a knife."

"Then teach me how to fight with a blade," he suggested.

"What, here? In the middle of the street?"

"No." He grabbed her wrist and pulled her down a narrow side street between two buildings. "Here."

His gargantuan shadow loomed against the brick wall, dwarfing hers. She shivered, pushing away the memory of another dark alleyway.

Another large shadow.

He might have the advantage of size but she was quicker.

She'd always been quicker, even when they were children racing through the woods, dreaming of buried treasure and making plans to travel the world in search of adventure.

Plans that he had abandoned. Dreams that he had extinguished.

Indy gripped the hilt of her knife.

"Very well," she said. "You sense I'm a threat. You raise your knife."

He lifted an imaginary blade.

She lunged, letting instinct take control.

He parried, a split second too late. Her fist slashed across his forearm and then slid home against his flat abdomen.

"If this were a knife you'd be dead." She slid a finger along the firm flesh beneath his rib cage. "Never parry with your unprotected hand. Always stay behind your blade."

She lifted his giant hand, wrapping his fingers around a pretend dagger, positioning his wrist. "Maintain a firm grip on the hilt. Keep the knife edge up and out, pointed toward the threat."

His eyes glinted in the dim light. "You're making a habit of touching me, aren't you, Indy?" he said in a husky whisper.

She dropped his hand as if it were a pile of hot coals and stepped away from him. "In your dreams, Ravenwood. And I told you not to call me Indy."

*In her dreams.*

Sweat-soaked, sheet-twisting dreams. Forbidden dreams.

Dreams she'd been having since he'd been a reckless boy with a disarming grin, daring her to jump her pony over the highest fence. She'd nearly broken her neck more than once.

He'd broken her heart.

He was her enemy. Her rival.

And she did want to touch him. Desperately. Every single time she saw him.

She'd always thought that reality would pale in comparison to her vivid dreams. After their kiss, she wasn't so sure.

Her dreams might be the paler, tamer version.

A tremor rippled between her shoulder blades.

"Shall we call that truce now?" he asked. "I can be pleasant."

She didn't want him to be pleasant. She relied on him to be infuriatingly arrogant.

Pleasant was dangerous.

Change three letters and pleasant became pleasure.

"We don't have to be pleasant to each other," she said. "At least when we're in private. All we need do is find the stone and return to our separate lives." She sheathed her dagger and headed back to the crowded street.

He followed.

She would find the strength to ignore him. That's what she'd do. She'd completely ignore six feet of overly confident, sinfully handsome former best friend during the two-day journey to Paris.

"I always stay with Sir Charles Sterling, the British ambassador, when I'm in Paris," Ravenwood informed her. "And you?"

"I always stay with Lady Catherine Hammond. She made Paris her permanent residence seven years ago and hasn't ceased trying to convince me to do the same. I visit her for several months every year when I'm able."

"I'm not acquainted with Lady Catherine but I've heard about her discovery of Bronze Age barrows in Yorkshire. I've also heard she's quite the eccentric."

Indy shrugged impatiently. "That's what people say when they don't have a box to fit someone inside. Lady Catherine is my archaeology mentor and my friend. I'll be glad to have the chance to visit with her. I received a letter from her recently that was rather worrisome."

"How so?"

"She wrote that she was in ill health and was experiencing heart palpitations and terrible vertigo. She consulted several medical doctors but only found a small measure of relief after hiring a Dr. Lowe, whom she calls a mesmerist."

"I've heard of mesmerism. It's all quackery."

"That's what I'm afraid of. It does sound as though Dr. Lowe has a powerful influence upon her. She's a very wealthy woman, and I only hope he's an honorable man."

They reached her town house and Indy opened the door with her key. She kept only a small household staff because she traveled most of the year. A piano symphony whirled into the air with a crashing of ominous bass notes.

"Who's playing?" asked Ravenwood. "It sounds like a man. Why is a man playing the piano in your house?"

"Don't be jealous. It's not a man, it's my friend Miss Beaton. She practices here as my piano is superior to hers."

"I wasn't jealous."

Odd that he would deny it in such a guilty tone. Had he actually been jealous at the thought of a man in her town house?

"We depart for Paris tonight at five o'clock. Meet me at The White Bear, Piccadilly," he said tersely.

She watched him walk away. Men and women alike turned their heads and stared as he passed. He was larger than life. Taller, more confident, more charismatic . . . with enough charm to woo the world.

She tore her gaze away. She must hide her desires more carefully.

Build her walls higher.

She could never let him see how he disarmed her.

# Chapter 7

✑

SAFELY INSIDE HER house, Indy collapsed against the solid wood door, her breath coming in short puffs.

*Holy mother of . . . what in the nine concentric circles of tormented Hell had just happened?*

She felt like her heart had been ripped from her chest yet again and pinned to her lapel, beating and bleeding for the whole world to examine.

This wasn't just an unexpected twist, or a plummet from a cliff. She had no idea what this was. She had no precedent in her experience for interpreting its meaning.

This morning she'd been on solid footing, and now . . .

Now she knew that Ravenwood kissed with his eyes open, as if he didn't want to miss a millisecond of her response.

She knew the muscular scaffolding of his torso, the lean lines of his abdomen, the marble-sculpted roundness of his buttocks beneath her questing hands.

The gruff, encouraging noises he made when he was pleased by the progress of said questing hands.

The sensation of being both supported and

overwhelmed by the sheer strength of his body, the force of his kisses. He'd always been larger than life in her mind, like a colossal sphinx carved from limestone.

But beneath that arrogant, mocking exterior she knew now that he had a heart that thumped against her breast, eyes that heated with desire . . . lips that played over hers with such teasing gentleness that it drove her to the brink of madness.

She unbuttoned her pelisse and removed her hat, setting them on the hallway table, moving heedlessly while her mind and heart still raced.

*You're in trouble, Indy. So much trouble.*

She couldn't simply unlearn all of this newly acquired knowledge. She was both an archaeologist and an archivist by nature. She not only wanted to make incredible discoveries, she wanted to pore over them until she'd classified them, until she understood their deeper significance.

The desires, fears, and forces that had driven the lives of ancient peoples. The mistakes that had destroyed them, the passions that had overruled their good sense, or the hope that had sustained them.

The kiss with Ravenwood had given her the exact same thrilling sense of discovery as uncovering an archaeological site. She wanted to know what it meant.

She wanted to know why he'd kissed her, why he'd lost control this time, when all the other times they'd clashed he'd remained mocking and emotionally removed. Yes, he'd wanted to frighten her, but she sensed it had been more than that.

For that matter, why had she kissed him? She couldn't help the detailed, wanton dreams she had about him, but she could have pulled away from his kiss.

*Because you wanted him to kiss you.*

*You want to learn him, understand him. Scratch his surface and dive beneath.*

What she must do was pretend it hadn't happened. Bury these new feelings just as deeply as the old ones. Lock up all of these questions and swallow the key.

Easier said than done.

When the *Observer* made its way to Paris, everyone in British society there would be asking them questions about those ludicrous, grandiose wedding plans she'd described.

She untwisted her hair from the knot her lady's maid, Fern, had fashioned that morning. She needed to loosen something. Unravel something. Because she was wound so tightly she might snap.

She ran her fingers through her hair, scratching her scalp with her fingernails. She was the owner of this body, this mind, this heart . . . no one else.

It was only a game. A diversion tactic.

Their mission was real and of paramount importance for her, and for England.

Viola's piano playing stopped abruptly and Indy heard the sound of muffled cursing.

*Enough thinking. What's done was done. They left for Paris in only a few short hours.*

Indy entered the music room and ducked her head to avoid being hit by the clothbound notebook sailing through the air.

She knelt and picked it up.

"Oh I am sorry." Viola swiveled on the piano stool. "I hope I didn't hit you."

Indy opened the notebook. "Symphony Number Ten in D minor, opus one twenty-six," she read aloud. "Number Ten's not going well?"

"Number Ten will be the death of me. Father's hearing is worsening every day. I can't tell precisely what he wants to convey and so I take stabs in the dark . . . but that's not why I threw the notebook."

Indy joined her by the piano. "What's wrong?"

"I was sacked today." Viola played a ferocious chord progression with her left hand. "Can you imagine? Sacked from the worst music teaching post in all of London. Attempting to finesse a melody from Lady Clara's fingers was a hopeless endeavor, I assure you."

"They let you go because she wasn't making any progress?"

"Lord Bent sacked me because he pinched me on the bum when no one was looking, as he's done so many times before, and something in me just snapped. I couldn't stand there in silence anymore, so I let him know in no uncertain terms that I was not a lump of dough to be pinched and that if he didn't keep his hands to himself I'd be forced to use mine to slap him."

"I suppose that didn't go over very well."

Viola's face fell. "I don't know what I'll do. It was a well-paid position. I'm a fool."

"No you're not." Indy put her arm around Viola's shoulders. "I should go over to his house and put my knife to his throat and see how he likes being at a power disadvantage."

"He would deserve that. Loathsome creature."

"You'll find another position. I'll ask my brother if any of his friends could use the best music instructor in all of England."

"Thank you." Viola smiled. "And thank you for letting me use your piano. This is such a pleasure to play." Her fingers caressed the gleaming ivory keys, teasing out a lilting melody.

Fern entered carrying a tea tray and set it on the table. "All your things are ready for Paris, my lady."

"Wonderful. Have a lovely time with your family while I'm away."

"Thank you, my lady. I do appreciate the extra time." Fern bobbed a curtsy and left.

"Paris?" asked Viola.

"I had a trying day as well," said Indy.

"Tell me what happened."

Indy opened a cabinet and produced a bottle of sherry. "I think we both could use a dash of this in our tea."

Viola sat with her at the table and Indy poured equal parts sherry and tea.

"Now, what's happened?" asked Viola. "You went to your brother's house?"

"It's going to be all over the broadsheets soon, so I may as well tell you. I've done something impulsive."

"You? Do something impulsive?" The feigned incredulity on Viola's face made Indy smile.

"It's shocking, I know."

"What did you do?" asked Viola with a curious glance as she sipped from her cup.

How to explain what had happened when she couldn't make sense of it herself? "While you were fending off boorish unwanted advances, I was succumbing to . . . temptation."

"What sort of temptation?"

*The wicked scoundrel sort.* "It's somewhat difficult to explain, but the heart of the matter is that the Duke of Ravenwood and I are to be wed."

Viola set down her teacup and liquid sloshed over the side. "Have you gone quite mad?"

"It's all hogwash. Don't believe what you read about it in the papers. We're not really going to be married."

"You're marrying . . . or you're not marrying?"

"It's only one of our battles. It's all a game. The Grandest Wedding that Never Will Be. We're seeing who will cave and bow out first." Indy swallowed more tea. "It won't be me."

"I need more tea." Viola poured herself more sherry, and no tea. "But how did this happen?"

"There was a misunderstanding."

"What kind of misunderstanding?"

"We were arguing."

"Arguing is grounds for marriage?"

"We may have been . . . argue-kissing."

"What on earth is argue-kissing?"

"It's when you're half arguing and half kissing. Maybe a better name for it would be hate-kissing. Keep your friends close, your enemies closer, and such. I'm sure it happens to people all the time."

"I'm not sure of that in the least. *I've* never been tempted to *hate-kiss* anyone."

"It's . . . complicated."

"I gathered as much. So . . . you were hate-kissing the Duke of Ravenwood and then what happened?"

"Then my brother, and Mr. Peabody from the *Observer*, walked in upon us."

Viola sprayed tea, which was mostly sherry by now, in an unladylike manner. "What did you say?"

"My brother Edgar was being interviewed about the steam races and he wanted to show Mr. Peabody a model of his steam engine. He didn't know what was happening in his library."

"Hate-kissing," Viola supplied helpfully.

"Exactly. And . . ."

"There's more?"

"There may have been some . . . arse-grabbing."

"Oh sweet Lord. Lady India Rochester. What exactly was occurring in that room?"

Indy bristled. "I don't even know, really. It just . . . happened. And then when we were caught I was so furious with myself and angry with Ravenwood. I didn't want the newspaperman to publish an account and have everyone think that the duke had won the war of the sexes, and so I said the first thing that popped into my head."

Viola groaned. "Oh no. That never ends well."

"I know," said Indy ruefully. "Sometimes I can't hold my tongue. I explained to Mr. Peabody that we had been betrothed since birth but that Ravenwood had finally agreed to set a date. I then proceeded to elaborate upon our wedding plans. I thought that if I made up enough outrageous details Peabody would be distracted from the hate-kissing."

"And did it work?" Viola poured Indy more sherry.

Indy swallowed it in two gulps. "I think so? We'll know when the paper is published. I won't be here because I'll be in Paris. With Ravenwood."

Viola's eyes widened. "Wait. First you were kissing, next there's a wedding to plan, and now you're traveling to Paris with him?"

"We're both searching for the same antiquity to . . . purchase."

Viola shook her head. "Are you certain you know what you're doing?"

The sherry tea was taking the edge off Indy's panic. Maybe it wasn't so bad what she'd done. Maybe everything would work out splendidly.

She'd ignore Ravenwood. They'd find the stone on the very first day. She'd verify the name of the temple and be off to search for Cleopatra's tomb within a week's time.

She downed the remainder of her tea.

"Do you have . . . feelings for the duke?" asked Viola, gazing into her teacup instead of at India.

"I do have feelings for him. Botheration, annoyance, rage, and . . . oh yes, the urge to strangle him most of the time. I haven't had the chance to tell you yet that he discovered my disguise when I infiltrated the Society of Antiquaries yesterday."

"He didn't," said Viola, her eyes widening. "Did he give you away?"

"No, but only because there was no personal gain to be had by doing so. I made a discovery that he was too dense to see and that's what started this whole antiquities quest."

"I still can't believe you snuck into the meeting. Your heart must have been pounding so loudly."

"It was a close thing with that moustache—the paste didn't hold very well."

"I might think about infiltrating the Royal Society of Musicians."

"I don't think your disguise would be as easily believed as mine." Viola was slender with an adorable button nose and large green eyes. Her personality was oversized, but her person was petite.

"The male societies are not all they're cracked up to be," said Indy. "It was actually really boring and staid. All they did was sit around a table and make lists."

"An all-female society would be much more fun, I'd wager," said Viola with a giggle.

"So much fun. We'd drink sherry tea and cook up schemes for female world domination."

"I like that. If they won't let us join their societies then we should start our own."

"A gathering place for all the females who've been barred from the societies they should by rights be eligible to join," agreed Indy.

"I could invite Miss Ardella Finchley to join. She's a brilliant chemist."

Indy didn't have many friends in London. Only her brother, Mari, and Viola. She was traveling so much of the time. It might be nice to associate with other unconventional ladies.

Viola lifted her teacup in a salute. "To the Society for Professional-minded Ladies."

"We can't name our society anything so obvious or we'll be shut down for seditious activities."

"You're right. I hadn't thought of that. It would be rather a perilous undertaking. Perhaps we could call it something domestic and innocuous, like the League of Lady Knitters? We could keep knitting and mending baskets at the ready as cover in case we're raided by the authorities."

"I do like that. Or we could call it something Greek or Latin. Very respectable-sounding, yet non-specific." Indy fingered the shape of the coin necklace beneath her bodice. "Like the Minerva Society, for Minerva, goddess of wisdom."

"I do like that." Viola clinked Indy's teacup with hers. "They'll never even notice us. We'll hide in plain sight."

"We'll do more planning when I return from France," said Indy.

Viola sighed. "I do envy you traveling so freely—I can't leave Papa these days. I love him dearly but he is trying to one's patience."

"Ravenwood would try the patience of a saint. I'm hoping we'll conclude our search swiftly and I'll be able to resume my plans for my next journey."

"He may try the patience of a saint, but please don't let him turn you into a sinner."

Too late for that. She'd been sinning in her dreams with Ravenwood for years now.

The hall clock chimed and Viola jumped. "Is it already so late? I must be going home." She rose from her chair and kissed Indy on the cheek.

"Promise me you'll be careful. I know that you and Ravenwood have a history."

"Not to worry. I don't trust him as far as I can throw him. If I could throw him. Which I couldn't. He's too large."

He was so large. He'd been thrillingly in control as well. Why had that been so thrilling?

Those hands of his . . . She was not a small woman, she had generous curves, and his palms had covered quite a lot of territory.

The sensation had been strange. He'd made her feel almost delicate, and she had to be so very strong and powerful all the time to achieve her aims.

And that kiss . . .

"Indy," said Viola. "I must leave now."

Her mind kept diving off of cliffs. She must grab hold of herself. "Not to worry, all will be well. You're welcome to practice here while I'm away. I should only be gone less than a fortnight."

She escorted Viola to the door before climbing the stairs to her bedchamber.

*You're making a habit of touching me.* He'd said the words flippantly but they'd cut her because they were true.

She'd never been able to shake the desire. The young girl who secretly loved it when he pulled coins from her ears was now the woman who dreamt of him at least once a week.

She'd tried everything: sleeping potions, counting sheep, long walks before bedtime . . . none of it helped.

The dreams started out innocently enough.

Everyday, ordinary Ravenwood interactions. They argued and hurled insults at each other, much as they'd done earlier today, and then . . . the heat of anger transformed into the heat of desire.

And not ethereal courtly desire—earthly, fleshly desire.

Dreams so far beyond the pale that when she woke, panting and soaked with sweat, she was certain that she'd been marked somehow and that the world would be able to see her forbidden longings written across her skin.

They weren't your garden-variety dreams.

Her wicked imagination invented things she was fairly sure she'd never even heard of.

The dreams could take any form, fantastical or mundane, but they always involved carnal pleasure. Probably because their rivalry was all about control and power, the dreams were about that as well.

One night she'd be on top, riding him, and the next time he'd have her down on her belly and he'd take her from behind.

Dream-Indy seemed to think she was far more sophisticated and worldly than she actually was. Sometimes she even experienced a pleasure spasm in her sleep and awoke with a sweet throbbing between her legs.

Even thinking about it made her feel a little tingly.

She'd very discreetly taken a lover once, a fellow archaeologist from Sweden, and it had been . . . nice enough. Safe and . . . rather boring, if the truth be told. She hadn't understood what all the fuss was about.

All that heaving and awkwardness.

There'd been no sparks flying, no racing heart and damp palms.

Since then she'd never even considered taking another lover.

She wasn't saving herself—she was devoted to her dream of becoming a world-renowned archaeologist. Which was the entire point of going to Paris to find the stone.

She spread the map out on a table.

*Where are you sleeping, Cleopatra?* Beneath a temple, in a stone chamber, with a mask of gold . . . she was somewhere. And Indy was going to find her.

She thought of Shakespeare's description from *Antony and Cleopatra*: "Age cannot wither her, nor custom stale her infinite variety. Other women cloy the appetites they feed; but she makes hungry where most she satisfies . . ."

Revered or reviled, Cleopatra had been without doubt one of the world's most powerful women. A fascinating character who educated herself in a time when women were kept ignorant, and overcame great adversity in her quest for power.

She'd also possessed a grand theatrical streak and hadn't been inclined to modesty. Her love affair with Antony was purported to have been both passionate and volatile.

Had Cleopatra and Antony kissed like Indy and Ravenwood had kissed today? She'd called it an act of war, and it had been. He'd advanced and she hadn't been intelligent enough to retreat. She'd launched her own offensive without any strategy and with no thought to the long-term consequences of her actions.

And now she was paying the price.

*You can't be trusted to keep your hands to yourself.*

*You must remain in control of your body and your emotions.*

Focus on the larger goal. Find the stone, finish her translation, and leave England.

Their journey was only a new branch of their deep-rooted rivalry.

The rules of engagement remained the same.

Never reveal her true thoughts. Never ask him searching questions. Never let him see her buried pain.

Guard against attraction. Parry with jokes and insults.

And, above all, guard what was left of her heart.

He'd wounded her once.

She would never allow him to wound her again.

# Chapter 8

❧

"A FEW INCHES TO the left and the bullet would have pierced your heart."

*Tell me something I don't know.*

Dr. Ackerman probed the scar tissue on his chest, checking to make sure there was no metal left under the skin.

There wasn't. Raven had used his own knife to extract the bullet and other fragments of metal.

If only he could extract Indy from his heart so easily. Take a swig of whisky, grit his teeth, heat his knife in the fire, and thrust it deep enough to cut out all the fragments of her that lived beneath his skin.

All through the brief carriage ride to Sir Malcolm's estate just outside of London, his thoughts had circled like buzzards.

He'd known there would be a confrontation—nothing could ever be peaceful or calm with Indy—but a passionate kiss, a counterfeit engagement, a knife fight in an alleyway . . . It wasn't like him to become embroiled in scandals he didn't expressly create for his own purposes.

Only one person in the entire world held the power to push his control so far off its axis: Indy.

When they were children hunting for buried

treasure in fields, he'd dreamed of traveling the world and discovering new antiquities with her by his side—his fearless companion.

He'd also believed that fathers could never be murdered, that life was filled with hope, and that good always triumphed over evil in the end.

Once upon a time he'd even believed in love. And love had seemed so simple to describe—a pair of light grayish-purple eyes, a quick smile, and an even quicker wit.

Now she'd sharpened that intellect of hers to a dangerous weapon.

If he weren't careful, she'd slice right through the veil separating his two lives.

He'd suggested she teach him how to use a knife so that he could assess her current skill level. She'd been extremely adept, with quick reflexes and a sophisticated understanding of how to best someone of superior strength.

Pretending to be inept with a dagger had proven surprisingly difficult for him, though. When she lunged for his chest every instinct he'd honed to deadly precision had leapt to the fore and it had taken every ounce of his control to feign a clumsy defense.

He'd been trained in the art of knife fighting on these very grounds, as well as the arts of fencing, bare-knuckle boxing, and other hand-to-hand combat styles.

He could have had Indy on the ground in three seconds flat.

Stretched beneath him, soft curves and muffled curses.

Arms pinned above her head. Entirely at his mercy. *You'd like that, wouldn't you?*

Gods, he was a fool. He never should have gone to Banksford's house looking for her. He'd only wanted to protect her.

*Wrong.*

If he were tied to a chair and his interrogator were torturing him and he supplied an answer as flimsy as that, he'd receive a lash across his back or his chest . . . or some other more sensitive area.

*Wrong. Try again. Why did you go to see her today?*

*Because I wanted to talk to her. Because sometimes I go for years only catching brief glimpses of her and I wanted more.*

*Better. But what did you want exactly?*

*I wanted . . . I want . . . her.*

In his arms, his bed, by his side . . . he'd always wanted her.

"The scar appears to be healing nicely and the bullet was removed cleanly," said the doctor. "You're a very lucky man."

"I don't believe in luck."

"Then believe that the Almighty has a purpose left for you, for he surely saved you from bleeding to death on the streets of Athens."

"In a church," said Raven.

"Pardon?"

"I nearly bled to death in a church. The brethren ministered to my wounds."

Everything had been going well until the night he met Jones in the public plaza. The ambush had taken them completely by surprise.

It had been a sunny afternoon. A public square.

Yet four of Le Triton's trained assassins had attacked with knives and pistols.

*Kill or be killed.*

Jones was dead.

Raven had been left for dead. He'd lain there with flies buzzing around his ears and people shouting at him. He'd played dead until he was sure his attackers were gone. Then he'd staggered into a nearby church, faint with blood loss, the sound of death ringing in his ears.

As the priests bathed his wounds, he watched his blood mix with water and run in rivulets across the stone floor.

Perhaps it had been the loss of blood, or the sun shining through the stained-glass window depicting a female saint with piercing eyes.

Faced with death, he'd questioned the choices he'd made. At thirteen, he'd been so certain of his destiny. Become a spy for the Crown, as his father had been before him. Become an agent and clear his father's name.

But he'd been so young when he made the choice and Sir Malcolm sent him away to the brutal, grueling secret training school in Scotland.

When Indy had made the quip about a thrilling assignment for the Crown he'd wanted to grip her by the shoulders and shake some sense into her. There was nothing glamorous or exciting about his work.

Long periods of tracking and surveillance, waiting for someone to make a mistake, to show their hand, followed by intense bouts of intrigue and combat.

Stop a war. Topple a despot.

The physician dug his thumb into a sore place on his back.

Raven made no sound, though it hurt like the blazes.

He avoided his reflection in the large glass mounted on the wall. He knew what he would see; a map of scars detailing every battle he'd fought.

The wounds belied his reputation as someone who hired others to do his dirty work.

Indy could never see him less than fully clothed. Not that she would ever have cause to see him unclothed. Just as he'd never see her less than fully clothed.

Or gloriously naked.

Tangled in his sheets and purring with pleasure.

His cock stirred. Dr. Ackerman glanced at him.

Let the man think that pain gave Raven pleasure.

There were brothels catering to that—men who wanted to be whipped with riding crops or even beaten with fists. He'd never understood the reasoning behind the fixation.

He absorbed too many beatings during the daylight to want one at night.

Thinking of Indy always stirred his blood, but it wasn't only erotic imaginings that captured his mind. What sometimes stirred him the most were far more objectionable thoughts.

What his life might have been like if he'd followed a different path. Married Indy and gained a partner in adventure . . . traveling, living, discovering together.

His hands never bloodied . . . his body never battered.

Sometimes, in the quiet moments between awareness and his fitful version of sleep, he pictured them standing before an altar. He painted their wedding night in vivid color and detail.

And then sometimes, when he wasn't being vigilant enough, a fantasy rose in his mind. The same fantasy that had filled his mind while he lay in that church, not knowing whether he would live or die.

Sitting with Indy in comfortable chairs in front of a fireplace in a house somewhere. He never knew where they were, and never cared, because she was there with him and that was all he'd ever wanted.

They were older. When she smiled there were faint wrinkles around her lovely eyes. He loved the way the firelight caught and held the first strands of silver threading her black hair.

They weren't alone.

There were two children at their feet. A girl of about four or five, playing with alphabet blocks, forming words already because she was clever like her mother, and a younger boy, who kept trying to steal his sister's blocks and put them into his mouth.

It was the worst sentimental claptrap.

Imagining that he and Indy were married and had children. An alternate path. The path that could have been.

"You must sleep more," said Dr. Ackerman. "Lack of rest can impair your judgment and dexterity."

"I'll sleep when I'm dead."

"You'll die sooner than not if you don't sleep."

Raven grunted. One day he wouldn't pass his physical and they'd put him out to pasture with the other retired agents. If he was lucky.

Or he could die with a knife in his gut or a bullet in his heart on a sunlit street in a public square.

Either way, there would be no warm smiles and peaceful family moments in his future. His brother Colin would inherit the dukedom when he was gone. Colin was an honorable, conventional man and he'd married a timid, conventional girl and they were already expecting their first child. Raven had received a letter from Colin inviting him to attend the christening, when it happened.

Raven never accepted Colin's invitations. It was better this way. Better to maintain the distance between them.

"You may garb yourself," the doctor said, gathering his instruments into a leather bag.

Raven dressed and headed for the shooting range.

His hands had been shaking badly since he'd nearly died in Athens.

He must stop thinking about anything other than the task ahead.

He must prove himself today.

RAVEN COCKED HIS brass percussion pistol and aimed at the row of small glass bottles arranged on the faraway brick wall.

*His Grace has just made me the happiest lady on earth . . . by finally agreeing to set a date for our wedding.*

Indy's words kept floating to the top of his mind.

He fired, but none of the bottles danced and shattered.

Not even close.

His concentration was the thing that had shattered.

No doubt Malcolm was watching from the house. Raven must banish all thoughts of Indy.

There were no servants here to reload a man's gun. This was a training ground for agents who must fend for themselves while in the field.

Here was the clandestine society Indy had imagined. Inside the house, there was a staircase concealed by a bookcase, leading to a secret subterranean espionage training facility where he was only a number, not a duke.

Dukedoms didn't matter inside these walls. The petty quibbling of the aristocracy over precedence and patrimonies—none of it mattered.

He reloaded and placed his forearm on the low brick wall, steadying his pistol.

*The taste of her lips, her tongue. The softness of her breasts crushed against his chest. Her perfume overwhelming his senses.*

*You know you'd do it all again. You'd risk everything for another taste.*

He fired, but the raw emotion of the memory skewed his bullet away from the target.

A spy must remain emotionless. Detached.

*Integrity. Intelligence. Courage. Selflessness. Resilience.*

These were the values at the core of his training. From the age of thirteen he'd been indoctrinated by his instructors, taught to separate his heart from his mind.

Love had no place on the path he'd chosen.

He was a soldier. A warrior. He knew his duty and nothing could distract him from it.

This was a mission, just like any other mission.

If Indy must go to Paris, he'd be there to protect her. It was the next best thing to her not going at all.

Finally, he hit a bottle, then another, until the entire row of bottles lay in pieces on the ground and the acrid scent of smoke filled his nostrils.

Miss Mina Penny, Sir Malcolm's niece, approached him from across the lawn. She was a pretty thing with honey-blonde hair and a sweet, delicate-featured face that betrayed her every emotion.

Raven had known her since she was a child, come to live with Malcolm after both of her parents died in a carriage accident. Now she served as Sir Malcom's secretary. She was also a crack shot.

"Good day, Your Grace," she said when she reached him. "Uncle Malcolm is ready for you now in the library."

"Thank you, Miss Mina. Lovely day for shooting, though there's quite a chill in the air."

She was wrapped in a gray fur-lined cloak. She set down the case she carried and opened it to reveal a gleaming brass sporting pistol.

"Is that one new?" he asked.

"It's the new Greener muzzleloader. I'm to test it for Uncle." She tapped the barrel. "There's a nice hardness to it."

Was that a naughty gleam in her eye? Time for Raven to leave. Flirtatious young girls were not his cup of tea. He preferred stronger stuff.

"Why have you never married, Your Grace?" Miss Mina asked abruptly, leveling the pistol at him.

It wasn't loaded, at least. "I'm not the marrying kind. My younger brother will inherit the dukedom and he's already working on producing an heir."

"I might not be the marrying kind, either, but I want to have a Season, nonetheless. I want to live in London proper instead of moldering away out here in the countryside. I want to visit the London Tavern and debate with all the radicals and poets and musicians. I want to . . . I want to do *something* besides stay cooped up here my whole life."

She led a sheltered existence, which was ironic, given that she was living in a hotbed of espionage. He'd often wondered if she'd guessed what really went on around here.

She pouted. "Uncle M never lets me go anywhere."

"He's protective of you."

"I'm nineteen—a woman grown. I know what happens around here, don't think that I don't."

She fixed him with an unnerving stare, still holding the pistol aimed at his heart. Surely she didn't know *everything*.

"A great lot of shooting and fencing," he said, "and—"

"I may be female but I'm not a dullard." She lowered the pistol.

He kept his expression bland. "You serve as Sir Malcolm's secretary, do you not?"

"Tedious paperwork; estate sales, antiquities behests and the like. I've been working on . . . other things." She leaned toward him. "I wonder if you might test something for me?"

She lifted a concealed compartment at the bottom of her pistol case and handed him a gold pocket watch. "This is something new," she whispered, glancing back toward the house. "If you're in a tight spot and you've no other way out, you open it here," she demonstrated. "And then you turn the face one half turn. No! Don't do it now—unless you want to fall unconscious."

Raven paused. He'd been given concealed weaponry before, ingenious devices such as knives hidden in walking sticks, and pistols small enough to tuck into the back of his trousers. But this was something new. And he'd certainly had no idea that Mina might have an interest or knowledge in the weapons of his trade.

"I'm not sure I should be encouraging you," he said.

"No," she said with a pert smile. "You should be thanking me. Because there may come a time when this watch will save your life. After you turn it, you press down. Then you'll hold your breath and fling it at the person you wish to incapacitate. It won't harm them, only tranquilize them, send them into Morpheus's arms for a good many hours. It's my latest invention. But don't tell Uncle. I'm still in the development stages."

Raven tucked the watch into his pocket. "You're going to be a whole lot of trouble for some man, someday, Miss Mina."

But she'd never be his trouble. She was aesthetically pleasing, like a sculpture carved by a master, but he preferred his women older. On the tall side. With breasts that would overflow his palms.

Slim hips, yet a generous arse. Limbs for days . . .

Black hair and grayish-purple eyes.

Her eyes sparkling, Miss Mina curtsied. "I'll take that as a compliment, Your Grace. You'd better go to Uncle now."

"I think I'd better. Excuse me." Raven made his bow and left.

He carried his pistol case back to the house, leaving Miss Mina to her target practice, her inventions, and her dreams of a London Season.

He found Sir Malcolm in the library. "Your niece seems a bit restless," he said.

Malcolm glanced up sharply. "Did she say something to you?"

"She asked me why I wasn't married, leveled a pistol at me, and told me she was nineteen and that you couldn't keep her cloistered here forever."

"Damnation." Malcolm struck his palm against his desk. "I can't stand the thought of letting her go. I know what's out there." His eyes were bleak.

He'd lost his wife and young daughter one year before Raven came to live with him.

"The world is a dangerous place," Raven said gently. "Especially for young ladies. But she wants to have a London Season. You must let her go."

He'd been trying to do the same thing with Indy—protect her from harm by telling her to stay home—and it hadn't done any good.

"Mina is different from other young ladies," said Malcolm. "She's far more inquisitive and inventive, she says whatever eccentric thing comes into her head. She has a genius for all things mechanical. Can you imagine her at Almack's Assembly, explaining to the Lady Patronesses about how to modify a pistol's firing mechanism to make it go off more quickly?"

"Surely you have a female relative who might guide her."

"There is my aunt. She never had children of her own. She might welcome Mina, but . . ."

"You don't want to let her go."

"She's such a comfort to me. And I don't want her to be hurt."

"You must allow her to have her freedom," said Raven quietly.

"I know. I'm just not ready yet."

"I think she was flirting with me."

"The deuce you say! I'll have you drawn and quartered."

"I didn't flirt back, but she could benefit from a woman's influence. She's surrounded by men here, and not the type of men you'd want her to be involved with, if you take my meaning."

"I hadn't thought of it. I still think of her as a child. But you're right. If she must be taken away from me, I'd rather have her find a perfectly ordinary man to marry, not someone . . ."

"Someone like me."

A man with too many dark secrets. A man with blood on his hands.

"Your words," said Malcolm. "Not mine."

"Lucky for you, I'm not on the marriage mart."

"Speaking of which, how did your meeting with Lady India go?"

"It was exactly as you said. I had no luck at all."

"So she'll be going to Paris as well. That's a complication, but it shouldn't be a hindrance. Could even be useful."

"Wait, there's more. I . . ." There was no easy way to say this. "We kissed. And a newspaperman may have walked in on us."

"Good God, man, how did that happen?"

"We were at Banksford's residence and Mr. Peabody of the *Observer* was there to interview him about his steam engine."

"Well this does complicate things."

"Complicated doesn't even begin to describe it. You're going to read some very unusual details about our upcoming nuptials in the paper. It's all hogwash. We're not really going to marry."

"I see."

Those two words held volumes of unspoken meaning.

He saw that Raven had lost control.

He saw that Indy was his weakness. His Achilles heel.

Malcolm studied the paper he held. "You've passed the tests. By the skin of your teeth, mind you."

"You've already had my debriefing. It was an

impossible situation. There were four of them and two of us. They caught us unawares."

"You've suffered an injury. No shame in taking a holiday."

"Save your concern for someone who needs it."

"I think you're ready to go back out but there are others who might question my decision."

"You mean Lord Grey." He was Sir Malcolm's direct superior at the Foreign Office and there were those who said he could become the next Secretary of State for Foreign Affairs.

"He's concerned about your stability."

"Just give me my marching orders and I'll see the job done."

"See that you do," said Malcolm. He handed Raven a dossier with the word CONFIDENTIAL printed across the front. "Here's the latest intelligence on Le Triton. Also profiles of Beauchamp at the Louvre, Ambassador Petrov and . . . Sir Charles."

"Why Sir Charles?" Raven was confused by his inclusion. He knew the British ambassador to France quite well.

"We're afraid he's gone somewhat feral. He's taken Margot Delacroix as his mistress and may be feeding her information."

Margot Delacroix, the most alluring of the Paris demimondaines, and the most dangerous. She was a French royalist agent who would stop at nothing to keep the Bourbon regime in power. She was also Le Triton's close associate. Because of her ties to the underworld, Raven had shared her bed once, more than three years past. She hadn't betrayed any confidential information, and Raven had admired the skill with which she had attempted to manipulate him to her purposes.

Sir Charles was playing a hazardous game.

Raven placed the dossier in his pistol case.

"Engaging Le Triton will require a bargaining chip," said Malcolm.

"The Wish Diamond. He's been after it for years."

"A rumor will soon spread through Paris that you've made bad investments and are in need of cash. Your cover is that you're in Paris to sell the diamond necklace but you won't go through an intermediary. You'll arrange a face-to-face meeting with Le Triton, inside his fortress."

"I'll make the deal, or I'll take his base by force."

"Don't be a hothead. There's a reason we haven't been able to bring him down. He owns the French police. And we've never been able to gain a clear picture of the layout of his fortress."

"I'll find a way inside."

"Just don't do anything stupid. You'd be one man against dozens. I'll have a team in place to help you—you'll receive my signal." Malcolm stood and walked around his desk. "Now that I think about it, your traveling companion will make a fetching model for the necklace. You can have her wear it to Le Triton's gaming establishment in the Palais Royal."

"Not going to happen, Malcolm. I won't use her as bait."

"You've used females as diversions before.

Treat this like any other assignment. You told me there was no attachment between you."

It wasn't just any assignment. Not when Indy was involved.

"Those women received compensation for their aid and they were aware of the risks involved," said Raven.

"I think having her there could be beneficial. She seemed eager for the mission. From what you've told me about her she's not defenseless."

"I won't use her as bait," Raven repeated.

Malcolm shrugged. "Maybe you'll reconsider once you're there."

A footman delivered a message. "Ah, from our friend Lord Grey," said Malcolm.

"Telling you not to send me on assignment, I'll wager."

Malcolm slit the letter open. "You're wrong. He anticipated that I would send you back to the field and he sent a message."

Raven lifted an eyebrow. "Well? What does he say? I know it's not Godspeed and good luck."

Malcolm chuckled. "It says 'Tell Ravenwood not to cock it up this time.'"

"Not a chance. This mission will be flawless. Smooth as silk." In and out with stealth and precision.

This was a test.

Fail this mission and they would force him to retire. It would be far more difficult to fully prove his father's innocence when Raven was no longer an agent. And then what would he have sacrificed everything for?

"Be careful," said Malcolm, shaking Raven's hand.

"I'm always careful."

"Don't let emotion color your judgment. I know that you and the lady have a history."

"That won't be a problem." Raven took his leave.

He had one purpose only. If he kept his gaze firmly locked on the target, his hand would never waiver. He must locate the stone swiftly and return it to England. So swiftly that Indy wouldn't have a chance to court danger.

He'd never allow her to be harmed by association with him.

He might never be able to extract her from his heart but at least he could continue to make her think the worst of him. She'd said she didn't wish him to be pleasant. He was prepared to be as tiresome as she desired.

Lewd, crude, and rude. The Ravenwood she knew and loathed.

A brick wall. A blunt instrument.

By the end of this journey she'd wish she were anywhere else than with him.

# Chapter 9

❧

INDY ARRIVED AT the coaching inn early that evening and waited while Ravenwood supervised the placement of their trunks atop the traveling coach he'd hired for their exclusive use on the overnight journey to Dover.

When all was arranged to his satisfaction, he handed her into the coach. "Where's your maidservant?" he asked. "We should be off immediately."

"I never travel with my maid. I'm accustomed to doing for myself. While Fern's a dear, she's forever scorching my hair with heated tongs, or attempting to wrestle me into fashionable gowns. I find her more of an encumbrance than an aid on archaeological expeditions."

His face registered shock and then censure. "Indy, I had assumed you would at the very least bring a maidservant with you on our journey. It would be prudent."

"Why, are you planning to ravish me?"

He frowned. "Don't be ridiculous."

Why would that be ridiculous? Of course she didn't *want* him to ravish her. But she didn't think it was so very strange to arrive at the conclusion that the lusty thoughts she had about him might be reciprocal, given the kiss they'd shared.

The kiss that could never have an encore per-
formance.

"Well I'm not planning to ravish you," she assured him, "so you may as well climb into this
carriage so that our quest may begin."

His eyes darkened to flat brown. "Are you certain you want to go through with this? Why don't
you travel to Egypt as you had planned? It's not
too late to change your mind."

"Good try," she muttered.

"I wonder, if I had begged you to come with me,
would you have stayed home out of principle?"

"Nothing could keep me from the relic we seek.
Not even the prospect of your irritating company
on the journey."

There went that sardonic brow of his, lifting over a mocking expression. "That's what I
thought you'd say, my super-dainty Indy, who
sings as sweetly as a nightingale."

Now he was quoting Shakespeare? "You must
be hard of hearing, my ruffian rogue," she rejoined. "Now if you don't mind I had hoped to
reach Dover early tomorrow morning." She patted
the seat cushion. "Don't worry, I won't bite."

A fleeting expression of something like panic
crossed his face. He doffed his hat and made a
slight bow. "I'll do anything for a woman with
a knife."

He climbed into the coach and a groom closed
the door.

The carriage left the yard.

The traveling coach he'd hired was by no
means as luxurious as one of her brother's car-

riages. The interior was commodious, built for six or more passengers, and the seats were covered in faded and cracked leather. There was a decidedly unromantic lingering odor of snuff and moldy cheese.

Which was perfect.

Stale snuff and lumpy leather upholstery was far preferable to sandalwood and soft, plush velvet.

Otherwise, this might be too much like the beginning of one of her bawdy dreams. Alone in a carriage with Ravenwood . . . on an overnight journey to Dover.

In one of her dreams, all manner of depraved and degenerate things would be bound to happen.

She was determined that nothing worse than a little ribald repartee was going to occur in this carriage tonight.

The best way to safeguard her heart was to pretend that she didn't own one. She was fully capable of out-maneuvering Ravenwood at his own game.

He drank like a fish? She'd guzzle him under the table—or under the carriage bench.

He was calm, cold, and collected? She'd be an iceberg with a side of frost.

Everything was a bawdy joke to him? She had dozens of off-color jests at the ready, learned from the sailors on her voyages.

And the number-one way she was going to win was this: she would never lose her temper. Not once. No matter what asinine things he did or said.

She unlocked her handsome mahogany traveling kit to reveal silver flasks, cups, and table settings gleaming against red velvet.

The carriage jostled but she expertly extracted two silver cups with handles shaped like sinuous dragons.

"What's your poison?" she asked Ravenwood.

He turned away from the window he'd been studiously staring out of since they left the White Bear coaching inn. "Pardon?"

"Old French cognac, Scotch whisky, rum, gin . . . I'm practically a traveling tavern."

"I'm partial to Scotch whisky," he said with a bemused look.

She selected the whisky and concentrated on pouring it into the cup instead of onto the upholstery.

She handed him the cup. "Peatmoor Old Scotch whisky." She poured a generous portion for herself. "If the bottle's to be believed it 'carries the wild rough scent of the Highland breeze.'"

"To your health." Ravenwood lifted his cup.

They swallowed at the same time, their gazes locked. She downed the fiery liquid without sputtering or saying any of the foul words that sprang to mind.

She'd been practicing.

She wiped her sleeve across her lips. "Another?"

Ravenwood arched one brow, shadows playing over the keen edges of his handsome face. "Why not?"

The whisky burned going down her throat but

she approved of the mellow warmth it spread through her belly.

"Ah." She swirled the dregs in her cup. "Puts one in mind of a good stiff breeze to lift a bonnie Highland laddie's . . . tartan," she said with her best Scottish burr.

Ravenwood choked on his drink. "Have you even been to Scotland?"

"No, but they make delicious whisky and the men wear skirts. What's not to like?"

"They're called kilts."

"Whatever they're called, I hear they wear nothing underneath. A Highland breeze might be the beginning of a very special show." She tilted her head, glancing lasciviously at his lap. "For a lady's eyes only."

The remainder of his whisky spilled down his cravat.

She hid a smile behind her silver cup. Her plan was off to a capital start. She was definitely out-rogueing him by a healthy margin.

"You really must be more careful, Your Grace. That's very expensive imported contraband."

"I've Scottish blood on my mother's side." He hooked one ankle over the opposite knee and leaned back in his seat, the very picture of aristocratic nonchalance. "I've been known to wear a kilt on occasion."

If he'd been wearing a kilt, the foot-propped-on-the-knee move would have given her a very entertaining show indeed.

*Devil take her wicked imagination.*

"Is it warm in here?" She fanned herself with the spy novel she'd brought to read on the journey. Actually it was quite chilly. She had woolen blankets tucked around her and heated coals in a brass warmer at her feet.

"When did you start drinking whisky?" he asked. "Doesn't seem up your alley."

"You don't know *what's* up my alley," she said archly.

"Apparently not." He ran the edge of the cup over his chin, drawing her attention to the stubble of whiskers already shading his angular jaw. Why did that faint, shadowy evidence of his masculinity make her want to kiss him again?

Must be the whisky.

He spread his arms over the back of the carriage seat. They stretched nearly the entire length of the seat. His eyes were the color of the whisky in her glass.

He caught her eye and his lips slid into a slow smile.

If she'd been the kind of woman who blushed, her face would have turned beet red.

"Seems to me that you might try to ravish me after a few more glasses of whisky," he said. "Women don't hold their spirits in the same way as men. Wait, wait—" he interrupted her indignant protests. "Before you accuse me of being an arrogant jackass, my observation is based strictly on scientific facts. My body mass is larger than yours. I've more surface area to absorb the spirits."

He certainly had a large surface area.

His hands were simply massive, his fingers long enough to wrap around the entire silver cup. She tested the girth of the cup she held. Her thumb and forefinger only stretched halfway around.

She caught him staring at her fingers with a strained expression. Perhaps he was imagining depraved things as well.

One wouldn't think a gentleman's hand would be such an object for erotic fixation, but in her dreams his hands did so many delicious things. They fondled her breasts. Stroked her between the legs. Lifted her by the waist and settled her down over his . . .

*Bollocks!* Maybe whisky hadn't been such a brilliant plan.

It was time for the unsavory jokes. They couldn't talk about their conflict, their past, or anything else that would be detrimental to her heart.

She poured another glass of whisky for him and a much smaller one for herself. "Have you heard the one about the sign on the bawdy-house door?"

"Come again?"

"While that would be a good sign," she admitted, "but this one said, 'We're not home. Take the well-beaten path.'"

He snorted. "Do you even know what that means?"

"Certainly I do. And there's more where that jest came from. I've a whole arsenal of bawdy jokes at the ready."

"Indy." He set his empty cup on the seat beside him. "This really isn't a competition, you know. You don't have to best me at everything. You can drop the bravura act."

"I'm merely being a congenial traveling companion. And maybe it's not an act. You don't know me anymore. This could be what I'm like with my intimates."

"What intimates? As far as I know your only friends are your brother and his wife. You're married to your archaeological work. Your idea of excitement is a fourteen-hour excavation in a dusty old burial site. You spend more time with skeletons than living society."

*Don't lose your temper. You're made of ice, remember?*

"At least my passion is for the betterment of womankind, not simply my own immediate gratification. And I've sacrificed much for my work—my reputation, for one thing. Mamas shield their daughters from me as if my independent spirit might rub off on their precious offspring like polish from a boot."

"I'm certain mothers shield their daughters more stringently from me than from you."

"But that's because you're fulfilling everyone's expectations, not flouting them. You're supposed to be an arrogant rogue whose collection of lovers is only eclipsed by his private collection of antiquities." Her shoulder bumped against the window. She was as far away from him as possible now. "It's so very unoriginal, Ravenwood."

And it still made her so furious.

Despite all her resolutions to remain emotionless, the all-too-familiar anger swelled up as if she'd hit her mind with a hammer by accident. He'd chosen such a useless life over the one they'd planned together.

She'd carried this pit of anger in her belly for so long, like she'd swallowed the pit of a peach. It felt like it could choke her. But she would never ever ask him why he'd changed. Why he'd stopped answering her letters.

*You can't walk backward into the future. What's done is done.*

She opened her novel, even though it was too dark now to see more than shadows outside the windows.

The words on the page were too blurry to read.

It was always like this when she was with him. One moment she wanted to jump into his lap, and the next she wanted to lash out and find a way to hurt him, as he'd hurt her.

The whisky seemed to make it worse, if anything.

Those feelings should be dead and buried. They shouldn't be haunting her still.

INDY'S STRAIGHT-SLASHING DARK eyebrows drew closer. He'd angered her, as he always did. She was tucked into one side of the commodious coach, no longer playing the out-rogue-the-rogue game. The severely cut blue wool coat she wore had epaulets, like a military captain.

She didn't need feminine adornments to be the most beautiful woman in any room. Her eyes were jewels enough. Her sable hair the only silk she required.

This was familiar ground. They were back to arguing. All was well with the world.

And yet . . . he wanted to make her smile, not frown.

He wanted to defend himself, defend his choices.

Tell her that he took pride in his work, and was one of the best at what he did. Or he had been the best until that day in Athens.

Until . . . but he wouldn't think of that now. He'd been having nightmares about it every night. Dreams where he didn't make it off the street and he watched himself bleed to death from somewhere outside of his body. He still couldn't fathom that he'd been communicating secrets to Jones, and Jones had been a traitor.

His specialty was controlling conflicts. He either resolved them, or he prevented them from happening.

The threads of a complicated conflict, the egos involved, the profit and fortunes to be made, the lives that would be lost—he gathered all of the intelligence and wove it into plausible scenarios and then he found the thread to pick to unravel the war before it began.

The Rosetta Stone theft could start a war, there was no doubt about it.

Indy was part of the plan to recover the stone, nothing more.

"We can't all be noble crusaders for a cause. Some of us like our world of familiar creature comforts," he remarked.

"I will always choose the road less traveled," she replied. "I'm trying to achieve something worthwhile with my life. I need the stone more than you do and that's why I'm here. I'm also here because I don't trust you not to sell it to the highest bidder," she said cuttingly.

That caught Raven off guard. "You think I'd betray my country?"

"I think you're on the side of Ravenwood above all else. It's your interests that drive every decision you make. Which mistress to take, which treasure to hunt, which velvet waistcoat to wear . . . it's all self-serving."

"I may be selfish, but I'm not a traitor."

The word hung in the air between them. Traitor. His own father had been accused of High Treason. Part of the reason Raven had become a secret agent was so that he could exonerate his father. The charges had never been proven, but they hadn't been fully dropped, either.

"Very well, you wouldn't sell the stone," she conceded. "But you do have items in your collection that belong in museums."

"You've never kept any treasure for yourself?"

"Never. I'm on the side of history. The stone should be in a museum, nowhere else. I don't much care which museum, as long as I have access to it. Although ladies never do have the access they deserve to educational resources."

"I didn't make the rules, Indy."

"But you profit by them. In your world the line between the sexes is sharply divided. Men are given most of the pie, and women are left to make do with a slender slice."

"You're an exception. You have to admit that many females simply aren't cut out for strenuous pursuits."

She set her book down on the seat with a thump. "Said every man who ever tried to justify denying a female an education or an opportunity."

*Lewd, crude, and rude. The Ravenwood she knew and loathed,* he reminded himself.

"What if all the women started chasing after antiquities?" he asked with a calculated smirk. "There'd be no one left to share my bed."

"That doesn't even deserve a response," she said scathingly.

"Are you going to tell me why you require the stone so badly? I gather you're translating a hieroglyphic."

"My aim isn't your concern. We share a goal for a few weeks and then I go my way and you go yours. You descend back into the murky hell you call a life and I go about the business of making history."

"Making history. Must be a prestigious prize you're after."

"I only have one life to live. I want it to mean something. I want to make the world a better place for young girls. A world where they're encouraged to follow their interests and talents. Where they're given the education to achieve their goals. Where their achievements are mea-

sured by the same criteria as their male counter-
parts. Someday that world will exist. I know it
will. And when it does, I want to have done my
part. I want the women of the future to look back
and know that I helped open one small door for
them by illuminating the lives of unconventional
females throughout history."

He wanted to shout *huzzah!* and raise his cup
to her.

As a young boy, he'd believed that all girls
could jump as high, run as fast, outsmart, outmaneuver, and generally best any boy they met.

He'd grown up knowing that girls were the
equals, if not the superiors, of boys.

Then he'd gone off to the secret spy training
school, where girls were excluded, and they'd
tried to make him believe that he was superior
because of the thing dangling between his legs,
but he hadn't bought what they were selling.

Indy had ruined him for that notion since birth.

He wanted to say these things aloud.

What he said was: "You've always had your
head in the clouds, Indy."

"And you weren't always such a horse's arse,
Ravenwood."

She opened her book and pretended to read
but he could tell she was fuming.

He didn't want her to hate him but he must
maintain a safe distance. A gulf of animosity and
mistrust. Otherwise he might be tempted to tell
her how amazing he thought she was. Or how
much he believed in what she was trying to do.

He had to be content with doing whatever

he could behind the scenes to make sure she achieved her goals. Several times he'd intervened on her behalf during her archaeological expeditions, remaining anonymous, of course.

"What are you reading?" he asked.

"*My Lady Spy*, by Mrs. Edgecombe." She held up the cover for him to see. "Spy novels are quite popular now since the Napoleonic wars. I thought this might prove useful for our expedition. Have you read any spy novels?"

*I live them.* This was a treacherous topic. "Can't say I have. I think I'll try and sleep now. You should as well." He turned away from her, balling his greatcoat into a pillow, and stretched out on the bench.

Spy novels were off-limits.

So was speaking his true feelings. Not that he had feelings. Brick wall. Blunt instrument.

He truly had assumed she'd bring a chaperone. He should have known Indy never did anything the conventional way.

This journey would be over soon. Recover the stone. See that no harm came to Indy.

Try to ignore how beautiful she looked in the gathering dark, how her lips turned the color of wine.

How he wanted so badly to taste her again.

# Chapter 10

~

INDY SHIVERED AS *he touched the base of her neck, his fingers following the bone-knots of her spine down her back.*

*She wore only a thin shift and it was pooled around her waist, her breasts bared for him in the cold air.*

*He was seated behind her.*

*Was he naked as well? She turned her head to see.*

*His white shirt hung open and he wore a kilt. A kilt? A tartan woven from reds and blues.*

*And his hair was . . . she snuck another glance. His hair was long. Grown past his shoulders, long and thick and tangled. My, it had grown so fast.*

*She shivered with desire.*

*"Are you wearing anything underneath that kilt?" she asked.*

*"Not a stitch, lass," he whispered in her ear in a thick Scottish brogue. He lifted the hem of his kilt and she quickly averted her gaze.*

*"You're not Scottish, Ravenwood," she scolded.*

*"Call me Raven," he whispered hoarsely.*

*She gulped. She'd known that his intimate friends called him Raven. Not Daniel, not Ravenwood. A new name. A new intimacy.*

*"Remove your shirt, Raven," she whispered boldly.*

*Solid arms folded around her, his head in the crook*

*of her neck, his breath rustling across her cheek like wind through the last remaining leaves of an oak tree in winter.*

*"You've always wanted to touch me, Indy, and I want to touch you," he whispered.*

*"Where?" Please let it be where she hoped . . .*

*"Here." His hand skimmed across to her belly and lower, cupping her mound through her thin shift. Exactly where she'd hoped.*

*The shift melted away and he flicked his fingers over her sex in the way she liked the best. He was so good at this part. He was good at all the parts.*

*She found her bliss quickly, arching backward into his arms, surrounded by his strength and consumed by passion.*

*She reached behind her, tracing the shape of his staff through the wool of the kilt. She slipped underneath the kilt, finding the hot silk of him, sliding her hand around him. He moaned into her ear, thrusting into her palm.*

*His hand moved to cover her throat, shifting her head to one side so that he could kiss her while remaining behind her.*

*Throat exposed and vulnerable in his large hands.*

*His kiss rough and uncontrolled.*

*She loved the way his fingers closed around her delicate throat. She knew he would never hurt her. That he only wanted to give her the most exquisite pleasure.*

*Again, and again . . . and again.*

*His lips tasted exactly like Peatmoor Old Scotch whisky. When he broke the kiss she giggled. "Mellow. Soft. Delightful," she quoted from an advertisement for the whisky.*

*"Mellow time is over," he said forcefully.*

*His hands closed around her hips, lifting her to her knees. His body fell across her back, his weight so heavy, his hardness nudging between her legs.*

*She fell forward onto her wrists, bum raised in the air. His arm curled around her waist.*

*"I'm going to take you from behind," he growled.*

*He bent her forward onto the carriage seat . . . only the carriage had disappeared. They were on an enormous bed with midnight-blue velvet curtains around them.*

*He pinned both her wrists with one large hand while he positioned himself behind her.*

*He moaned, louder this time. It didn't sound like a moan of pleasure. Had she hurt him somehow?*

*"Raven . . . ?"*

*A low growling, like a cornered animal.*

Indy lurched awake. She brushed damp hair away from her eyes.

Raven was moaning in his sleep. In the darkness he was only a huge shape curled on the carriage seat, one arm flung over his head.

He moaned again, louder this time. He must be having a nightmare.

She jostled across the coach and sat down near his head. His skin was clammy, his forehead hot. He was sweating.

Maybe he had a fever.

He formed no words, only that low moaning in the back of his throat.

His body was so tense. She kneaded his shoulder, the one she could reach. Taut, solid muscle.

"Shhh," she whispered. She soothed a hand across his brow.

Suddenly his body shifted, sliding up the seat toward her. He settled his large head in her lap with a contented sigh. His arm settled around her hip.

He stilled, and his breathing quieted.

She didn't dare move.

She brushed her fingers through his thick hair, stroking his brow. What had he been dreaming of to make him so agitated?

His father had died when he was so young. She knew everything about him before that moment, and she knew the letters he had sent her from school, and then, after the letters stopped coming, she knew next to nothing substantial.

What had changed him? What had transformed him from the mischievous, yet honest and kind-hearted boy she'd known into this immoral scoundrel?

In the darkness of the carriage his shadowed face was less sculpted—more vulnerable, so like the young boy she'd known.

What demons made him cry out in his sleep? She'd always pictured him sleeping soundly, limbs sprawled wide, with a beautiful woman in his bed to cater to his every whim.

He must have unknotted his cravat and yanked open his shirt in his sleep. One button was missing, causing his white linen shirt to gape open at the neck.

*You're making a habit of touching me, Indy . . .*

She couldn't help herself. She slipped her hand inside his shirt to touch his breastbone, expecting to meet smooth flesh, dusted by hair. What she found was a ridged scar, very close to his heart.

With a feather-light touch she explored more. He had other scars, raised lines as if from the slash of a knife. Round knots of scar tissue in two places that could be bullet wounds.

How had he received such scars? It didn't add up with what she knew about his life.

He'd been knifed. Shot. Was the stolen-antiquities business so dangerous? She'd never heard of him fighting any duels or being involved in any altercations.

The hard knot of recent scar tissue near his heart made her feel protective. The thought that this huge, strong man beneath her fingertips had stopped a bullet with his muscle and bone. He'd survived an attack, several attacks, and he'd hidden it from the world . . . from her.

This man she thought she detested . . . and definitely desired.

She thought she knew him.

Maybe she didn't know him at all.

He'd hurt her feelings and betrayed her, but she'd never once considered that perhaps he'd been hurt as well. Perhaps he had motives she may not have considered. There could be more to his story, more to him than met the eye.

He lifted his head suddenly. She tried to remove her hand from his chest but strong fingers trapped her hand in a firm grip, just like in her dream.

A rush of heat flooded her belly.

He was awake. And she'd been caught with her hand down his shirt.

RAVEN'S HEAD WAS cradled in Indy's lap. She had her hand down his shirt.

She'd touched his scar.

*She knows everything.*

*Don't be foolish. All she knows is that you have a few scars. Laugh it off.*

He released her wrist and sat up. "I knew the whisky would make you want to seduce me. I didn't know it would be while I slept."

She clasped her hands in her lap. "You called out in your sleep. You were having a nightmare. Are you feeling well?"

He'd been dreaming about Athens again.

"Quite well." He buttoned his shirt. "Did you rip open my shirt?" he asked incredulously, realizing that the top button was missing.

"Of course not!" She searched the seat cushion for the missing button. "You must have torn open your shirt while you slept."

"Are you sure about that?" he asked, just to needle her. "Perhaps I should have brought a chaperone."

"Quite sure. Your shirt was hanging open when I approached. I . . . was checking to see if you were feverish." She glanced at him from under her lashes. "How did you come by those scars? The one near your heart is still quite fresh. I thought you were lounging on the beach in Greece last month."

*Damn.* He betrayed nothing. "Duel with a jealous husband," he lied.

"I didn't hear about any duels."

"We kept it quiet."

"It's difficult to keep such matters quiet."

"Not so difficult abroad. I bribed the various parties to stay silent."

"And the ridged scars on your abdomen? Are they knife slashes?"

"You certainly had a good feel, didn't you? Next time wake me up first so I can at least enjoy it as well."

"I didn't mean to . . . touch you. I . . ."

"Your hands strayed of their own accord."

"I told you, I was seeing if you had a fever. And then I found that knot of scar tissue. Tell me how you received the wound."

"I did tell you."

"And I'm not satisfied with your answer. I think there's a story behind these wounds. I'm an archaeologist and a historian. I like digging for answers. I'll discover your secrets eventually, if I put my mind to it."

This entire conversation must be put to an immediate halt. He'd do whatever it took to stop her inquisitive mind from probing any further.

There was enough attraction smoldering between them to set this carriage on fire. Her touch so close to his heart had undone him completely.

He could only think of one way to divert the conversation, and that was by doing the thing he wanted to do most.

*When an enemy discovers a vulnerability, elimi-*
*nate that weakness. Shore up your defenses. Go on the*
*attack.*

"Why don't you just tell me the truth?" she
asked.

"Because I'd rather do this." He drew closer to
her and kissed her neck. "And this." He kissed
the corner of her mouth.

She responded by turning her mouth and kissing him full on the lips. He answered by parting
her lips with his tongue and delving inside her
mouth with confident strokes.

The arguments, the rivalry, all of his shadows
and secrets and her indomitable pride. Their tangled past. The hurt and the betrayal.

If he could, he would kiss it all away.

She was meant to be adored and treasured.
Pull her close, don't push her away.

She pulled back slightly and he immediately
broke the kiss.

She stroked the back of his hand where it
hugged the contour of her cheek. "I know what
you're trying to do."

"Please do explain it to me." He tried so hard to
keep his voice light, his expression teasing.

She couldn't know everything.

She had no idea that he'd nearly died a month
ago and it had shaken him to the core and now he
was questioning every decision he'd ever made.
Especially the ones that had kept them apart.

"Before, we were hate-kissing. This is evasive-
kissing. You don't want me asking questions
about your scars, about your past, and that's why

you kissed me. You want to distract me from your secrets."

"Did it work?"

"It worked." She moved his hand closer to her lips and kissed the center of his palm. The light touch of her lips sent shock waves reverberating through his body.

Shaken to the core.

The bedrock of his life cracking and shifting.

"Why did you stop?" she asked.

"I thought you . . . you pulled away."

"I only wanted to do this." She dipped her head and kissed the base of his throat. He tipped his head back and allowed her to explore his throat, his collarbone, her lips and tongue tracing a path that led dangerously close to his scarred heart.

"My turn." He kissed behind her ear. Greedy for the skin of her throat, the pulse at the base of her neck, her soft earlobes. Lingering perfume behind her ears. Where else did she apply the scent?

Her lips were so soft and she smelled so damned good. And she still tasted like whisky.

He'd been having the nightmare . . . the one where he rose above his body and watched the blood drain away and his skin turn blue . . .

He kissed her to drive away the memory of the nightmare.

She was so warm and supple in his arms. Not the Indy he'd placed on a pedestal, like a saint in a stained-glass window. The imperfect, contradictory woman in his arms. She made his blood sing a new song. A song about wanting to live.

Wanting to build something new.

She made a sudden movement with her head and his teeth jarred against her teeth. She pulled back, laughing softly. "That wasn't very pleasant."

"Don't worry, we'll find our way. Evasive-kissing requires practice." He nipped at her lower lip with his teeth and she responded by giving him a love-bite on his lips.

Give and take.

Fire and ice.

He'd known it would be like this. Too perfect. He'd known her heat would start to melt away the layers of ice his heart was preserved inside.

Her hands at the nape of his neck, fingers tangling in his hair.

His hands surrounding her throat, his thumbs stroking the proud lines of her jaw.

"I dream about you sometimes," she whispered. "I had a dream tonight."

He'd lain awake so many nights thinking of her. He'd imagined her in his bed. Heard her moaning his name. No one else had the same low, seductive voice.

And no one else had her unique smile, that knowing curve of her lips that he'd been searching for on other faces and never found. She had the smile of a Roman goddess, immortalized in metal and stamped onto a coin.

Stamped onto his heart.

He brought her face closer and kissed the tip of her nose. "What did you dream about?"

"This. Kissing. And . . . more."

*More. Yes, please. Much more.* He kissed her

cheekbone, her chin, the vulnerable curling of her ear. Held in check by reverence . . . and by the knowledge that this couldn't go too far.

"This is innocent compared to my dream," she said.

He stroked a long lock of glossy black hair away from her forehead. "Tell me more."

"You were wearing a kilt. I suppose that's because we were talking about kilts. And you weren't wearing anything underneath the tartan. I know because you . . . you lifted your kilt and showed me."

"I showed you?" He smiled against her lips, surprised by the bold admission. "I'm such a scoundrel."

"A bad, wicked scoundrel."

"I suppose you slapped me in your dream and told me to go expose myself to the devil."

She laughed softly. "Actually, I told you to remove your shirt."

He swallowed hard. He'd sell what was left of his soul to the highest taker for the opportunity to do her erotic bidding.

*Careful now. Don't allow this to escalate into something you'll both regret. It's late, and whisky was involved, and . . .*

"That could be arranged," he said. Because he was a scoundrel. And that's what a scoundrel said when a beautiful woman spoke of ordering him to remove his clothing.

"I think it *should* be arranged." Her eyes glittered in the darkness. "I'll go first," she said in a throaty whisper.

She reached behind her and undid something and her bodice slid lower, exposing the upper curves of her breasts.

He nearly groaned aloud.

He'd pictured her naked too many times to count. Cock in fist while he thought about what it would be like to have her in his bed. A potent blend of soft curves and sharp intellect that would go straight to his head and make him drunk with desire.

A lifetime of imagining the pleasure of this moment, countered by a lifetime of justifying why it could never happen.

The balance of those scales was tipping fast.

Indy undoing her bodice and presenting herself to him was simply more than he was able to refuse.

Just a small taste of paradise.

He lowered his head.

Spiced floral scent that infiltrated his mind and stiffened his body. She applied her perfume between her breasts. Every day? Or only on days she knew she'd be in a carriage alone with him?

Her breasts were full and heavy in his hands, filling his palms to overflowing with soft satin flesh.

She arched her back. "Raven," she whispered. "Yes."

Just like his fantasies.

She wore a necklace with a thin gold chain around her neck, the round pendant nestled over her heart.

He lowered his lips to her breast again, shaping the darker areola with his tongue and lapping in narrowing circles to the tip of her breast.

He sucked on one nipple while he stroked her other breast, lightly pressing the nipple between his thumb and forefinger.

The pendant around her neck caught his eye, glinting in the gloom inside the carriage.

Round. Copper.

He stopped worshipping her breasts and lifted the pendant. There was something very familiar about the design. "Is this . . . the Minerva coin I chose for you?" he asked, his heart filling with pride that she wore his parting memento around her throat, hidden between her breasts.

She snatched the coin away from his hand and backed away, pulling up her bodice. "Yes. But I don't wear it for sentimental reasons."

Gown fastened now, necklace hidden. Heart hidden. Her expression solemn and face shadowed.

*You hurt her. You betrayed her.*

*Stop wishing that she remembered you as the boy who believed in love and happy endings.*

She smoothed a hand over her hair. "I wear the coin to remind myself never to trust anyone ever again."

Her voice so flat and emotionless.

"Good." He adjusted his shirt. "People aren't to be trusted."

"Believe me, I don't trust anyone except myself. And I have the coin and the scar to remind me of why." The bitter edge to her words sliced through his heart.

Literal scar. He'd traced the edge of the faint ridge along her breastbone as they kissed.

"I have a scar along my breastbone," she clarified.

And because he had to feign no knowledge of her life, even though he knew far more than she thought he did, he asked, "You have a scar?"

"Yes, and I'm happy to tell you how I received it. I'm not ashamed of it. It happened in London. I was nineteen, walking by myself through a marketplace in Whitechapel, proudly carrying the dagger that Lady Catherine had gifted to me. I'd been to see a bookseller and I was on my way to the British Museum to deliver several antiquities. I thought I was so invincible with that dagger at my hip." She laughed briefly. "I was dreadfully young and naïve."

She fell silent.

"If you don't want to relive the memory you don't have to."

"A man appeared out of nowhere, dragged me down a side alley and pulled the knife from my belt and turned it on me. Held it to my throat and demanded the contents of my pockets and purse."

Again, he had to feign ignorance. "That must have been terrifying."

"It's true what they say." She lifted her hand in front of her face. "Scenes from your life do play before your eyes like a theatrical production when you face the prospect of death. I remembered Edgar holding my hand and leading me into the bathing pond when we were children and I was frightened of the water."

When Raven had lain in that church in Athens he'd seen Indy's face but it hadn't been a memory. It had been a fantasy from a different life.

"I didn't want to die," she whispered.

He reached for her hand. He couldn't not touch her when her voice was laced with so much suffering. He wanted to fold her into his arms.

"I thought about all of the things I would never do." Her grasp around his fingers and the antiquities strengthened. "I surrendered what little coin I had. I asked him not to kill me. I'd like to say I had a plan to break his hold and make my escape, but I didn't. I did try to run but he caught me easily and dragged me deeper into a narrow passageway between two buildings. Just like the alleyway we were in yesterday."

"Perhaps we shouldn't have been mock fighting in an alleyway."

She shivered. "He sliced a line across my hairline, here." She lifted the hair from her forehead. "And one along my collarbone. Deep enough to draw blood. I thought it was all over for me. I prepared to fight as hard as I could but I knew I didn't have the skill or the strength to throw him off. Blood dripped into my eyes and I couldn't see anything."

He stroked her fingers. "It sounds like a nightmare."

"It was. Until something wonderful happened. My assailant lifted into the air like he'd suddenly learned how to fly. Just flew into the air and smacked against the opposite brick wall."

Raven made a sympathetic sound. He knew how the story ended.

"Someone threw him off me," she continued. "I wiped the blood from my eyes but I couldn't see my savior. My assailant lay on the ground. My savior shouted at me to run in a deep, gruff voice. I ran and I didn't stop running."

Raven remembered that day so well. He was rarely in London but when he was, he couldn't help but shadow Indy, just to be close to her.

He'd lost sight of her for a moment, in the crowded marketplace, and he'd panicked. And then he'd seen the flash of her dagger in the dark alleyway.

He'd intervened. How could he not? She'd been in grave danger. He hated to think what might have happened to her if he hadn't followed her that day.

He'd wanted to reveal himself, tell her to be less careless. Instead he'd watched her race away.

It had nearly killed him to let her go, knowing that she could have died.

She gave a little shake of her head. "So that's why I learned to wield a knife properly. The next time I was accosted, in London again, I successfully fought off the attack. I know I'm not invincible. I try not to take foolish risks. I've been given this second chance and I'm going to make something of my life."

"I understand how you could feel that way."

"Your bullet wound—did it have a similar effect?"

"More the opposite effect, I'm afraid. My brush with death reaffirmed my belief that life is short and should be lived to the fullest. I'll ring it like a bell, live fast and hard, and probably die young."

She removed her hand from his grasp. "Do you truly believe that? Do you believe that your life is worthless?

Not worthless. He served his country. He prevented mass bloodshed. And he pursued his own aim on the side, to clear his father's name once and for all.

Even though the charges had never been proved and Raven had inherited the title and holdings, his father had been tried in the court of public opinion. They said he'd been sleeping with an enemy agent, a spy with the code name of Le Fleur. They said he'd betrayed his king for the love of one of Napoleon's spies. It had been harrowing for Raven's mother most of all.

Raven knew his father had been honorable and that he never would have turned traitor.

Raven placed honor and duty above all.

He was a good soldier. When he had to, he put his head down and plowed through the enemy line.

"Raven?" she asked.

"What did you call me?"

"You always call me Indy so why shouldn't I be allowed to shorten your name? Raven's what your close friends call you, I believe. We used to be friends."

*We used to be friends. We should have been lovers. Life companions.*

"That was a long time ago," he said. "Another lifetime."

"Why did you . . . change?" she asked.

She didn't ask him why he'd betrayed her. He knew she was too proud to ask. This was as close as she would come to the subject.

He'd relied on her prickly pride all of these years. On her hatred.

It all seemed so wrong, now. He questioned everything. Especially the reasons he'd pushed her away. And the reasons he had to lie to her right now. One more lie to add to the ocean of lies that his profession required.

"I'm ruled by my baser instincts, Indy. The world has accused my father of the same. I don't have the ethical framework that you do. I travel where the warm winds of fame and fortune blow me." The hedonistic, fortune hunting cover he'd constructed.

"Do you? I hear this cynicism in your voice and I'm not sure whether I believe it fully. I find it so difficult to reconcile my memory of you as a boy with the man you've become."

He gave people what they wanted. He was a glassy surface, reflecting back what the world wanted to see.

"What you see is what you get. All the world loves a rogue."

"That's all you show me, that's all you show the world."

"I'm all surface, Indy, there's nothing to find, nothing to uncover."

What he wanted to do was tell her everything. Just spill it all out and ask her forgiveness. But a man like him never asked for forgiveness. Never admitted to any wrongdoing.

They could torture him and he'd never admit to anything.

Withstanding torture had been part of his training, so why couldn't he withstand the torment of the disappointment he saw in her eyes?

"My life is already open and closed," he said. "I'm already a citation in an encyclopedia. Daniel, Duke of Ravenwood: hedonist, mercenary, dies alone, brother Colin inherits and restores the respectability of the family name."

Her silence was deafening.

"All right, Raven. If that's how you want to play this." Her tone was resigned.

He'd won another round. A victory as hollow as a rotten tree trunk.

"How is Colin?" she asked. "I haven't seen him, or your mother, in such a long time. I believe he married?"

"Colin is fulfilling all of my mother's dreams. He distinguished himself at Cambridge and then found a shy, sweet-tempered lady to marry. They are expecting their first child early next year. He'll be a fine duke after I drink myself into an early grave. He's sober minded and civic-minded. Cares for improving the conditions of the tenants on our estates and all of that."

He'd made the choice to become a spy for his family. Because of Raven's investigations, his father had not been formally charged with high treason, and Colin had a title and a fortune to inherit. Raven had to remember that when his choices began to feel wrong.

"And how is your mother?" he asked Indy. "I saw her last at the wedding breakfast for your brother and his duchess."

"The dowager duchess is doing surprisingly well. I believe she is experiencing something of a second girlhood. She's dressing her hair differently and wearing less plumage. And she spends a lot of time with Mari's father, Mr. Lumley."

"My mother never remarried, though she could have." He looked out the window. Fog rolled around the carriage in a mist of mauve and gray.

She shivered and his first instinct was to drape his arm around her. He stopped himself with his arm half outstretched.

She was cold. He wanted to warm her.

She was in pain. He wanted to comfort her.

He noticed that she hadn't moved back across to the opposite seat. She rested her head against the wall. "I'm so tired," she said.

He tucked his greatcoat around her shoulders. "We've changed horses several times. We'll be there soon. If you want to sleep more, you should."

Her eyes closed and her breathing slowed. The carriage jostled and she moved away from the wall, tilting toward him and dropping her head onto his shoulder.

Brave, knife-wielding, independent Indy, resting against him while she slept.

With her head on his shoulder and her warm breath against his neck, he was happier than he'd ever been. It was the happiest damned moment of his cold, blighted life.

And it was all kinds of wrong.

He could never let her know how perfect it felt to have her in his arms.

He was glad they'd be staying in separate residences in Paris. He didn't trust himself anymore. Nearly dying in Athens had shaken more than his confidence. It had shaken his soul.

She made him want to stop putting one foot in front of the other, marching down the dutiful path.

When he was with her, all he wanted to do was touch her, hold her, taste her lips.

Raise his face to sunlight pouring through a stained-glass window.

Watch firelight find strands of silver in her hair.

Live another day. Find a new path.

# Chapter 11

❧

*H*ER PLANS TO outmaneuver Raven had misfired spectacularly, Indy reflected as the carriage they'd hired when they arrived in Paris rattled down the rue Notre Dame des Victoires.

It was half past six in the evening. Parisians were gathered by the hundreds in the coffee-houses and cafes to drink Burgundy wine and gossip over a game of chess or billiards.

Raven stared out one window, Indy the other.

They had scrupulously ignored each other on the brief passage by steam packet from Dover to Calais. They'd taken luncheon in Calais at separate tables. They'd followed an unspoken agreement to place more distance between them.

Instead of hiring a private conveyance, they'd traveled by diligence from Calais to Paris with several other passengers. Raven had entertained the group with card tricks and jests during the long overnight journey. She'd done her best to finish her novel but she hadn't been able to con-centrate.

She'd been thinking about what had happened in the carriage on the way to Dover. How she'd told him about her dreams. Talk about giving the man more fodder for his already over-sized ego.

There was no trusting herself around him, and doubly so when there was Scotch whisky involved.

When she'd seen his troubled sleep, a welling of sympathy and emotion had threatened to ruin all of her plans for remaining aloof. And when she'd found the knot of scar tissue, so close to his heart, she'd known his life could have ended.

And that knowledge had hit her like a bullet to the heart. Lodging itself in her conviction, her confidence, that life was better without him. He'd betrayed her, yes. But she relied on him to be there. She relied on their rivalry.

What if he had died? She couldn't imagine life without him.

Maybe there was more beneath his surface. Some complicated reason that he'd betrayed her. A morality and a purpose to his actions that she'd never envisioned.

Maybe there was a chance that they could be friends again. Maybe there was a chance . . . She pressed her forehead against the window, watching the tide of humanity swirl along the avenue.

A strapping young sailor threw his arm around the shoulders of a beautiful girl with laughing dark eyes, and ushered her inside the warmly lit doorway of a café.

They weren't so afraid in Paris to openly show their feelings.

There were so many lovers in the world, so much hustle and bustle of humanity, and she was removed, always removed, by choice.

She studied history and she studied the lives

of others and those lives were always filled with complications. While she lived an unconventional life, she didn't have the traditional complications: a spouse or a lover, children, responsibilities beyond her work.

She'd had a privileged life on the one hand, wealth and social standing. Her father had terrorized her childhood and her mother had never succeeded in imposing her will on Indy because she'd learned to fight early. Her mother had softened after Edgar's marriage, after their reconciliation—still, Indy had never had a heartfelt conversation with her.

Indy had few friends. She had Lady Catherine in Paris. Mari and Viola in London.

She was alone most of the time by choice; because she was mistrustful of opening herself to anyone, and wary of being hurt.

For good reason.

She mustn't dig into Raven's past any deeper. No more questions.

Asking questions left her exposed and vulnerable. He'd crush her heart all over again and she didn't know if she could survive a second time.

Knowing his reasons wouldn't lessen the sting of his actions.

"I read somewhere that Paris has more than seven hundred coffeehouses and cafes," said Raven.

Indy inhaled slowly. She could do this. Converse pleasantly like strangers. Remark upon the weather and the sights.

"Sounds about right," she said lightly. "There

seems to be one on every corner. And they're incessantly crowded from nine o'clock in the morning until midnight. It's so different here. Respectable ladies are free to sit in the cafes, conversing with their male companions with perfect ease."

"I like that about Paris. The ladies don't labor under such repressive strictures of propriety and modesty."

"I visit Lady Catherine every year and stay for several months. Every time I visit, she tries to convince me that I would thrive here. I'm sure she'll renew her campaign during this trip."

"You had no time to inform her that you were coming—are you sure she's at home?"

"I have a standing invitation to visit with no advance notice necessary. If she's not at home, the doorman knows me by sight."

"We'll go to Sir Charles's residence first and engage one of his carriages for your use while you're in Paris, just in case Lady Catherine is not at home. I don't trust these public conveyances for a woman traveling alone."

"I won't argue with that. My trunk was stolen once by an unscrupulous outrider."

"Tomorrow morning we'll begin our search by visiting the Louvre and speaking with Beauchamp."

"I've been thinking about potential scenarios," she said. "If Beauchamp is involved, though I highly doubt he is, the Rosetta Stone would be a wonderful centerpiece for the new Egyptian exhibit at the Louvre. After Napoleon was defeated, the French were forced to return so many of the artifacts he'd pillaged."

"I don't think they would display it so boldly. If Beauchamp is behind the theft, he'll keep the stone secret."

"Perhaps. But if France had the provenance to support a claim that Beauchamp purchased the stone from an anonymous party with no questions asked because he wanted to save it from being lost to a private collector, what claim does Britain truly have to the Rosetta Stone?"

He gave her a searching look. "Our monarchy won't see it in that light."

"Then I return to my theory that the Russians orchestrated the theft as a means to end the peace between England and France and they are waiting until an opportune moment to pin the deed on France and sow discord."

In other words, they could be engaged in averting a war, which was no trivial matter.

The fate of the peace between France and England could hinge upon the success of their search.

It was nearly dark when they arrived at the Hôtel de Charost, the British ambassador's residence, on the desirable rue du Faubourg Saint Honoré. After Raven identified himself to the gatekeeper, their carriage was allowed to pass through the carriageway that connected the street to the courtyard.

"Such commodious stables," Indy remarked as they alighted. "One wouldn't think a residence in the heart of Paris would have room for dozens of horses."

"Two dozen horses, I believe."

"And the house is quite grand. To whom did it belong before it became the ambassador's residence?"

"Wellington purchased it from Napoleon's sister Pauline after she joined her brother in exile on Elba. These *hôtels particuliers* are built to house multiple generations at the same property. Sir Charles only has himself, his wife, and their daughter, Lucy."

They approached the main house between two stone pavilions and across the grassy *cour d'honneur*, which was separated from the kitchen and stable service courts on either side by arcaded screens of five arches each. The façade was mostly windows illuminated by lamps that cast a soft glow across the hard planes of Raven's face.

A British butler with an appropriately dignified manner showed them to a spacious drawing room, hung with green silk and oil portraits.

A young girl of about seventeen, very slender and brunette with a long, swanlike neck, burst through the door. "Oh there you are. Finally! I've been on pins and needles waiting for your arrival."

"Greetings." Raven laughed. "Lady India, this is the Honorable Lucy Sterling."

"Just Lucy, thank you very much, Your Grace."

"How do you do, Lucy?" said Indy.

"I've been longing to meet you, Lady India!"

"You have?"

Lucy bobbed her head and the fan-shaped braided hairpiece attached to the top of her head waved back and forth. "Mrs. Bertha Featherstone arrived an hour ago from London. She only stayed for a half hour but she told us all about your wedding plans. It's ever so romantic!"

"News travels swiftly, I see," said Indy. She'd hoped to avoid the topic for at least a day or two.

"Oh we hear about everything in Paris. I do miss my friends in England quite dreadfully. You're arrestingly beautiful." Lucy walked in a circle around Indy. "I've never seen eyes that shade. If I were mixing the colors I would have to use blue, red, white and a hint of black, I believe. You must let me paint you while you're here." She turned to Raven. "Everyone is simply dying to see the lady who captured you at last."

"Lucy, pray do not importune our guests," remonstrated a handsome older woman as she entered the room. She had the same graceful posture as her daughter.

"You're the one who said it, Mama. You said the Duke of Ravenwood will never be caught for he is a confirmed bachelor and enjoys his freedoms far too much."

"Did I say such a thing? My apologies, Lady India, you've given the lie to my words."

"We met once, Lady Sterling," India said. "A chance encounter at the Palais Royal."

"So we did." Lady Sterling clasped India's hand.

She turned to Raven. "Tell me, Your Grace, how did this delightful turn of events come about?"

He grinned mischievously. "'She hung about my neck, and kiss on kiss she vied so fast, protesting oath on oath, that in a twink she won me to her love.'"

Lady Sterling looked puzzled.

"His Grace is quoting Shakespeare," Indy explained. She had to give him credit. He kept using her weapons against her. She was amazed at his ability to memorize Shakespeare.

As a boy, he'd always teased her about her love for the Bard.

"I've never known him to do so," said Lady Sterling.

Lucy's eyes sparkled. "Love changes everything, Mama."

"I suppose so." Lady Sterling stared out the window for a moment, her expression sad. "Well," she said with a smile. "I'm certainly glad you'll be staying with us, Lady India."

"No, no I'm not staying here," said Indy. "I'll stay with Lady Catherine Hammond on the rue Louis le Grand."

"Lady Catherine? Impossible." Lady Sterling waved her words aside. "Haven't you heard? She sold her residence in Paris and purchased a crumbling old chateau near Montrouge."

"Really? How strange. I haven't heard anything about it."

"It was all quite sudden," said Lady Sterling. "Lady Catherine said she was moving away from the unhealthy environs of Paris upon the advice of her physician, Dr. Lowe."

Indy exchanged a glance with Raven. She'd told him of her concern about Dr. Lowe's troubling influence on her friend.

"You must stay here," cried Lucy. "You simply must. We've a whole wing for guests and no one staying at the moment."

Indy and Raven exchanged a glance fraught with tension.

"I'll go to Meurice's Hotel," Raven offered.

"Nonsense. I won't hear of it," exclaimed Lady Sterling. "We're rattling around in this enormous house, just the three of us."

Lucy brushed Indy's hand. "You must come and meet my friends. They're simply expiring of curiosity to meet you. We were having a musical evening when you arrived."

There was a question in Raven's eyes. He wanted to know if Indy had any objection to sleeping under the same roof with him.

It wasn't ideal.

She should probably insist on going to stay at a lady's school that took in female travelers. That would be the prudent course of action. But they did have a job to do, and it would be expedient to be in close proximity to go over the plan of action and modify their list of suspects as events unfolded.

And then, of course, there were all the new varieties of kissing that they hadn't discovered yet besides argue-kissing and evasive-kissing. For instance, what would Paris-kissing be like?

She mustn't think such thoughts. Especially when she didn't have whisky to blame.

Lady Sterling would place them in opposite wings of the house with herself in the middle to act as chaperone. Not that Indy required a chaperone.

There would be no more intimate conversations. A complete moratorium on dreams.

And absolutely no Paris-kissing.

She squared her shoulders. "Thank you, Lady Sterling, I'll gladly accept your hospitality. And there's no need for you to run away to a hotel, Your Grace. I'm sure you want to converse in private with Sir Charles."

"My husband is in the library," said Lady Sterling. "I'll escort you to him, Your Grace."

"Hoorah," cried Lucy. "The lovebirds in our nest! If you're here in Paris to have your wedding costumes designed, I hereby nominate myself as your willing servant. Anything you wish, anything at all—"

"A bite to eat and a bed will be most welcome," Indy said, cutting off Lucy's rhapsodies.

"Of course," said Lady Sterling. "You must be fatigued after your long journey. Lucy will show you to your chamber."

"Please say you'll allow me to paint you," said Lucy. "I'm having lessons from Master Rossetti and I'm becoming quite proficient with portraiture." She turned glowing eyes to an oil portrait of her mother that hung on the wall. "That's one of mine."

"Modesty, Lucy," said her mother.

"But it's beautiful!" her daughter replied.

"It is indeed," said Raven. "Both the subject and the painting."

Lady Sterling smiled. "Flatterer."

"Will you sit for me?" Lucy pressed Indy.

"We'll see," replied Indy noncommittally.

"Before you retire you must visit the music room to meet my friends."

"I—"

"No excuses. Only for a moment. There's something I want to show you."

Indy exchanged a helpless glance with Raven as she was borne from the room by a tide of chattering femininity.

Lucy clutched her hand as if she were afraid Indy was a mythical unicorn and might bolt if the maiden relinquished her golden tether.

Her friends were arrayed in the music salon in gowns of yellow, pink, and pale blue: a wash of pastels like a rainbow glowing with shimmering life, all chattering at once, their coiled, braided, and beribboned coiffures bobbing atop their youthful faces, all big eyes and rosy cheeks and dewy lips.

Only three of them—four with Lucy—but Indy felt surrounded by an army of girlish charms.

"Here she is," announced Lucy, presenting Indy to the young ladies. "Lady India Rochester, she who hath brought the Rogue Duke up to scratch."

Sighs and giggles met her dramatic pronouncement.

"Miss Lydia Wright, Lady Susan Granville, and Miss Francoise Pelletier." The young ladies performed graceful curtsies as Lucy introduced them.

India bowed to them; she wasn't much for curtsying, and her masculine greeting was met with more giggles and the tinkling chimes of eardrops and arm bangles against graceful necks and arms.

Indy had been young and carefree once, but she'd never been one for adornments or giggling.

Miss Francoise possessed the innate elegance and self-possession Indy had observed in many Frenchwomen, and her dark brown eyes assessed Indy with interest, and a hint of condescension. She'd obviously decided Indy, in her travel-worn cotton gown with messy curls piled atop her head, was no threat to her beauty.

Indy had never understood the constant rivalry certain females engaged in—always measuring their attractiveness and charms against their sisters. *It isn't a war, ladies,* she wanted to say. *We're all in this together.*

Miss Lydia, whose eyes were as blue and wide as a field of cornflowers, drew closer. "We've been speaking of nothing else since we heard the news."

"We have wedding fever!" cried Lucy, gripping Indy's hand fervently.

"However did you manage to keep the circumstance of your engagement secret for so long?" asked Miss Francoise.

"And how did you induce him to set a date at last?"

"It was simple," said Indy with a shrug. "I told

him that if he didn't wed me soon, I'd perforate him with my dagger."

"You didn't," exclaimed Lucy with a shocked expression.

"You have a dagger?" asked Miss Lydia, her eyes widening even further.

Indy drew her blade from under the fitted coat she wore.

The young ladies gasped and drew closer, the enormous puffed sleeves of their gowns fluttering like butterfly wings.

"Sometimes men are such fools. They don't really know what they want. All he required was a little nudge in the right direction," said Indy confidingly. "In Mr. Shakespeare's time, the males dressed as ladies to perform the plays. I merely reversed the roles. I played the Petruchio to his Kate and forced his hand. If there's a gentleman you want to bring up to scratch, I advise you to purchase a blade and learn how to use it."

Lady Susan, with ginger-colored hair and pale eyebrows, tilted her head to the side, like a bird. "Oh, I don't know if I could do that. It's terribly shocking."

"Time waits for no woman," said Indy. "Grab destiny as though you want it. That's my motto."

"I simply couldn't," repeated Lady Susan.

Indy held out the hilt of her knife. "Here, take it. See how it feels in your hand."

Lady Susan accepted the knife gingerly. "It looks wickedly sharp."

"I have many daggers, but this one is from Norway. The handle is made of polished birch and the blade is steel. Isn't it beautiful?"

Lady Susan handed back the knife. "Ah, yes. Very beautiful." Her expression said the exact opposite.

"Speaking of beautiful," said Lucy brightly, "we want details about your wedding gown."

"We heard from Mrs. Featherstone that you are to be wed in cascading layers of canary yellow frills from your neck to your toes."

Indy sheathed her knife. She eyed the exit. If she made a run for it, the young ladies wouldn't be able to catch her. She was wearing boots and they were wearing silk slippers.

Miss Lydia glanced at her friends. Lucy nodded at her encouragingly. "I wish to . . . that is . . . are you quite certain such a gown will be the most becoming for your figure and complexion?"

The girls crowded closer, cutting off her access to the exit. "I'm quite attached to my pineapple dress," Indy said firmly. "Now, if you'll excuse me—"

"We know everything," said Lucy. "The pine-apple dress, the duke's pink silk doublet, the champagne fountain."

"The swans." Miss Lydia sighed, clasping her hands. "They mate for life. It's so romantic."

"I daresay so many swans might produce some rather *unfortunate* consequences upon the lawn," drawled Miss Francoise in her charming French accent.

"Hush, Fran," said Lucy with a frown. "There

will be footmen following after the swans to control any . . . situations."

"Your attendants must wear pale yellow," said Miss Lydia.

"No, they must wear pink," said Lady Susan.

"You must carry orange blossoms," said Lucy.

"She must carry rosebuds," disagreed Miss Lydia.

What was it about young ladies and weddings? Their eyes shone with a nearly fanatical fervor.

"I was thinking of carrying flowering thistles," said Indy. "The flowers will match my eyes."

Lucy's brows knit. "Thistles? Aren't they rather . . . prickly?"

"I'm quite prickly, so they'll be appropriate. Or I could carry an arrangement of artichokes."

That silenced them. They all looked aghast.

"Artichokes? They eat them quite often in France, you know," said Lady Susan. "Steamed and dipped in a melted butter. They're delicious, but as a wedding bouquet? No, no, it won't do at all."

"Wouldn't you rather have a nice bouquet of rosebuds?" asked Miss Lydia hopefully.

"Let her carry artichokes if she wants to," said Miss Francoise. "And wear her pineapple gown. I for one think it will be quite charming."

"About the gown . . ." said Lucy. "We had thought you might wish to see these fashion plates from *la Galerie des Modes*." She caught Indy's hand and pulled her toward a round table that stood near the gleaming pianoforte in one corner of the music room.

Miss Lydia turned the pages of a large cloth-bound book filled with etchings of ladies' fashions. "Now *this* is a wedding gown." She stared lovingly at a print of a simple white gown with puffed sleeves, a narrow low-cut bodice, and an overlay of delicate leaf-patterned embroidery.

An inexplicable welling of emotion and fatigue swamped Indy's mind. "How about a compromise, dear ladies? Why don't you choose three gowns from the fashion plates and I promise to take them into very careful consideration . . . tomorrow. Now I must retire for the evening."

"You promise to take them into consideration?" asked Lucy.

"I solemnly swear."

"Don't leave just yet. You haven't had a pastry." Lucy gestured to a tray piled with pastries and tarts.

Indy's stomach grumbled, reminding her that she hadn't eaten enough today. That must account for why the sight of the simple, elegant wedding gown had made her feel so queasy.

As she sampled the refreshments, the girls conversed about weddings they'd attended and which bride had been more breathtaking than the others, and which groom more dashing.

Something about discussing her wedding with Raven, even though it was all a huge fabrication, had her craving solitude. Or buttery French pastries.

Pastries would do for the moment. She ate her way around the top layer of the tiered tea tray and proceeded to the next.

Must be all this talk of becoming a bride. For these girls it was the height of their ambition in life. To become a beautiful young bride and marry the most handsome and gallant of gentlemen.

When her own naïve hopes had been ground to dust, she'd vowed never to be defined by her association with a man.

She'd achieve her ambitions alone, and on her own terms.

She'd never be a duchess. She didn't *want* to be a duchess.

What a lot of trouble that would be. She was barely upholding the standards of lady-hood. Actually, she wasn't upholding them at all.

She was far too ambitious and adventurous. She'd never become anyone's wife and give up her life of daring and freedom.

All the pastries were gone now and most of the tarts. Yet she still had a craving for more treats. "I don't suppose you ladies keep a bottle of sherry in the music salon?" she asked hopefully, interrupting their sentimental recollections of weddings past.

"Heavens, no," said Lucy. "You'd have to go to Father's study for sherry."

India sighed and popped the last flaky pastry into her mouth.

Raven was probably smoking a cheroot and drinking an excellent aged Cognac at the moment. He would be pressing Sir Charles for information about their suspects, conducting important investigations while fanatical ladies on the hunt for wedding details interrogated Indy.

She could have brought her fake moustache, trousers, and Hessian boots to Paris and embarked on her own search for the stone wearing a masculine disguise.

Instead, she was staying in the same house with Raven and pretending to be his fiancée in truth, instead of merely on a meaningless piece of paper.

# Chapter 12

❧

"*Y*OU SLY DEVIL, hiding your engagement all these years." Sir Charles poured Raven another glass of wine. "Are you sure you're man enough to tame that one? She seems a right spitfire."

"I've no interest in taming her."

"You like her unpredictability and spirit, eh?"

"It does keep life interesting."

"I'll wager it will keep the marriage bed interesting as well," said Sir Charles with a lascivious wink.

*Not going to think about marriage beds. Beds with Indy in them. Beds in general.*

Sir Charles had always been one of Raven's best contacts. As a diplomat he was their eyes and ears in Paris. Charles knew Raven worked for the Foreign Office but he wasn't privy to the secret nature of his position.

Malcolm had said not to trust Charles, that he'd gone rabid and must be leashed. There was something slightly off about his demeanor. A grayish tinge to his skin as though he'd been indulging in unhealthy nights on the town.

Still, Raven found it difficult to believe Charles would help Le Triton steal the Rosetta Stone. What could he possibly gain from it? He may have taken a notorious French mistress, and he was burning the candle at both ends, but to betray his country in such an ostentatious manner would end his career ignobly and open him to being tried for treason.

Though there was always the possibility he'd been blackmailed into helping orchestrate the theft.

"What brings you to Paris?" asked Sir Charles. "I know it's not wedding shopping. I heard something about the Wish Diamond?"

"You heard correctly. I'm here to find a purchaser for the necklace. Lady India doesn't want me to keep it. Though she'd rather I donated the priceless antiquity to a museum." He shrugged. "Weddings are expensive. Especially the outrageous affair she's planning."

"Heard about that. Making you pay for your indiscretions, is she? You're not really going to wear a pink doublet and silver spurs on your shoes?"

"Not a chance."

"Didn't think so."

"She spoonfed the newspaperman humiliating details to bring me down a notch or two."

"I know the feeling. Lady Sterling has become increasingly difficult of late. A fellow needs his diversions, am I right?"

Which must be a reference to Margot Delacroix. Charles didn't yet know that Raven was aware of the affair.

"You're not wrong," said Raven with a practiced grin. "I'm sure you'll be able to help connect me with potential buyers for the Wish Diamond."

"I have the perfect venue. I'm hosting a small diplomatic affair here at the residence the day after tomorrow."

"Splendid. I'll attend with Lady India."

Raven had read about the plans for the diplomatic affair in the dossier. It was the perfect safe activity for him and Indy to attend together. A safe diplomatic event would keep her out of harm's way. She'd be occupied with evaluating every attendee for possible culpability while he prepared to infiltrate Le Triton's lair.

"I'll have my valet help with your evening attire," said Charles. "These formal occasions are so strict on protocol."

"Thank you."

He probably knew more about Sir Charles right now than his own wife did. He knew that he was up to his red-rimmed eyeballs in gambling debt, he knew that Margot Delacroix had him twisted in knots around her dainty finger, and that he hadn't shared the marital bed with his wife in over a year.

"Lady India's décolletage will be the perfect setting for the diamond, if I may be so bold as to say so," said Sir Charles. "Everyone will be salivating over her . . . necklace. I'd consider buying it myself, as a gift for a lady friend, but I'm sure I won't be able to afford your price."

Raven didn't move the smallest muscle, but the crude remark grated on his nerves. And yet Sir Charles was only mimicking the sorts of shameless things Raven used to say.

*Did say.* There was nothing different about

him. He was the same cold-blooded agent with the same careless, hedonistic persona. He wasn't changing or metamorphosing in any way.

"No doubt she'll spark a bidding war," said Raven. "Will Le Triton attend the affair?" He already knew that he hadn't been invited, but he wanted to watch Sir Charles's reaction.

Sir Charles obliged by turning one shade grayer and developing a slight tic at the corner of his left eye.

Interesting.

"He won't attend the diplomatic event, but we can visit him at his gaming house, La Sirène. I have an engagement there tonight. Le Triton has been pouring funds into the Louvre's new Egyptian exhibit. He's made several large gifts of antiquities from his collection. I purchased several items of furniture from him for the residence."

Even more interesting. A connection between Sir Charles, Le Triton, and the Louvre.

Raven remained silent. Sir Charles was agitated about something, and listening quietly sometimes caused people to divulge secrets.

"You wouldn't believe the deals I've negotiated on exquisite French antiquities recently," said Charles. "I have whole warehouses filled with sixteenth-century windows and medieval carved stonework that I purchased for a song. I'm planning to ship it all to England and rebuild my castle in Dorset in majestic style."

*If you live that long*, thought Raven. Associating with Le Triton tended to shorten men's lives. "I'd love to tour your warehouses while I'm here," said Raven casually. "You know what a delight I take in such things."

"Oh, ah . . ." Sir Charles cleared his throat. "I suppose that could be arranged."

Raven would tour the warehouses secretly this very night. It would be a simple matter to find the warehouse records in the locked drawers of the handsome escritoire behind them.

"Where do you find your architectural pieces?" asked Raven.

"I have my contacts, just as you have yours."

Which was another way of saying that Charles hadn't acquired his antiquities in an honest way. "Aren't you worried about the French mounting a protest if you take too much of their country home with you?" asked Raven.

"Not a bit." He puffed out his chest. "I do what I please. I control things around here."

Raven added *delusional* to his list of Sir Charles's rapidly growing list of suspicious traits.

"I think I'll retire for the evening," said Raven. "Where have you placed me?"

"Your usual chamber on the first floor. Lady India is in the one next door." Another suggestive wink.

"Uh . . . isn't this a large house?"

"Thought you'd want to be close to her. Besides, Lady Sterling is refurbishing the guest quarters and those are the only two rooms available. Are you sure you want to retire so early? Why not come with me to La Sirène?"

Le Triton's gaming house in the Palais Royal was a notorious hub for criminal activity. Raven didn't want to engage Le Triton until he'd done more investigating.

Sir Charles was hiding something. Raven would spend his evening searching the man's warehouses and going through his other records.

"A quiet evening's what the doctor ordered," Raven said.

"Not going soft on me, are you?" asked Sir Charles. "Does your charming fiancée have you on a short leash?"

Raven smiled. "Absolutely not. I'll accompany you to the gaming house later this week." He rose and took his leave.

On his way upstairs, he heard the sound of female voices. He stopped outside the music salon. Indy must still be inside. He heard her low voice, and then the soft, high giggles of her companions.

Curious. He thought she would have retired by now.

The door stood ajar. He moved closer to hear what they were saying. He heard his name and paused, listening intently.

"When I was your age I wanted a very simple wedding," he heard Indy say. "Only Ravenwood and our closest family. I was going to wear a white gown, very similar to the one you showed me, Miss Lydia. For our honeymoon we would have journeyed to Athens to view the Parthenon."

The wistfulness in her words jabbed at his heart like a doctor searching for bullet fragments.

He'd wanted the same thing. And everything had gone so very wrong.

Learning that his father had been a spy . . . that his dying wish was for Raven to become one as well.

Learning to detach from his emotions. Losing the desire for personal fulfillment and existing only for the mission.

"Why did you not marry the duke when you were our age?" one of the girls asked. "Why did you wait so long?"

"Life is a long and winding road, if we're lucky," said Indy. "Sometimes paths diverge, and then they align again. So it is for the duke and me. We weren't ready for marriage then. He was too wild and restless, and I . . . I didn't know it at the time, but I needed to strike out on my own. Find my own way in the world."

"How thrillingly unconventional," was the reply.

"Now I really must leave you, ladies. I'm very tired. Thank you for the refreshments."

Raven rapped on the door so Indy wouldn't catch him lingering outside, eavesdropping on her. He entered the room.

Indy was surrounded by a bevy of young girls, like a queen with her attendants. "Your Grace." She nodded regally.

The girls giggled softly.

"We've kept you too long," said Lucy. "The duke is restless."

More giggles and sidelong glances.

"Will you join me, Lady India?" he asked.

Indy nodded. "With pleasure. It was lovely to meet you, ladies."

"Don't forget your promise," called Lucy as Indy left with him.

"I won't," said Indy over her shoulder.

"What promise?" Raven asked.

"They don't approve of the plans for the pineapple gown. They want me to choose from their French fashion plates."

"Most ladies take these matters quite seriously."

She glanced at him from under her lashes. "They do, don't they?"

"I'll escort you to your chamber. Have you had supper?"

"Only pastries."

"I'll have something sent to your room." They walked up the stairs. "Here we are."

"Where are you, in the other wing?"

"I'm right," he pointed at the next door. "There."

"Surely not." Her eyes widened with alarm. "That can't be. Surely Lady Sterling would never allow such an impropriety."

"The guest wing is being refurbished and these are the only two rooms ready."

"Splendid," she muttered. "Just perfect. Tomorrow I'm finding new lodgings."

"Or I'm happy to leave."

"These are your friends, you should stay. I can't take much more of Lucy's wedding fever, so I'll be the one to leave."

A maidservant passed by and bobbed a curtsy, keeping her head down as she walked past them.

"I've something to tell you," said Raven. "About our search."

Here was where he diverted her attention away from Le Triton and toward Beauchamp and other less likely and far less dangerous suspects.

Indy entered her chambers and Raven followed, shutting the door behind him.

She traveled the perimeter of the large room, opening doors and sweeping aside curtains. His training in espionage had taught him to do the same in a new environment; map every potential entrance, exit, and hiding place.

"What are you looking for?" he asked.

She moved to the fireplace and warmed her hands over the flames. "I was making certain that there was no adjoining door between our chambers."

"If there was a door I would keep my side locked in case you decided to drink more whisky and rip my shirt open again in the middle of the night."

"I didn't rip open your shirt—you did. In your sleep." Her gaze lingered on his cravat and collar. "Have no fear, Raven." One side of her full lips slid into a smirk. "Your virtue is safe with me. Now what did you want to tell me?"

"Something Sir Charles told me tonight made me suspicious. He said that the Louvre has received several recent shipments for the Egyptian exhibit. When we go to the Louvre tomorrow, I want you to interview Beauchamp alone, while I slip away and search the premises."

"Why don't you do the interviewing and I'll do the searching?"

"I don't think my pretty ankles will distract

him long enough for you to conduct a thorough search."

"Why does your plan involve me standing around looking pretty?"

"It's not that, and you know it. You're the one who knows Beauchamp so well. Didn't you study hieroglyphics with him for several months? I hear he's infatuated with you." Why wouldn't he be? She was the most beautiful and fascinating woman on earth.

"You make it sound improper. Lady Catherine and I merely attended a series of his lectures."

"I've only met the man in passing, so it makes more sense for you to interrogate him."

"Oh very well," she said testily. "I'll keep him talking while you search."

"And don't fall for his glib flattery. He may be a brilliant linguist and antiquities expert, but he's also a notorious libertine."

"No need to warn me. I know all about notorious libertines."

Ouch. Her words kept wounding him when he thought himself impervious to feelings of any kind.

"Beauchamp did ask me to become his lover once," she said. "He told me that he admired my brilliant mind."

"That's not all he admired, I'll wager," Raven muttered.

She laughed. "Why my dear duke, are you jealous?"

"Of that conceited dandy? Hardly." Raven wasn't prepared for the ferociousness of his reaction. He wanted to shout that Beauchamp wasn't worthy to kiss the hem of her gown but he wasn't supposed to betray his emotions. He was a brick wall.

He was a brick wall who had to know whether she'd accepted Beauchamp's offer. "Did you accept?"

Her lips flattened into a line. "I don't think that's any of your business."

"You're my fiancée," he said gruffly.

Stupid thing to say. He was betraying too much.

She rolled her eyes. "Do I have to remind you that this is only a farce to hide our true purpose for being in Paris? You have no rights over me. I could take dozens of lovers if I so chose. You certainly haven't been chaste."

True. But the rumors of his conquests had been greatly exaggerated, mostly by him, in order to maintain his roguish cover story. He hadn't had a mistress in more than a year.

He should tell her that he had no objection to her taking lovers, that he wished only happiness and fulfillment for her, but the words stuck in his throat. The thought of her in another man's bed made him feel like a bull in a china shop.

He wanted to stamp his hooves and start smashing things.

"Take a lover," he said through gritted teeth, "just please don't let it be Beauchamp."

She tossed her head, and a lock of hair escaped from her simple coiffure. "Why do you object to him so much? Oh." She nodded her head. "I forgot. He published that scathing article about fortune hunters stealing antiquities for private collections. It was a thinly veiled attack on your unscrupulous methods."

"The man's a sanctimonious prig."

Raven hadn't cared about the article. What he'd cared about was hearing that Indy was attending Beauchamp's Paris lectures. Beauchamp and Indy spoke the same languages and shared so many of the same passions.

"Beauchamp invited me to accompany him on his upcoming expedition to Egypt under the patronage of King Charles."

Another stab of pain, as if she'd jabbed her dagger into his heart. "Will you go with him?" he asked, striving to keep his voice casual and uninterested.

"Traveling with Beauchamp as brilliant as he is, as limitless his resources, I'd be nothing more than his assistant." She shook the stray lock of hair away from her cheek. "I don't want to be a footnote in history. I want my very own chapter."

"And you'll have it, too. Probably not just a chapter. A whole set of volumes devoted to Lady India, the intrepid explorer."

She glanced at him with a puzzled expression.

That had been too intimate, too approving. *Back away now, Raven. Back to your jokes and your innuendoes.*

"Good night, then," he said hastily.

"Good night."

They stood there staring into each other's eyes, neither one of them moving.

"Good night," he repeated foolishly.

A good night for more kissing. A fine evening for bedsport.

He left her chamber and walked the few short steps to his own room.

At least there was no connecting door between their chambers, because if there were one, and if she came to him in the night and told him more about her erotic dreams, he wouldn't be able to turn her away.

He'd survived torture. He'd been shot at, knifed, hunted like a dog.

But Indy would make short work of his defenses.

That's why he had to find the stone. It could even be in one of the warehouses Sir Charles had been so furtive about. More likely, it was already with Le Triton.

If he didn't find the stone in Charles's warehouses that night, he'd talk to his usual contacts. Surprise a few ruffianly types. And if no one told him what he wanted to know, he'd bloody them up until they started talking.

He'd find the stone. Indy would identify it as the real one. And this mission would end.

He'd be a hero for the Foreign Office, his reputation reinstated. He would continue his quest for definitive proof of his father's innocence, with access to all of the resources of the Foreign Office.

Indy would leave on her next expedition. Alone. Without that lecherous Beauchamp.

And Raven would . . . well, he'd find some fresh trouble to get into.

Put his head down, and follow the dutiful path.

# Chapter 13

❦

*I*NDY LIFTED HER eyes. "I've always loved this view." She shivered in the chilly air. October usually began sunny, but soon the temperature would drop precipitously.

She and Raven stood on the Pont Royal. To their left was the impressive colonnade of the Tuileries and the Louvre, hugging the banks of the Seine. In front of them the river branched into two channels bordered by bustling quays, with the spires of Notre Dame rising majestically in the distance.

"It's a magnificent view," agreed Raven, but he wasn't looking at Notre Dame. His gaze was fixed on her face.

Excitement drew curlicues in her mind, embellishing her thoughts with hope. Today she and Raven could solve this mystery. In some ways this journey was the fulfillment of their childhood dreams; the adventurous partnership they'd envisioned.

Searching for treasures in foreign lands with Raven by her side.

Even though he'd been a royal pain in her arse all through breakfast, amusing himself by calling her ridiculous endearments for the benefit of the delighted young Lucy.

He'd called her his tough on the outside yet delectable on the inside pineapple, to which she'd responded by calling him her petite cabbage, in the odd manner of the French, who thought cabbages were adorable.

The endearment battle had only escalated from there, leaving Lucy and Lady Sterling gaping at them, not knowing whether to laugh or call for the French police.

His mask of joking reprehensibility was firmly back in place, which made it easier to maintain a safe emotional distance from him, but also gave her an odd feeling of loss. A hollow sensation in the pit of her stomach.

He tucked her hand into the crook of his arm. "I've always thought Paris to be one of the most romantic cities on earth, my fine feathered swan of a fiancée."

"Enough." She removed her hand and pretended to realign the fingers of her gray gloves. "We don't have to continue the act when we're alone. And what do you know about romance? Your dalliances are more transactional in nature, I believe."

"Ah, but *chérie*, I'm looking forward to driving Monsieur Beauchamp wild with jealousy. I'm practicing." He caught her hand and brought it to his lips.

"Kindly pull yourself together, you're acting like a complete ninny."

"I'm the Ravenwood you know and loathe."

"You can say that again."

"I'm the—"

"Not literally," she huffed. "Come along now. We have an antiquity to hunt."

They entered from the Place du Museum on the ground floor of the Old Louvre, which housed the Museum of French Sculpture and the Museum of Antiquities. Indy had brought Beauchamp's catalogue of the Gallery of Egyptian Antiquities, which listed in detail the more than nine thousand pieces they'd acquired from private collections including those of the former King Louis XVIII.

"It says here that they have recently acquired a very interesting mummified cat," said Indy, leafing through the booklet as they waited behind another tourist at the front desk.

The museum was only open to the public on Sundays, but foreigners with passports could enter by writing down their names and addresses.

"Is Monsieur Beauchamp on the premises?" Indy asked the bored-looking clerk in French when it was their turn.

"Yes, Madame, he is here but he is very busy at the moment."

"Please inform him that the Duke of Ravenwood and Lady India Rochester are here to see him."

"Dukes and ladies," said the clerk, as if those were two of the things he found most annoying in life. "Dukes and ladies do not take precedence over very large, very heavy, and fragile shipments of antiquities that just arrived today."

Indy met Raven's gaze. This could be it. Beauchamp could be unpacking the Rosetta Stone as they stood here.

"Monsieur Beauchamp knows me," Indy said firmly. "Don't mention the duke part, only the lady. He'll want to see me."

The clerk's eyes traveled over her plain attire. "Lady . . ."

"Lady India Rochester. We'll walk through the Antiquities rooms and wait for him in the Egyptian gallery."

"Oh very well. I'll inform him you're here." He snapped his fingers and a young page scurried to the desk to do his bidding.

They walked through the rooms of the Gallery of Egyptian Antiquities, Indy pointing out items of particular interest.

"It's built on a grander scale than the British Museum," remarked Raven.

"It's one of the most ancient palaces in France," she replied.

"What does the name *Louvre* mean? I've never bothered to research it."

Indy thumbed to the beginning of the catalogue. "Some have derived it from Lupara, a wolf, because it was formerly surrounded by a thick forest, much infested by wolves. Others have derived it from the Saxon word *Lower*, a chateau; and others, with more probability, from the ancient Gaulic word *Ouvre*," she read aloud. "Signifying the beauty of its architecture."

"It is magnificent."

"Outside of archaeological expeditions, the place I feel most at home is in museums. Every painting, sculpture, and relic has a complex story that isn't readily visible to the untrained eye."

Communing with the art and artifacts of people long dead was endlessly fascinating. It was also her safe haven.

Usually museums made her feel calm and peaceful.

Today she was on high alert.

In the Salle de Candelabre Indy stopped in front of one of her favorite pieces, a towering marble statue of a goddess. "Have you seen her yet?" she asked Raven. "They call her Venus de Milo, because she was found on the island of Melos by a Greek farmer."

"I've heard of her but never had the pleasure. She's very beautiful. But where are her arms?"

"They never found them. Personally, I don't think she's a Venus at all. I think if they had found her arms, she would have been holding a spear and leading a charge as Victory."

"Or she could have been holding an apple, the symbol of her victory in a beauty contest presided over by Paris before the Trojan War began."

"I see a warrior, you see a beauty contestant. There's the difference between us in a neat encapsulation."

"Or she could be both," said Raven. "A great warrior and a great beauty. Like you."

His mask had slipped and he was being nice to her again. "I'm not a classical beauty like my mother. I have too much of my father in my face."

"No one can look away when you're in the room. You've a strength and beauty to you. And

so does she." He gazed at the statue. "What sepa-
rates the great works of art? An artist who has
a story to tell. Every brushstroke or chisel mark
has an urgency to it as if the artist knew his own
mortality and was trying to create something to
outlast himself."

And now he was inside her head. *Bollocks.* Why
couldn't he be despicable 100 percent of the time,
like he used to be?

"I agree. The great works of art tell the story of
the artist. The sculptor is long dead, the hand that
created this crumbled to dust, but the stone en-
dures. And inside the stone, a song to be heard."

Her two worlds were colliding.

Her safe, peaceful place invaded by the man
who made all of her lonely, mistrustful choices
feel like they had been made not out of any grand
or higher purpose, but out of fear.

The man beside her was sculpted not from
stone but from flesh and blood and bone, and
there was a heart beating beneath his ribs, a body
she wanted to run her hands over to learn his
shape. To find his story. Listen to his song.

She could see that he was hiding something
from her.

She caught glimpses of another man behind
his eyes.

She wanted to know why he donned the mantle
of the unprincipled rogue. Was he hiding something painful? She thought of what Mari had
said. An anger so strong can only be born of pain.

If she chiseled away at him would she find
something new underneath?

She could spend her entire life researching the past and ignoring the present. But would she wake up one day and already be old and frail, with only her books and memories to keep her company?

Would she look back on her life and regret the risks not taken, the kisses not kissed?

The anger she'd nursed for so long. Would she regret that as well?

"What are you thinking of?" he asked. "You have a thoughtful expression, as though you're working out mathematical equations in your head."

"I was wondering what I might find if I chiseled away at your disguise."

Alarm flitted across his face. "I told you I had no deeper layers. I'm all surface. We should go and find Beauchamp."

"We should," Indy agreed.

A man's voice startled her. "She's beautiful, isn't she?"

They both turned around to find Beauchamp had entered the room while they were speaking.

BEAUCHAMP WAS STARING at Indy instead of the Venus when he spoke of beauty.

There'd never been any love lost between Raven and Beauchamp. If the man didn't take his eyes off of Indy and move them to the statue soon, there could be bloodshed.

"Lady India, what a surprise." Beauchamp bowed over Indy's hand, giving her a limpid, admiring gaze.

Indy smiled widely. "Victor, it's delightful to see you."

She called him Victor? Raven barely restrained himself from ripping the man's throat out with his bare hands.

"It is an unexpected pleasure to see you, my lady." He inclined his head in Raven's direction. "Your Grace."

"Monsieur Beauchamp," Raven growled.

He wasn't in a very charitable mood at present.

He'd found absolutely nothing of interest last evening in Sir Charles's desk drawers, or his warehouses. And Le Triton's servants were proving remarkably un-bribable.

"What brings you to the Louvre, my lady?" asked Beauchamp, in an insinuating tone of voice that clearly implied that she was here to see him.

"I wanted to show His Grace the new gallery. I've been reading to him from your excellent catalogue. It's quite an accomplishment. Over seven thousand new pieces."

"Over four thousand from your Mr. Pepper's collection alone. The British Museum turned him down, I hear. Said his collection was too expensive. King Charles was happy to pay the ten thousand pounds he asked."

"It was our loss," said Indy.

"You had to purchase something to replace all the pieces plundered by that marauding despot and then returned to their rightful owners," said Raven, though he was supposed to keep quiet.

Beauchamp raised his eyebrows. "And what of your Lord Elgin's marbles? Clearly they belong back in the Parthenon."

"Perhaps," said Indy, darting a questioning glance in Raven's direction. "Will you be hunting for the missing pieces of the Rosetta Stone when you return to Egypt this year?"

"What would I want with the dessert when the main course is in the British Museum?" asked Beauchamp.

"My mistake," said Indy. Clever how she'd turned the conversation to the stone. "It would be marvelous if the stone could be made whole."

"Marvelous," agreed Beauchamp, though he didn't sound enthusiastic about it. "I hope you'll allow me to give you a personal tour? I want to show you around my new collection."

Indy placed her hand on Beauchamp's arm. "I'd be delighted."

*Overly whiskered, pompous windbag.* Raven stewed as the man waxed eloquent about this sarcophagus and that collection of weaponry.

Beauchamp was probably considered to be a handsome man. He was nearly as tall as Raven, with dark hair and dark eyes. He wasn't of Indy's social status, but he was a brilliant linguist.

She seemed quite happy leaning on his arm.

He'd instructed her to flirt with Beauchamp, but did she have to hang on his every utterance? It was twisting his gut into knots. She never had told him whether she'd accepted Beauchamp's offer, or not.

Beauchamp touched her arm and Raven saw red.

Indy laughed at something Beauchamp said and Raven nearly crashed his fist into a display case of ancient golden tableware.

Enough. He sidled closer to Indy. "Have you heard the news?" he asked Beauchamp. "We've set a date for our wedding. We will be married as soon as possible."

The astonishment on Beauchamp's face was nearly enough to counter the displeasure on Indy's fair visage.

He was cocking everything up. He was supposed to keep quiet and slip away unobtrusively. But he couldn't just stand there and let Beauchamp slobber all over her.

Indy glared at him. "Sometimes one does wish for a little more *privacy*." She deliberately took Beauchamp's arm again and they walked away, leaving Raven trailing behind like a bloody attendant.

Now Raven was wishing he'd used his usual methods to make Beauchamp talk. He could have cornered him on his way home. Placed a hood over his face so he couldn't identify Raven. He would have asked him questions about Le Triton's involvement with the Louvre, and given Beauchamp gentle . . . nudges . . . if he didn't answer.

It would have been so much easier, and far more satisfying.

He must stop being so possessive of Indy and make his escape to search the premises, though he was nearly positive the stone was with Le Triton. He was about to leave when a guard approached and whispered something in Beauchamp's ear.

A look of consternation crossed his face. "I'm afraid I must leave you, my lady. Please do enjoy the exhibit." He hurried away with the guard.

Indy rounded on Raven, her eyes flashing. "I can answer my own questions, thank you very much. And what was all that about? Did you have to be so rude to him? You were like a dog marking your territory."

"He was the dog. He was practically slobbering on you."

"He was being a gracious host. It's a good thing this is only a charade—I would never tolerate being overly protected in such an odious manner. Now you've lost your chance to search."

"Beauchamp didn't leave in the direction of the area where newly arrived antiquities are stored." Raven pointed to the arched doorway in the center of the wall. "The loading area is through there. We can still search, but we'll have to be careful."

"How do you know where to search?" she asked.

"I studied the architectural plans for the building last night."

Raven kept a watch for guards as he guided her down a corridor toward the courtyard where packages were received.

The heavy metal door swung open with a loud groaning sound. There were guards on the outside, patrolling the courtyard, but the large storage room was unoccupied.

When his eyes adjusted to the gloom, he saw that there were several large crates, one of which was sitting on rollers so as to be easier to pull up the ramp. Sarcophagi and crates were piled everywhere.

"Everything's in the process of being classified," Indy whispered.

A guard passed in front of one of the outside windows.

"We must hurry," whispered Raven.

"There." Indy pointed to the large wooden crate near the outer door. They moved soundlessly, stepping in tandem to the unopened crate.

The problem would be prying it open without making too much noise.

Raven searched the room and found a metal pry bar. Indy wrapped her shawl around the metal edge to muffle the sound. He wedged the bar under the lid and pushed with all his might.

The creaking sound of the wood pulling away from the nails seemed deafening, and Raven hoped the guards outside couldn't possibly hear the noise unless they opened the door.

The lid came free and Indy helped him lift it off and set it to the side.

The crate was filled with shavings of wood. He brushed them away, digging downward. "I feel something solid."

She thrust her arm into the shavings and found his hand. He guided her hand to the edge he'd found. "Rough," she said. "Not smooth like a sculpture." She continued her exploration.

"Raven." Her eyes caught his in the dim light, gleaming like a twilight sky. "There's an inscription carved into the surface. I think this could be the stone!"

# Chapter 14

*INDY TRACED THE* jagged edge, her breath catching. What a triumph it would be to find the stone so swiftly.

Raven dug deeper into the wood shavings, piling them to one side of the crate.

Her heart raced. A black edge emerged. Black basalt.

She brushed wood shavings away and leaned over the edge of the crate, sticking her nose close to the stone so that she could read the inscription.

"Well?" Raven asked. "Is it the stone? Don't keep me in suspense. We must hurry—there are guards outside and they could decide to patrol the room at any moment."

She traced the hieroglyphic for Ptolemy. "It could be the stone," she said.

"Really?" he asked incredulously.

"Could it really be this easy?"

"Obviously we make a good investigative team. Me and you. Not you and Beauchamp."

She smiled. "I'm getting the feeling that you really don't like Monsieur Beauchamp."

"He stole the stone."

"We don't know that for certain yet." She

brushed away the shavings to reveal more of the inscription. "It could have been sent to him without his knowledge."

"Hogwash! Don't defend that pompous windbag. I'm going to see that he's brought to justice for this."

"Calm down, Raven. We don't know all of the facts. Let's uncover the rest so I can make a thoroughly informed identification."

They brushed away more of the shavings.

The search could be over. She could translate the name of the temple. It was all so thrilling and wonderful. So why wasn't her heart lifting with joy?

*Because this means you won't have an excuse to spend time with Raven.*

She stroked her hand across the surface of the stone, pushing deeper, and then . . . the stone ended. Far too abruptly.

"It's not big enough," she blurted.

"What do you mean?"

"It can't be the stone. It's not long enough."

His hands scrabbled faster, clearing away the shaving.

The stone ended abruptly in a jagged, blunt edge. "You're right," he said, his face falling.

"It's only a fragment of a tablet." She sat down with a thud on the wooden lid of the crate. "It's not the Rosetta Stone."

Raven placed a hand on her shoulder. "I'm sorry. I know you need the stone for your research." He turned back to the crate. "Could it be one of the missing pieces from the stone?"

She perked her head up. "It could be, at that." She examined the tablet, tracing the blunt edge. "It might be the right shape. If it's a missing piece, then Beauchamp has even more of a motive for stealing the rest of the stone. And it would explain why a replica was placed in the museum. He could have been arrogant enough to think that no one would discover the deception."

Raven's gaze searched the room. "But there's no other crate big enough to house the stone."

"Back to the hunt," said Indy. "We can—"

A loud bell alarm sounded. Indy jumped. "They know we're here. They've raised the alarm."

"Don't panic." Raven helped her replace the shavings and the lid. She took his hand and they raced for the door.

"There's no one here," she said, scanning the corridor.

She heard the sound of footsteps but they were running away from them, not toward them.

No one tried to stop them or arrest them for trespassing.

A guard raced by but he paid them no attention. The clanking of the alarm sounded again.

"What's happening, do you think?" asked Indy.

"I've no idea but they're not after us."

"Thank heavens."

They returned to the Egyptian gallery not a moment too soon. Seconds later, Beauchamp walked through a door with a stricken expression.

"Victor, what's wrong?" asked Indy.

"You'll have to leave now, Lady India. Your

Grace. The entire museum is being shut down. The police are on their way."

"Why, what's happened?" she asked.

"I'm not sure I can tell you until the authorities have completed their search." There was a coldness about his demeanor now, a reserve that hadn't been there earlier.

"Why don't you tell us, perhaps we can help?" said Raven.

"Something's gone missing."

"Something important?" asked Raven.

"Priceless and irreplaceable. Now if you'll excuse my haste, I'll escort you out."

Indy had noticed something earlier. "Could it involve the chair? The one with the blue lion's-paw feet?"

Beauchamp stopped abruptly. From his reaction Indy could tell that she was right.

"*Mon dieu*, how could you know this?" asked Beauchamp.

"Because she's very clever," said Raven.

"I read your description of the chair and noticed it was missing from the exhibit. I thought perhaps you had it out for repair," she explained.

"A chair?" asked Raven. "You're so upset about a chair?"

"Not just any chair," said Beauchamp. "A three-thousand-year-old Egyptian chair, preserved in nearly perfect condition in the chamber of a tomb. One of our most popular displays at the moment because its lines are so close to the fashionable Directoire style with its feet and curved roll back.

The chair proved to be a powerful curiosity. This is quite a blow for the museum. And . . . it's not the only item missing."

"Who would steal from the Louvre?" asked Indy. "And for what purpose?"

"That's a very good question." Beauchamp's eyes traveled over Raven's face challengingly. "Why would anyone want to gloat over another's misfortune?"

"We won't tell anyone," said Indy.

"Please don't," said Beauchamp.

"You have our word." Indy inclined her head.

Beauchamp nodded distractedly and hurried away.

As they left the Louvre, Indy spoke in a low whisper. "It can't be Beauchamp. Why would he stage that whole episode? The chair went missing and he was completely surprised."

"Then why did he lie about the missing piece of the stone? He said he wasn't keen to find it."

"I can't be certain that's what we uncovered. It looked like a shape that might be right but the lighting was low and . . ."

"Don't sympathize with that puffed-up buffoon."

"What's he ever done to you?"

"Nothing, I don't like his attitude. I don't like his smarmy smile and the familiar way he put his hand on your arm."

"I put my hand on his arm."

"Well, I didn't like it."

"You don't own me."

"I told him we were to be married and he still placed his hand on the small of your back to steer you. And don't say he didn't. I saw it clear as day. Don't ever become his lover. You can do much, much better."

"Oh I suppose you would be a better choice." She said it angrily, but the second the words left her mouth she wished she could take them back.

"As a matter of fact, yes. Beauchamp would probably require a guidebook and a map to find your . . . uh . . . never mind."

"The pearl in my oyster?" she supplied.

He snorted. "Not the euphemism I would have chosen, but yes."

"And you're such a masterful lover."

"It just so happens that I am. The world's best."

"Of all the arrogant . . . you're a jackass, you know that?" she sputtered.

They marched side by side, separated by a gulf of tension. Their world order restored. Slinging barbs and innuendoes.

*He declares himself to be the world's best lover. She calls him an arrogant arse.*

"I think you're wrong about Beauchamp," said Indy as they walked back on the rue du Fauborg Saint Honoré. "I think we can safely cross him off our list. Whoever stole the stone was the same one who stole the lion's-paw chair."

"The odds are good," he said grudgingly.

"So what else has been stolen? That's the question. We should find out whether anything else is missing from other museums in other countries. This could point firmly in the direction of your antiquities thief, Mr. Le Triton."

"Or not," said Raven. "It could be anyone,

really. Especially the Russians. We'll be able to make subtle inquiries at the diplomatic event tomorrow evening."

"What event?"

"Didn't I tell you?"

"No, you did not." She stopped walking. "What event?"

"Sir Charles is hosting a small gathering of diplomats tomorrow and I said you and I would attend."

"Well thank you for accepting the invitation without telling me about it."

"It slipped my mind."

"I've nothing to wear to an affair of state."

"It's Paris. You can purchase something ready-made."

"A duke's sister does not wear ready-made," she said disdainfully.

"Then have a seamstress make you something."

"Overnight?"

"I'm relying on you to gather intelligence on our suspects."

She walked in silence for a few moments, resentment simmering. If she was attending an affair at Sir Charles's house tomorrow evening there was no point in moving to a lady's school or hotel. "I suppose I could make a new list of suspects and we could start crossing them off tomorrow," she said.

"That's the spirit."

When they arrived back at the house, Lucy was waiting in ambush. "Oh there you are! I have a surprise for you. Madame Victoire is here to garb you for the soiree tomorrow evening!"

A slender woman in an elegant jet-black silk dress came forward. She curtsied to Raven. "Your Grace, it would be such an honor to dress your future duchess."

"She also has several sketches for your wedding costume," Lucy enthused. "And don't worry, there are still mounds of frills, just artfully arranged."

Raven grinned at Indy. "Problem solved, my dear." He turned to Madame Victoire. "Lady India was just bemoaning her lack of a suitable gown to wear tomorrow and I said she should purchase something ready-made."

"Ready-made," huffed Madame Victoire. "Certainly not. I do have a dress made already, but I will modify it entirely to suit your queenly figure, my lady. And as for the wedding costume, I have several sketches already complete. If you'll perhaps consider a softer gold instead of the canary . . ."

"I'll leave you ladies to your work," said Raven, making a hasty departure.

Traitor. Leave the ladies to their work. Frills and silk and stitches. But she did want to look her best tomorrow. For intelligence-gathering purposes, only, of course. Not because she wanted to see Raven's jaw drop when she appeared at the top of the stairs.

She'd be a *femme fatale*, as the French said. *My Lady Spy.*

She'd use all the weapons at her disposal.

RAVEN DIDN'T EVEN bother to attend supper that evening.

During the meal, Indy had asked where he was and Lady Sterling had said the gentlemen had gone out. From the resigned way she said the words Indy understood that Lady Sterling's husband abandoned her quite frequently in the evenings.

He and Raven were probably visiting gaming houses and bawdy houses, doing all manner of foolish things that could expose their secret. Raven thought she was the indiscreet one? She was going to give him an extra-sharp piece of her mind when he returned.

Some partnership.

Indy paced up and down her chamber, peering out the window from time to time to see if any carriages had arrived. When she wasn't pacing, she made lists of suspects and marked up the map of Paris that she'd brought with her on the journey.

She should have gone to a hotel.

Being in the same house with him was like dousing a fire with oil.

This entire elaborate ruse of theirs—and the events that had led up to it—the hate-kissing, the faux wedding plans . . . the whisky incident. Was it all in the name of archaeology, all in the name of her noble goals? Or was it purely selfish?

Had she done it simply because she wanted to be near him?

Was that why she was here, in this house filled with family, pushed and pulled by their whims, when she could be in a quiet, lonely room in an anonymous hotel?

*You know the answer to that question,* her heart whispered.

She curled up in a chair. The Minerva coin was still around her throat. Her talisman against the dangers of love. Or was it something else?

She unclasped the gold chain and held the coin in her hand. Was she wearing this for another reason?

The thought skirting the edges of her mind was nearly too terrible to contemplate.

Did she still have some pathetic hope that Raven would suddenly come to his senses and . . . what? Declare that he loved her?

And if she secretly hoped that he might love her still . . . did that mean . . .

*Bollocks!*

She gripped the coin in her palm, the edges digging into her flesh.

She couldn't love him. What a ridiculous thought. She would never be that stupid.

The noise of carriage wheels made her jump out of her chair and run to the window.

Raven alighted from the carriage but not Sir Charles.

She waited for the sound of Raven in the hallway. She thought he might stop by her chamber to explain where he'd been, but his footsteps passed her door.

No explanation. No apology.

They were supposed to be equal partners and she had a right to know what he'd been doing. She would not be excluded, or relegated to the role of silent observer.

She would not be his footnote, and she was going to tell him as much. Why should she be afraid to go to his chamber? She'd faced cut-throats in dark alleys. She was afraid of nothing.

Not even her own treacherous heart.

She shut the Minerva coin necklace in a small compartment in her traveling case. She didn't need to wear it anymore.

She rolled up the map and stuck the list of suspects down her bodice.

His door was literally five steps from hers. Five confident, purposeful steps.

A business meeting between two professional colleagues with the same goal, nothing more.

The door was ajar. She knocked loudly and pushed it open.

She stopped cold.

*Turn around. You're not equipped for this.*

Raven lounged in a chair by the fireplace in only trousers and a shirt. No boots. No coat.

His shirt hung open, exposing his neck and a breathtaking view of his upper chest.

Firelight glinting in copper eyes. Shadows playing across the delineated muscles of his chest.

Just like in her dreams, but even more beautiful.

She swallowed.

"What's this?" he asked with the devilish grin

that used to melt her heart. "I didn't ask for a curvaceous lady with amethyst eyes to be delivered to my chamber."

"And I didn't expect to find a half-clothed rogue waiting for me," she said indignantly.

# Chapter 15

♋

RAVEN STRETCHED HIS arms over his head and cradled the back of his neck with interlaced fingers.

He didn't have to hide the scars on his chest because she'd already seen them.

"I thought you were Sir Charles's valet bringing my formal attire for tomorrow's diplomatic event."

"There's a chill in the air, Raven." Her gaze lingered on his chest. "You should be wearing more clothing."

"That's why I'm sitting by the fire. No point in dressing when he'll only undress me."

The heat in her eyes made his stomach muscles clench.

The way she stared made him want to give her a better show. He flexed his pectorals and her gaze intensified.

"Don't you have a night robe?" She stopped staring at his chest and searched the room. "Ah ha! I see one there. Do put it on."

He grinned. "Why, are you going to ravish me?"

"Certainly not. I'm here for a meeting between colleagues on a shared mission, and it won't be much of a professional meeting if one of the participants is practically naked."

"The valet could come at any moment. Do you really want to be caught in my room?"

She closed the door. "I'll hide if anyone comes."

He stood. "Can we make this a breakfast meeting?"

"No we cannot." She unrolled the map she carried and spread it out on a table, weighting the edges with books she found on a shelf. "I don't want to be teamed with you any more than you want to be teamed with me, but we must develop a plan of attack. In tandem."

"In tandem usually implies that one of us will be in front of the other."

"Together, then," she said impatiently, touching the simple knot of hair at the nape of her neck. "As equal partners."

Together.

The problem was that he liked the idea of being together with her far too much. Together as in . . . *together.*

Joined. Connected.

As in . . . his hands connecting with her hair and pulling that simple knot free so he could see her black hair tumble around her shoulders.

He buried the idea as quickly as it arose.

"I thought we *had* developed a plan," he said lightly. "We attend the diplomatic event tomorrow and find out whether any other country has reported missing antiquities so that we may eliminate more suspects."

"I thought we'd decided on a plan as well, but then you snuck out of the house earlier with Sir Charles, going Lord only knows where."

So that's why her eyes sparked brighter than the fire in the hearth. "You didn't like being left alone this evening."

She crossed her arms. "I did not."

He wasn't going to apologize for going out with Sir Charles. He'd done nothing wrong. They'd visited his club and Raven had talked to several European diplomats. "You didn't enjoy your evening with Lady Sterling?"

She made an impatient noise in the back of her throat. "That's not the point, Raven. Here's the crux of the matter. You knew precisely what I was doing this evening. A quiet repast with genteel ladies. I, on the other hand, have absolutely no idea how you spent your evening. And I must say that my imagination ran away from me. You accuse me of being theatrical, impulsive, and unguarded, but you could say something in the heat of passion in a bawdy house and you could expose the entire mission and I won't have—"

"Indy, I didn't go to a bawdy house." He hadn't even thought that she might make that assumption.

She sniffed. "I don't care if you did."

She was lying. She did care. And he cared about making her think better of him. He was sick to death of trying to make her hate him.

He put on the robe and knotted it loosely around his waist. "I went with Sir Charles to his club with an eye to assessing whether any other diplomats might be aware that the stone is missing. All anyone could talk about was the theft of the chair from the Louvre."

"Well you could have informed me that you

were going out," she said stiffly. "If I'd been the one sneaking off like that you would have scolded me for being reckless."

"You're right. I should have told you where I was going. I'm not accustomed to having to answer to anyone for my actions." The Foreign Office left him mostly to his own devices. No questions asked if he achieved the desired results.

He approached her. "I won't leave you alone again without an explanation."

*During the day*, he amended silently. At night he would continue his preparations for the raid on Le Triton's stronghold.

He needed to confirm the exact number of guards patrolling the estate.

Malcolm had said he would assemble a team to assist with the mission, but Raven hadn't yet received any sign.

He bent over the map. "What's this, a map of Paris?"

"I've circled the residences of all the key players, as well as other locations that could conceal the stone." She tapped her finger on the map. "Let's approach this like an archaeological excavation. We know the item is in Paris, but we must narrow our search. We know it's not at the Louvre, so that leaves the Russian ambassador's residence, here." She pointed it out on the map. "Or Le Triton's estate, here."

Why did she have to be so damnably intelligent? He had to throw her off of the Le Triton trail. "You didn't circle the palace?"

"I don't suspect the French monarch. I think

he's too busy suppressing the rumors of an uprising in his own court."

"Agreed. But you haven't yet consulted Lady Catherine. Doesn't she know every antiquities enthusiast in Paris?"

"Lady Sterling informed me that Lady Catherine is on the guest list for tomorrow, as she's a well-connected British citizen living in Paris. I'll consult with her tomorrow."

She'd thought of everything. "Excellent work."

"Thank you. I also have a list of suspects." She extracted a tiny scroll of paper from her bosom and handed it to him. The paper was still warm from being next to her skin.

He'd never envied a scrap of paper before.

She'd listed four suspects: Le Triton; Beauchamp (crossed off and replaced with "other antiquities party?"); the Russians (Ambassador Petrov); and . . . He scrutinized the list again. "Why did you include Sir Charles?"

"You may be too blind to see it, but his wife is extremely unhappy with him right now and that leads me to believe he may be having an amour with a courtesan, which would open him to blackmail and to being influenced on behalf of the French."

Remarkable.

She'd just handed him the exact same list that Sir Malcolm had given him in the confidential dossier.

"I agree. These are our primary suspects." He strode to the fireplace and threw the list into the flame.

"What did you do that for?" she asked indignantly.

"One of the first rules of . . . sleuthing." He'd been going to say espionage. He was losing his edge. She made him careless. *She made him care.* "One of the first rules is leave no evidence to be found. The list could have fallen into the wrong hands."

"You never make lists when you're hunting antiquities?"

"I keep everything here." He tapped the side of his head.

She snorted. "Forgive me if I'm skeptical. I've seen how much brandy you consume. Do you even have a strategy . . . or are you just hoping for luck?"

"I don't require a strategy. I use my intuition. I know when I'm on the right trail, I scent antiquities like a bloodhound."

"Intuition," she scoffed. "Sounds to me as though you just don't like preparing or planning for anything. You hate anything that might mean forethought, responsibility, or commitment."

"My instincts and intuition have served me well. I found the Wish Diamond necklace in that rusted trunk in an abandoned farmhouse in Provence, remember?"

"You've been extraordinarily lucky, that's all. But sooner or later, luck runs out. Then what will you fall back upon?"

"My good looks and charm."

"I've had to rely on hard work and persistence." She moved restlessly toward the window. "Why do you keep the diamond, anyway? Aren't you afraid someone will try to steal it from your London townhouse?"

"I carry it with me."

She stopped moving. "Right now? You have it with you, in Paris?"

He indicated the black velvet case sitting atop the escritoire. "It's right there."

"Are you serious? You keep a diamond that used to belong to Alexander the Great out in the open? I thought you would have it under lock and key and guard watch."

"Sometimes hiding something in plain sight is the best way to ensure it's overlooked. You didn't notice it, did you?"

She opened the velvet box, lifted the sparkling necklace, and held it toward a lamp. She touched the enormous purple diamond at the center of the necklace. "It's breathtaking. Such a true purple. This really should be displayed in a museum for the delight of the world."

"It really should be displayed around your neck." He said it without thinking. Probably because he'd pictured her so many times wearing the necklace.

Indy clad in the Wish Diamond and nothing more.

"I've never cared for jewels," said Indy.

Despite her professed disinterest, she lifted the necklace and clasped it around her neck. The motion thrust her breasts toward him in an entirely distracting manner, even though she wore a modestly-cut gown of an olive-green hue.

She moved to the standing glass in the corner of the room and looked at her reflection.

She dangled the necklace against the base of her throat. The large purple diamond found a resting place over her breastbone. Not even a hint of curving bosom to be seen, but for some reason the innocent swath of skin was the most erotic sight he'd ever beheld.

Raven held his breath, attempting to prolong the moment. Indy watching herself in the glass, her eyes nearly the same color as the diamond.

He wanted to make her eyes spark with desire.

He wanted to give her joy.

Give her the necklace. Give her his dried-up husk of a heart.

"If Lucy saw you with that diamond around your neck, she'd insist on painting your portrait," he said, moving closer, drawn by her beauty.

She wasn't looking at him; she watched her own reflection in the glass, so he allowed himself to gaze at her with all of the longing and regret filling his mind, expanding his heart.

"Isn't the necklace in high demand by collectors?" she asked.

"Many have attempted to purchase it from me."

She turned abruptly and he struggled to mask his emotions. "I have an idea," she said, her eyes shining. "You said that Le Triton's estate is impenetrable."

Had he said that? He thought back to their conversation in her brother's study. She'd accused him of being friends with Le Triton, and he'd responded by saying that Le Triton ran a criminal organization from his impenetrable stronghold in Paris . . . Gods! What was wrong with him? He really was cocking this up.

"Ah," he cleared his throat. "I think you're right to focus on the Russian ambassador, Mr. Petrov. He'll be here tomorrow and—"

"Raven, I have an idea." Her smile glowed with excitement. "I know how we can solicit an invitation to visit Le Triton's estate. I'll wear the Wish Diamond to his gaming house at the Palais Royal. He'll see me wearing it, you'll offer to negotiate a sale, but only if he shows you his prized collection."

"Absolutely out of the question." Raven stalked to the fireplace and rested his hands on the mantelpiece. "I won't use you as bait."

Malcolm had made the same suggestion and Raven had refused. The word was already out that he wanted to sell the necklace.

Indy approached him from behind. *Don't turn around.* She could persuade him to do anything with those eyes of hers. *Don't look at her.*

"You're right, Raven. You won't use me for anything. I won't be *used*. Ever. I demand to be respected, listened to . . . trusted. I'm asking you to meet me halfway in this endeavor. You keep making these decisions that you think are for my own good and I will not have decisions made on my behalf."

"I won't put you in danger."

"Put me. Use me. You seem to think that you control everything and I control nothing."

He turned around and then wished to hell he

hadn't. The hurt in the depths of her eyes made him want to bash his head against the marble mantelpiece.

She wanted him to meet her halfway, to trust that she knew what she was doing and that her skills on this mission were as valid and valuable as his own.

She demanded his respect and he could give that to her. She demanded that he trust her enough to involve her in the plan to topple Le Triton. As much as his entire being railed against the idea, perhaps it was time to trust her skills, and her ideas.

"Indy," he began, but had to pause for breath, for calm. "You're drawn to these powerful women in history because you're proudly carrying their standard into the modern era. A queen such as Cleopatra would have worn a jewel such as this into battle."

Her challenging gaze faltered. "You're agreeing to my plan?"

"I'm saying that I . . . that I trust you." And he trusted himself to protect her. They'd go to the gaming house for an hour, no more. She'd display the diamond, he'd bring her home safely.

The pain in her expression receded. "The necklace will dazzle everyone into spilling their secrets tomorrow."

"You'll dazzle them."

"Not I. I'm not much of a seductress. I don't have any feminine wiles, as my mother loves to remind me."

He drew another deep breath. Move this conversation back to surface topics. Keep everything light and joking between them.

"You don't require feminine wiles with a bosom like yours," he said in a joking voice.

She glanced down at her chest. "That's not enough. I may have to use flirtation to encourage the suspects to talk. I should practice the art of seduction. I know that's one of the tools in the espionage arsenal."

"No, no." Not a good idea. "You don't require practice. You're quite seductive enough already."

"Flattery will get you nowhere, Raven. You know that's a load of horse droppings. I'm about as seductive as a porcupine." She tilted her head to one side. "Though with the right accoutrements . . . perhaps I could pass for a coquette."

"I really don't think such artifice is required for—"

"Picture me in a low-cut evening gown with my bosom thrust up by my corset," she said with a wicked little smile.

*Whatever you do, don't picture that.*

She advanced. Raven retreated until his back hit the heated marble of the fireplace.

The blaze in Indy's eyes was far hotter.

She wriggled her shoulders and thrust out her chest. "I should practice playing the helpless female, fluttering my lashes, exposing my décolletage, and saying flattering things. Insinuating myself into a man's confidence, all the while asking probing questions."

Exposing. Insinuating. Probing.

These were not things he wanted Indy to be doing.

Or things he wanted to do to Indy.

He cleared his throat. "You possess more feminine wiles than you may be aware of and you really don't need to practice. In fact, what you should do is get some sleep so that you're well-rested for tomorrow's adventures."

"I think I do need practice." She moved closer, widening her eyes and . . . damn it . . . fluttering her long, black eyelashes. "Now I'm going to give you a searing glance that is supposed to communicate that I'm picturing you entirely naked. Which should elicit a reciprocal imagining on your part."

She gave him a searing glance.

"Did it work?" she asked.

He gulped, unable to form words. He was still imagining her completely naked, wearing only the Wish Diamond around her neck, nestled between her sumptuous breasts. He'd also imagined grabbing her by the waist, flinging her over his shoulder, and carrying her to the velvet-curtained bed, which suddenly seemed to occupy most of the room.

Bed. Indy.

Bad combination.

"I'll take your silence and labored breathing as a yes," she said triumphantly.

"Why don't you take yourself back to your room," he managed to say.

"I'm not finished practicing yet. I must move slowly, sensuously. Nothing too brusque or bold.

A coy glance, like this. I've seen how courtesans behave. I'd show a little bit of flesh. Not too much. Just enough to tantalize." She slipped her sleeve off her shoulder.

She shimmied her shoulders and the other sleeve slid down as well, exposing her chemise and the upper curves of her breasts.

He dragged in a breath. "That's enough, Indy."

"I won't go too far, don't worry. Only to the . . . edge." Her gown slipped lower, her breasts nearly exposed now, the fabric caught on her nipples. She shivered, her nipples stiffening.

He couldn't take his eyes away from her.

"You're still upset with me for leaving without telling you where I was going. You're punishing me," he said. "Showing me that you're in control."

"Am I? Does this feel like a punishment?"

If the sight of her breasts straining over her low-cut corset was a punishment, then he'd been a very bad rogue and he'd pay penance for the rest of his life.

He licked his lips. "Indy, I don't think you require lessons in seduction. You're a natural. You could teach a master class."

"Then perhaps you should wear the diamond instead." She unclasped the necklace and draped it around his neck.

She was so near now that he could smell her perfume. Raven's entire body lit like a lamp wick touched by a flame.

"It . . . doesn't fit around your neck," she said, biting her full lower lip.

Her arms circled his neck, and her forearms

rested on his shoulders. Her luscious lips were so close.

"The diamond will look so much better against your décolletage than my chest." He moved the necklace back to her neck and fastening the clasp. He arranged the diamond over her breastbone.

It occurred to him that she wasn't wearing the copper Minerva coin around her neck anymore.

At least she wore the Wish Diamond. At least he could give her a lavish gift to make up for the hurt he'd caused. After they found the stone and left Paris, he'd give her the diamond. She'd probably donate it to a museum but he would always have this memory.

The pale purple diamond flickering with light, reflected in her eyes.

His fingers didn't want to leave her skin.

"Will I be enough of an enticement?" she asked.

"You'd give a marble statue a cock-stand, Indy."

She chuckled. "Is that right?" Her gaze traveled down his body.

He didn't even attempt to hide the power she held over him. The silk robe had parted to reveal his trousers, which were fitting very snugly at the moment.

"Now, listen here," she said, tilting her head down. "We need to have a chat."

Was she talking to his *cock*?

"Women are good for so much more than bedfellows alone. I know that's all you're interested in, but your master does possess an intellect, however diminished by debaucherous pursuits, and he must learn to treat females as equals and include them in his plans and speak to them as more than just ornaments. He mustn't make decisions on their behalf."

She lifted her head and smiled devastatingly. "Men are always underestimating me." She moved away, the smile dropping from her lips. "Don't make that mistake again, Raven."

So this had all been a lesson. She'd been toying with him. "Believe me, I won't."

He'd never underestimated her. He'd had to hide his admiration and respect. He'd been cheering for her this whole time, exulting in every one of her achievements.

"All I want from you is your respect," she said. "Stop treating me like a female to shelter and protect, and treat me as an equal partner."

"Equal partner. Understood. Er, the valet will be here any moment. I think I should have a moment to . . ." He waved a hand at his genitals. "Compose myself."

She smiled wickedly.

*Gods. Not another wicked smile. She had to leave.*

There was a knock on the door.

"Too late," she whispered, and dashed toward the large oak wardrobe, climbing inside and pulling the door closed.

*Perfect.* Now he had a stiff cock, a voluptuous woman hidden in his wardrobe, and a valet who was here to disrobe him.

"Enter," Raven called. He'd make sure the encounter was brief.

"Good evening, Your Grace."

"Harris."

"I've come to fit you for your evening wear, and I'll be happy to perform any other little duties you may require, since you've not brought your own valet."

*There's a whip-brained bonfire of a seductress in my wardrobe. Would you mind taking her away and giving her a good dousing with ice-cold water before she burns the house down?*

Harris held up a measuring tape. "May I take your measurements?"

Raven was about to send the man packing when a roguish thought occurred to him. Indy had been teaching him a lesson. A lesson in seduction.

Perhaps it was time he taught her one as well. A lesson about hiding in wardrobes.

"By all means." Raven shed the silk robe and flung it over a chair back.

Next he lifted his shirt over his head.

Harris approached. "If you'll just lift your arms, Your Grace."

"Happy to." He stood, legs and arms spread wide, in full view of the wardrobe.

The valet began measuring his shoulders and back.

She'd played him just now, deliberately teased and seduced him.

*Two could play that game.*

If she wanted a private show . . . he'd give her one.

INDY HAD AN excellent view through the keyhole of the wardrobe. In her crouched position she was right at eye level with Raven's nether regions.

The valet unbuttoned Raven's trousers with practiced movements and Raven stepped out of them.

Rather suspicious how his crotch was so perfectly framed in her view. Had he moved closer and turned his body in just the right way to give her a show?

She could clearly see the outline of his formidable male organ through the thin cotton of his undergarments.

The valet made his measurements, reciting numbers that made her head spin a little.

Goodness his thighs were massive. And the vast length of his arm span . . . and the thickness of his neck.

If he were a statue in a museum she would examine him unabashed. Think of him as marble. Think of him as . . . well, that wasn't bloody well going to work. She couldn't think of him as anything but Raven, the man she wanted to seduce.

There, she'd admitted it. All of that practicing her feminine wiles so she'd be able to question Russian ambassadors and French criminals.

That had all been about seducing Raven.

Because she always felt so off-balance around him. She wanted him so badly and he remained impassive. She wanted him to lose control again, as he had in Edgar's study and in the carriage. If he lost control, then she wouldn't have to abandon her own tenuous hold on propriety.

She could be the ravished one, the one who kept her integrity and her boundaries and her emotional distance.

The valet moved behind him, measuring his back.

*My word*, the muscles in Raven's stomach. What did he do to keep so fit and firm?

One, two, three . . . six ridges of hard muscle rippling down his narrow waist and over the base of his abdomen.

The scars on his chest lent him a dangerous air. She wondered again how he'd ended up with those scars.

The scars led her on a trail across his taut stomach and down to his thinly covered shaft again. Had it swollen in size? She stared in amazement. His male organ appeared to be . . . was it *twitching*?

She tore her gaze away from his crotch.

A disastrous mistake. He was staring directly at the keyhole. He knew she was watching. This was all a show, for her eyes only.

The valet was still measuring his back, oblivious to the game Raven played.

Raven winked at her.

She jerked her head back, muffling a curse as a heavy woolen garment fell on her head.

"Did you hear something, Your Grace?" asked the valet.

"Perhaps a rat in the walls?" suggested Raven.

*Oh ha ha. Very funny.*

"It wouldn't be the first time, Your Grace. These drafty old Parisian houses . . . I do long for the day when Sir Charles will take up residence in England again."

Indy leant forward again, daring another look.

Raven's hand brushed his thigh. A light touch where her fingers wanted to roam. It was unbearably erotic, being enclosed in the warm, dark womb of the wardrobe and watching him tease her so shamelessly.

It was like one of her dreams.

But in her dream the valet would leave and then Raven would pull down his smalls and he'd . . . he'd cup himself with his hand and . . . pleasure himself.

*Don't imagine it. Stop that immediately.*

The valet didn't even notice anything odd. He went about his business of measuring.

Raven stared directly at the wardrobe. He knew she was watching. He trailed his fingers down over his abdomen, beneath the buttoned flap of his smallclothes . . . exposing a trail of dark hair that led . . .

She was beginning to feel slightly faint. It must be all the wool. The air was too close in the wardrobe.

"I've taken all the measurements," said the valet. "I'll have your garments delivered tomorrow by mid-afternoon."

Raven nodded and the valet left the room.

Raven moved out of eyesight. She was about to open the door when she heard Sir Charles's deep voice.

Bollocks! The wool draped around her head and over her shoulders was making her feel like sneezing, and now she must remain completely silent.

"Did Harris see to your clothing for tomorrow?" she heard Sir Charles ask.

She peered through the keyhole but couldn't see them. They must be near the door.

"I'll be presentable," Raven answered. "Let's talk tomorrow, shall we? I'm tired."

Raven tried to dismiss Sir Charles, but the man lingered. Indy noticed that he was slurring his words, which led her to surmise that he must be inebriated.

"You're not turning in already, old friend?" asked Sir Charles. "You're really no fun anymore. Come out with me. We'll visit a certain establishment I know will restore your vigor."

"You go. I need my beauty rest."

The voices faded as if Raven had led Sir Charles out of the room. Now was her chance to escape. There was very little air in this tiny space with coats and clothing hung all around.

She tried to open the door of the wardrobe but it wouldn't budge. Must not be able to open it from the inside. She'd have to wait for Raven.

No, she never waited for anyone. She could find a way out of this predicament. Raven might have trouble convincing Sir Charles to leave and she needed more air.

She worked a few of her metal hairpins loose from her coiffure. She'd read about how one might be able to open a lock with a hairpin.

She wiggled the hairpin around in the lock but the only thing that happened was that the end broke off. Finding a few more hairpins, she put them together to make something thicker and jiggled the end around.

Something was happening. The end of the hairpin caught a piece of the lock and she heard a promising click. If she could only . . . push a little harder. The lock finally released.

She tested the door. It moved a little. Placing her entire shoulder against it she heaved with all her might and . . . tumbled directly into Raven's arms.

He must have opened the door from the outside at the same time she was pushing against it.

"Oof," she said as his arms wrapped around her and held her against his lean, hard frame.

# Chapter 16

❧

*I*NDY IN HIS arms. Right where she belonged.

She didn't attempt to right herself; she held still, balanced against him, her arms around his neck. His arms around her waist. Right where they belonged.

"Is Sir Charles gone?" she whispered.

Raven nodded, not trusting his voice to make much more than an awkward croaking sound.

"You were teasing me," she admonished, wrapping her arms tighter around his neck. "I know several ladies who would pay a small fortune to watch you strip off your clothing."

That made him smile. Her gaze was light, teasing, and sensual.

"You liked the show, did you?"

"It was entertaining." Her gaze flicked to his lips.

When he had her in his arms there was nothing on earth, no loyalty, no duty that could keep him from taking anything she'd be willing and eager to give him. Right now all he wanted to do was cup her bum and lift her.

Wrap her long legs around his hips and back her up against a wall.

"You didn't have to watch," he said. "You could have closed your eyes."

"I wanted to watch. It was quite stimulating."

She fit her hips to his hips, her weight supported by his chest and thighs.

"There was one part of you the valet neglected to measure," she murmured in the sexiest, huskiest voice he'd ever heard. "Too bad he didn't leave his tape or I might be tempted to remedy his omission."

"Indy," he groaned. "Don't say things like that. You'll be my downfall."

"What I want to know is whether these," she brushed her fingertips lightly over the waistband of his smalls, "might be convinced to fall down."

What was he supposed to do, tell her he would never drop his smalls for her? That was a lie. He'd do whatever she wanted if it meant he could continue holding her like this.

Her hips against his hips.

Her breasts crushed against his chest.

"I'm yours to command, Indy," he said.

"Finish the show. Drop your undergarments," she growled.

He grinned. "Why, are you going to ravish me?"

"Absolutely," she said, with the most devastatingly provocative smile he'd ever seen.

Just like that, his scruples ran for the hills, abandoning him completely.

Duty be damned. Honor be hanged. He'd risk everything for one more taste of her lips.

"Then let's move over by the fire. It's too cold here." He lifted her into his arms and carried her across the room, his eyes never leaving her face.

If she hesitated, if a shadow crossed her eyes,

he was fully prepared to end the encounter before it began. But that teasing smile remained on her lips and her gaze was warm with desire.

He'd locked the door after Sir Charles left. They wouldn't be disturbed.

He knelt in front of her. He unlaced her boots and set them aside. He undid her garters and rolled her stockings down.

"May I remove your gown?" he asked reverently.

She answered by reaching for the hem of her gown and lifting it over her shoulders in one practiced wriggling movement.

He loosened her corset, lifting it over her head, and then removed her petticoats. Now she wore only a short cotton shift and the Wish Diamond at her throat.

His wildest fantasy come to glorious life.

She slipped her shift down her shoulders, exposing her full breasts and her dark rose-colored nipples.

He'd been trained in the art of seduction.

She had no need for training. She seduced him with every breath she took.

She did something to her hair and suddenly it was tumbling down over her shoulders, spreading in waves over the red of the rug, catching the firelight and glinting with blue black.

He rose to his feet and stood over her for a moment, drinking in the sight of her. Long, black hair and sensuous red lips. Rounded breasts and long, long limbs. Arrayed in front of the flickering fire for him.

The most beautiful sight he'd ever seen.

He didn't touch her, not yet. Simply feasted his eyes on the swell of her breasts, on the swooping indentation of her waist. The bunched-up shift covered her only from her hips to mid-thigh.

Her gaze slid down his body. "Didn't I tell you to drop your undergarments?"

Slowly, teasingly, he undid the buttons of his smalls.

She watched his movements with a rapt expression, her eyes half lidded and smoky.

He pushed the garment down his abdomen, past his hips, over his thick, hard cock, until he stood completely naked.

She licked her lips, staring at his cock. "Now that's what I call a good show."

He fell to his knees and covered her with his body. He needed to feel her soft breasts against his chest. Her hips cushioning him.

Her legs parted slightly. She lifted her hips and pressed her mound against his cock through the fabric of her shift.

He kissed her, finally allowing himself that luxury. Her lips yielding to him, tongue rising to meet him.

His hands were made to shape her waist. His thumbs brushed the under swell of her breasts.

He left her lips and found her breast.

"That was a different sort of kiss," she said breathily. "We've hate-kissed, and evasive-kissed, but that was . . . pure seduction."

He sucked on her nipple until she gasped. He lavished attention on her breasts, cupping them with his hands, teasing her nipples with his tongue and lips.

She urged him on by threading her fingers into his hair and pulling him closer.

He grazed his teeth over her nipple and she squirmed in his grip.

He ran his hands down her arms. She had lithe muscles beneath the satin of her skin. She wasn't one to sit in a parlor all day. Her body had been shaped by activity—walking, climbing, archaeological excavations.

He pulled up the hem of her chemise and dipped his fingers into her wet heat and rubbed the moisture over her sex.

"How do you touch yourself, Indy? Slow and gentle?" He matched his movements to his words. "Or light and quick . . ."

From her responses she wanted a firmer pressure. She lifted her hips in little circles.

Her hand brushed his belly. Drifted lower. Settled, tentatively, over his cock.

Gently, he lifted her hand. As much as he was dying to feel the pleasure her hand could give him, he wanted her to come first.

"How am I doing?" he asked. There was always guesswork involved the first time. And he wanted this to be amazing for her.

"A little to the right, a little . . . more forceful . . ." She gasped.

He loved that she was confident enough to give him orders. "Like this?" He stroked faster, harder.

"Y-yes." Her voice shook and her breathing grew heavy and labored.

"Raven," she moaned, tensing.

The most beautiful sound he'd ever heard.

Her fingers curled around his biceps, digging into his flesh.

The crackling sound of the fire burning through wood, commuting it to nothingness and ash, filled his ears. Her moans burned through him, melting the ice around his heart to water that ran in rivulets inside his chest.

The feel of her softness and heat beneath his fingers drove him wild. The sight of her face, lips red and swollen from his kisses, black hair wild and untamed around her cheeks, filled his heart with a mixture of pride and joy.

"Come for me, Indy," he urged.

*Come with me. Let's find a new path together.*

HE TEASED HER, bringing her close to the brink and then easing off. Indy couldn't take much more teasing.

She couldn't speak because they were kissing, their bodies, tongues, minds, intertwined, interchangeable.

Her body. His body.

He was learning her secrets and there was no shame. This driving need, like a hard rain, pelting her body with sensation, little pinpricks and moisture sliding and soaking her.

Saturating her.

The rest of the household slept. Lamps extinguished. Fires dying. Cozy under the covers with bed warmers at their feet and flannel nightdresses against their skin.

While she lay on her back on the carpet in front of a fire with her legs spread and Raven's fingers inside her, moving over her sensitive flesh, his tongue stroking inside her mouth.

The pleasurable tremors she experienced in her sleep were pleasant little bursts of sensation. This was going to be something much bigger. Perhaps even of earthquake proportions.

She might shake the foundations of this venerable old house.

She didn't have to tell him what to do anymore, he had divined what she needed and he wasn't holding back.

He didn't stint.

Only a few more passes of his finger. Flying now, so fast, massaging more than just her most sensitive spot, manipulating the whole hood of her sex.

Sensation narrowed to a pinpoint concentrated between her legs, pulsing like a star in the night sky.

She reached a plateau and flung herself over the edge, alleviating the nearly unbearable tension, sending pleasure spiraling outward in widening concentric circles.

Her whole body alive with sensation.

Raven folded her into his powerful arms, cradling her head against his chest while she moaned softly, not quite believing how good it had felt, how the pleasure still coursed through her mind and body, fizzing like champagne bubbles on her tongue.

How she wanted to make him lose control as well. She needed him to moan in abandon.

She wanted to cradle his head against her breast as he came apart in her arms.

She nudged her hips against him, feeling her softness and wetness yield around the outline of his hard male sex.

She moved a little harder, experimentally.

He eased backward, allowing her more access to his body. She parted her thighs and shaped herself around him, rubbing shamelessly back and forth, enjoying the sensation of his hardness sliding against her sensitive flesh.

When he caught her hips in his hands and stilled her movements, she let out a small, frustrated moan.

"Indy," he said, gazing into her eyes. "What are we doing?"

"I think perhaps there's an attraction between us."

He grinned. "Do you think so?"

"I have a theory. It's like an itch I must scratch. It's like . . . well, I think it's like the first time I had escargot in a French restaurant and it was brought to the table with great pride, as the most decadent of delicacies, all smothered in butter, and everyone was oohing and aahing. I took a few bites and realized that escargot was definitely not my cup of tea. I couldn't get past the thought that until recently those snails had been crawling and oozing along the ground."

He stroked her hair back from her cheek. "Uh . . . what are you saying exactly? I'm not following you. What am I in this story—the slimy distasteful mollusk?"

She laughed. "Yes."

"I don't like this analogy."

"Once I sampled the snails I had no further curiosity about them. I prefer a nice haunch of beef."

"Indy?"

"Yes?"

"This restaurant's closed. Time for bed. Separate beds." He lifted her shift, attempting to put her arms back through arm holes.

"I don't want to be so damnably obsessed with you anymore, Raven," she blurted. "I need to sample you to get you out of my system for good."

He stilled. "If you're suggesting what I think you're suggesting, we can't. I won't. I mean to say that I don't think it would be right to take this any further. You've proven your skill as a seductress. You won this round."

"Then why do I feel as though I was the one who surrendered?"

"You didn't surrender, you gave me a gift. I loved making you come—it made me feel powerful."

"I want to know that feeling of power." She rolled on top of him, flattening his torso to the hearth rug with the palms of her hands. "I want to make you come."

She dipped her head and kissed his nipples, as he'd kissed hers, using her tongue to tease them into hard little peaks.

What would it feel like to brush her sensitive nipples against his? She tested the motion, supporting her weight with her palms and gliding the tips of her breasts over his chest.

"Indy," he moaned. She'd never heard that voice before. It trembled slightly and the tremor gave her a rush of satisfaction.

Not so impervious. Not completely made of stone.

She shook her long hair over the hills and valleys of his muscular torso, swirling the ends of her hair against his flesh. He seemed to like it, because his hands curled into fists.

He was slack-jawed, watching her every motion with a hungry expression.

She loved this feeling of power.

She was drunk on controlling his responses. She slid down his thighs, trailing her hair along his taut abdomen and lower, over his cock.

He had a very nice cock. Long and thick and hard as iron. She ringed his cock with her fist.

His eyes closed.

She moved her hand experimentally, down, and then back up, applying a light pressure with her fingers. He moved with her, his hips showing her what he wanted her hand to do.

Now then. To the sampling.

She bent her head and kissed the tip of him.

His eyes flew open. "What are you doing?"

"What does it look like I'm doing?" She kissed him again, opening her lips a little wider, licking the rim with her tongue, watching his expression the entire time. She'd heard about this act from Lady Catherine, who could be quite bawdy when plied with sherry and pressed to tell stories of her misspent youth.

Indy pressed more of her mouth around him, making sure her teeth were covered so she didn't hurt the soft, thin skin. She didn't want to injure him.

The muscles in his neck strained into ropes. He watched her with a possessive expression. He wrapped his fingers into her hair, where they rested lightly, his touch making her scalp tingle with sensation.

Her nerves were jangling with desire. Giving him pleasure aroused her more than she'd thought possible.

Maybe he'd been dreaming of her, pining for her. She'd do this so well he'd pine for her the rest of his life.

"That feels so good, Indy," he said jerkily. "Wrap your lips tighter, I'm not going to break. But I am going to explode. Yes. Like that. Gods. *Indy.*"

She loved the way he said her name like an invocation. Like a prayer.

Heeding the gentle pressure of his hand on her scalp she moved down, nearly taking all of him into her throat, and then back up.

He reached for her hand, found it, wrapped her fingers around the base of his cock. He was showing her what he liked.

He shifted his body and his fingers moved between her legs. How was he even able to think about her pleasure? But his movements weren't controlled, not like the first time when he'd skillfully manipulated her to a climax.

His fingers fumbled over her this time. He

wanted to give her pleasure and that was sweet but she was in control, although . . . it did feel quite nice when he slid one of his fingers inside her.

She lifted her head. "That feels good."

"I'm glad. How about this?" He fit another finger inside her. She rocked against his fingers. This is what it would feel like to have him inside her. The act of love that she longed for and feared at the same time. She feared it because she knew that with Raven it would be different. It would be devastatingly good.

She resumed her work, taking him back into her mouth and sliding her lips around his length.

His belly tensed. "Indy," he said.

She stilled. Lifted her head.

His shaft popped out of her mouth, quivering in the air.

"I'll die if I can't taste you as well," he said hoarsely. "Slide around my body, place your limbs over my chest."

"I don't understand."

He showed her what he wanted, lifting her body and turning her bum toward him, settling her thighs down around his neck. He used his tongue to open her sex. She squirmed and turned her head toward him. "Oh. I see. I'm to . . . pleasure you at the same time you are tasting me."

She'd never dreamt of anything like this. It was depraved, dirty, and . . . delicious.

There was a moment of embarrassment, to think that her legs were spread wide over his face and her breasts brushing against his thighs. But then she forgot all about the embarrassment because it was so delicious when he stroked her with his tongue, his large hands gripping her thighs and holding her in place.

She took him back into her mouth, her movements less controlled now because it was far more difficult to concentrate when his tongue was doing such wicked things.

Pleasure built so quickly that she knew she must hurry. She redoubled her efforts, taking more of him into her throat.

He swept his tongue across her most sensitive place and she trembled, her intimate muscles contracting. So close now.

On the next down stroke of her lips he rose to meet her, his body bucking in an uneven rhythm. Her pleasure spasm was smaller this time, less earth shaking, but the knowledge that he was so close to finding his own pleasure made her feel powerful and seductive.

She moved upward, away from his mouth, because her body was too sensitive now.

"I'm going to come," he growled.

He half-sat behind her, lifting her chin away from his sex. He wrapped one long arm around her torso, underneath her breasts, and sat up, pulling her with him. He remained behind her. Her thighs were spread wide on either side of his hips. She had an excellent view as his hand gripped his cock.

Her sex slid against the base of his cock as he pumped himself with his fist. She watched in fascination as he finished with a few swift, hard strokes.

He groaned and his seed spilled over his fist and onto his thighs and the carpet.

He collapsed back and she climbed off of him, turning her body, fitting her head to his shoulder, and kissing his neck.

She should probably be embarrassed by whatever they'd just been doing, but for now she wanted to recline by the last embers of the fire with his arms around her, limp and worn and still fizzing with pleasure.

# Chapter 17

❦

THE GLOWING EMBERS of Raven's orgasm faded, leaving his whole body light and heavy at the same time. He'd been with other women, what seemed like a lifetime ago, memories like ancient manuscripts faded by the sun.

Sex had been just a physical function. Sometimes a means to an end, a way of extracting information, a method of giving pleasure and receiving it in return.

He'd had willing partners, women who traded in secrets.

"Gracious," Indy murmured against his neck. "My dreams are lewd, but I certainly never imagined simultaneous . . . feasting. Your tongue in my . . . oh. Do you think that's what Mr. Shakespeare was referring to?"

"You make me want to do wildly inappropriate things, Indy."

"There was certainly nothing appropriate about it, I must say."

"We should talk about this . . . about why we keep succumbing to this attraction between us."

"What's there to talk about?" She laughed shakily. "I tried the buttery escargot. Now it's out of my system. I'll order something else next time."

"I should have been able to resist. You're my weakness. I don't want you to have regrets about this. I swear to you that I'll be stronger. That it won't happen again."

"We keep making these promises, don't we?"

"We do."

Probably he should ease her up to a seated position. Find their clothing. Bundle her back to her own bed.

He fit her more closely into his arms, brushing his lips against her forehead.

"Life takes such unexpected twists and turns," she murmured. "I'm a fallen woman, I have been for years, but I don't feel as though I've fallen. I feel like I've been climbing a steep incline, and each one of my experiences shows me where to find the next foothold."

He kissed the top of her head. "I'd rather be your mountain than your escargot."

He had to make jokes, because otherwise he was going to come completely undone.

"Was it Beauchamp?" he asked.

"No, it was an archaeologist from Sweden. And only the one time. It was . . . underwhelming."

Raven hid a smile. He was relieved to hear it hadn't been Beauchamp, and that the experience had been underwhelming.

He wanted to kiss her. Fold her into his arms and ask her to sleep with him in the bed with the blue velvet curtains. He had the strongest urge to spill all of his secrets.

But his secrets weren't his alone to tell. Other lives would be harmed, other covers compromised.

She nestled her head more firmly into the crook of his neck. "At the private girls' academy I attended in North Yorkshire we were warned so often about the dangers of losing our virtue, of falling from the path of righteousness. I never subscribed to the fear and guilt they tried to instill in my breast."

"My boarding school was equally manipulative and controlling." He couldn't tell her the nature of his training, but he could speak to the topic she had raised. "The instructors believed that harshness and discipline were the only methods that would produce men in their own mold."

"I've always wondered why you went to school in Scotland?"

"Sir Malcolm chose the school."

"He was almost a father to you, wasn't he? After your father died."

"Yes. He welcomed our family into his home for many reasons. He'd been a friend to my father, and he had lost his wife and daughter recently in an accident."

"I didn't know about that. How tragic. No wonder he took an interest in you."

He'd taken more than an interest. Sir Malcolm had groomed Raven to become a spy. At the time, Raven had been eager to follow in his father's footsteps.

"My mother chose my academy," Indy said. "She wanted to shape me in her image but I rebelled. I hated the constant preaching on propriety and domesticity. The day I turned sixteen I ran away. I had no plan, I only knew I must leave that place because it was killing my spirit. I wandered over the moors, cold and half starving, until I arrived at a house. It was Lady Catherine's house. She sheltered me, fed me. She provided a refuge when I needed one most."

This was the first Raven had heard of it. "You could have died wandering around on the moors," he scolded. "What were you thinking?"

"I wasn't thinking, I was feeling. I was sixteen. You stopped answering my letters. I hated my life. I've always had a dramatic streak. Wandering the moors fit my desperate thoughts. Why did you stop answering my letters?" she whispered. "I thought it was because you'd grown callous, shallow, and selfish. But I don't think that's true anymore. I think there's some reason, some secret you're keeping from me."

Gods, he longed to tell her the truth. That he'd made the decision to distance himself because he cared for her, because he hadn't wanted to hurt her.

"I want to tell you, Indy. I want to tell you what you want to hear."

"No." She shook her head against his neck. "Don't tell me what I want to hear. Tell me the truth."

"I was a fool." He could admit that much. "Indy, I've made so many bad choices, and I have to live with them. I know I hurt you, and I didn't want to hurt you. But . . . as you said, life takes these twists and turns sometimes. I chose a dissipated path."

"You could have become a diplomat, like your father. Why didn't you?"

"They did offer me the post in Bern, Switzer-land." A post uniquely positioned to keep an eye on the larger political framework of Europe. "I declined. Too boring, too tedious. I'm a rogue, not a representative of the law. I hate the formality and protocol."

She blinked. "Are you?"

"Am I what?"

"A rogue."

"You're lying in my arms, aren't you?"

"Because I seduced you."

"You did."

"I'm not convinced that you are a rogue. I still think you're hiding something. You're not at all who I thought you were. Sometimes your mask slips and I glimpse . . ."

The boy who used to love her? He glimpsed him as well.

"For all I know you could be a spy." She sat up abruptly. "Wait . . . is that it? Is that what you're hiding?"

It was high time for seductive, inquisitive ladies to be ushered back to their own bed-chambers. "Ha ha," he laughed heartily. "You've guessed it. I'm a spy. I'm a highly trained, lethal, ruthless clandestine operative who lives for a higher purpose."

She stared at him for a few awful moments. He didn't dare to breathe.

She rolled her eyes. "Oh what was I thinking, of course you're not a spy. You're a trophy hunter, a mercenary. You keep the Wish Diamond on your desk as if it were a piece of glass and not one of the most priceless treasures in the world and worthy of its own room in a museum."

He forced himself to grin at her. "Can we please not rehash the tired subject of our ethical differences? I'm little more than a pirate, and you're going to change the world. I think we've established as much."

"Have we?" She tilted her head and fixed him with that searching gaze again.

"Do you trust me enough to tell me what you're looking for?" he asked. "How you're going to change the world?"

She smiled. "It's funny, but I do trust you now. You said earlier that Cleopatra would wear a jewel like the Wish Diamond and you had no idea how appropriate your comment was. I need the stone to corroborate my translation of a map that I believe may lead me to Antony and Cleopatra's long-lost tomb."

"I'm not surprised. I knew you must be on the trail of a grand prize. You've been obsessed with Cleopatra since girlhood. I remember you draping yourself in sheets and quoting from the Shakespeare play. You always took such a long, dramatic time to die."

She raised her head. "'Die where thou hast lived. Quicken with kissing. Had my lips that power, thus would I wear them out.'"

Raven kissed her lips. "'I am dying, Egypt, dying. Give me some wine and let me speak a little.'"

"'Noblest of men, wouldst thou die? Hast thou

no care of me? Shall I abide in this dull world, which in thy absence is no better than a sty?'"

"That's when you'd start staggering around, clutching your chest and moaning." He chuckled. "I always thought if you didn't become an archaeologist, you'd become a stage actress and truly scandalize London society."

"All the world's my stage," she declared.

"And all the men merely players."

"When did you start memorizing Shakespeare?" she asked. "You always refused to when we were children."

He'd memorized Shakespeare's plays during his assignments because it made him feel closer to Indy. "Perhaps you don't know what's up my alley."

"Apparently not." She shivered slightly.

"You're cold. The fire's gone out."

"I think I should go to my bed now." She shrugged into her shift.

He'd been hoping she might suggest warming herself in his bed. But it was better this way. They'd already gone too far.

Good God. The things they'd done tonight. The oaths he'd already broken.

He helped her rise and then found her gown and boots.

While she dressed, he donned a robed and rolled up the map of Paris she'd brought to his room, fastening it with a piece of twine.

"Here," she said softly, holding out her hand. The Wish Diamond sparkled against her palm.

"Keep it," he said. "Wear it tomorrow."

"I'm confident that tomorrow evening our search will bear fruit."

"And then you can start your quest for the tomb."

She nodded, her eyes shadowed and unreadable. "Yes. One search leads to the other. Good night."

She left.

He lay awake, waiting for her to fall asleep. He'd go out again as soon as he was sure she slept soundly.

He imagined what her breathing sounded like in sleep. The little noises she made.

He'd been denying himself any real and meaningful connection with another human being for so long. He'd been so wrong to think that this journey with her could be kept on a surface level.

She was his weakness. But she also gave him a new strength of purpose.

He'd been so busy resolving conflicts on the world stage that he'd created this war between them. Now all he wanted to do was lay down his weapons.

Being with her made him want to strive toward different goals. Selfish goals that had far more to do with making her happy than finding the damned stone.

When she'd looked up at him in the museum, her eyes shining and said, "This could be the stone, Raven," an overwhelming sense of rightness had flowed into his heart. He hadn't been elated about the possibility of ending the search. He'd overflowed with joy because she was happy.

The foundations of his life had been shaken in that church in Athens. And the new footing he'd found, the only thing that seemed to make sense or feel right in any way, was to give her joy.

INDY LAY AWAKE, unable to sleep.

What had just happened? All of her resolutions, all of her promises broken.

Apparently when she saw Raven strip off his clothing, all bets were off.

She'd turned her dreams to reality in the most wanton, shameless way imaginable.

What exactly had they done? She'd certainly never heard of, nor imagined, such an act.

What would one even call such a thing? Simultaneous ministrations? Double the pleasure?

His cock inside her mouth, while he licked her intimate places. Truly depraved.

She wanted to do it again.

She wanted to feel him inside her body, and not only with his fingers, or his tongue.

She loved him. There was no other explanation for this madness.

She loved him, she wanted him, and he made her a fool. While she'd bared herself completely, he'd remained in control of his emotions and his secrets.

Shite. Balls. Damn his topaz eyes! Why must she love him? Why couldn't she remain impassive?

She rolled onto her side, curling around a pillow. Tomorrow she'd spend the day alone. She needed space to breathe and time to think.

RAVEN HAD TOO much time to think as he crouched in the darkness.

The crenelated wall of Le Triton's fortress rose before him, piercing the night sky like the spines along the back of some mythological beast.

Four guards patrolled the perimeter of the property. They passed at regular intervals, stopping to exchange a few words before resuming their diverging paths.

He'd seen several more guards atop the walls. No doubt there were at least a dozen in total. Le Triton would employ no less.

The main entrance was watched by a gatekeeper whose lamp was still burning. These were no ordinary servants. They were trained, lethal operatives.

Attempting to scale the wall, or enter the fortress by force, would be foolhardy in the extreme.

He must wait for Sir Malcolm's signal and rendezvous with the attack team. He'd give them the details he'd gleaned and they'd form a plan. He was confident that Malcolm would contact him by tomorrow afternoon.

Then, Raven's job would be to solicit the invitation to enter Le Triton's house as his guest. The Wish Diamond was his entrance fee.

And Indy his enticement.

Tomorrow the game would commence.

He sat back on his heels, remembering their night of passion. The sight of her with her hair tumbling around her shoulders and a purple diamond glittering between her mauve-tipped breasts.

He would remember the sight for the rest of his life. And he would remember the sound of his name on her lips. The exquisite touch of her fingers along his jaw.

The softness of her lips. The silk of her hair brushing across his belly.

When he lay dying, his last thought would be of her, of the heaven he'd known on earth.

The balm of her smile.

The temple of her eyes.

# Chapter 18

**❧**

THE DIPLOMATIC EVENT was to be held in the ground-floor ballroom. When Harris finally pronounced him elegant enough, Raven knocked on Indy's door. He hadn't seen her since the previous night's glorious madness.

He'd been reliving every word, every glance, every kiss . . . when he was supposed to be solidifying all of the details for the raid.

Everything was in place. Sir Malcolm and his team had arrived and were waiting for Raven's signal. He'd told them the number and location of the guards on the outside of Le Triton's property. Now his job was to elicit the invitation from Le Triton to visit his fortress.

With Raven striking from the inside, and the team of agents from the outside, they could retrieve the stone and bring down Le Triton in the process.

Raven had a pistol concealed beneath his coat, and Miss Mina's unusual timepiece in his waist-coat pocket.

Indy's door opened and a lady's maid emerged. "She's nearly ready, Your Grace," the maid said with a curtsy. "She bids you wait inside."

The maid left and Raven entered Indy's chamber.

"One moment," Indy called from behind a carved wooden screen.

Various rustling noises emerged from behind the screen and the floral-vanilla-pepper scent of her perfume lingered in the air.

He adjusted the diamonds at his cuffs and rearranged the chain of his pocket watch, unaccountably nervous. He was never nervous.

Nerves implied the ability to envision potentially disastrous outcomes. He never doubted or questioned his abilities. He plunged headfirst into the unknown with the confidence that he would win against all odds.

He contemplated offering to help her with any hooks and then gave himself a stern mental shake. Tonight would be all business.

Le Triton would take one look at the Wish Diamond sparkling against Indy's luxurious bosom and be willing to do anything to purchase the necklace. Raven still didn't like involving her, but she'd insisted, and he had to trust her.

She'd asked him to meet her halfway, and he was fully there.

That must be why his nerves were jangling a discordant tune, why he'd been on edge all day.

If Indy appeared from behind the screen with fresh hurt and pain behind her smile and buried in her eyes, he was going to hate himself even more.

*You don't regret even one kiss. One touch. You would do it all again in a heartbeat.*

She walked out from behind the screen.

Time slowed. His heart forgot how to pump blood through his body.

Curves poured into a gown the color of mulberry wine. The purple diamond at her throat sparkling the same color as her eyes, glossy black hair piled atop her head and fixed with a jeweled clip.

"Raven." She stuck out her chin. "Would you please stop staring at me as though I've sprouted a second head? I know it's ridiculous." She tugged at the ruffles at the neck of her gown. "I can't abide voluminous sleeves and tiers of ruffles. Lucy latched on to me and she wouldn't let go until I agreed to wear this purple silk monstrosity."

It wasn't the gown that made his brain feel like it had sprouted a layer of mushrooms like a damp log in a forest.

It was Indy.

The memory of her satiny smooth skin and her long hair tangling around her shoulders, brushing over his chest as she rose above him.

"Say something, please," she urged. "If you don't say something this instant I'm going to go and change back into one of my everyday gowns."

He said the first thing that came to mind. "I wish I had something to give you."

She tilted her head. "What did you say?"

"Gentlemen give ladies bouquets of flowers, don't they? Or maybe flowers would have been too conventional? You would prefer something more unexpected, I'd wager. A rare relic from a curiosity shop. Or a heavy book about antiquities. The heavier the better."

He was babbling. He never babbled.

The look on her face made his heart ache for all of the normal, everyday milestones in life that he'd given up when he became a secret agent. Courting Indy—properly courting her—would have been such a grand and unpredictable adventure.

"Never mind gifts. Let's go downstairs and find a thief," she said.

He smiled. "I'm glad you're on my side, Indy. Tonight you're the big guns. They won't know what hit them."

She'd blasted straight through his defensive line. *You're heart-stoppingly beautiful*, was what he should have said. *Forget-any-other-reason-for-living beautiful.*

She snorted. "Men are so easy to bedazzle. A low-cut gown, a shiny diamond, and you're like babes with a rattle: you can't look away." A smile played at her lips. "You're not so bad yourself."

He stood up straighter. "You approve?" He couldn't help preening a little. Harris had fussed and hovered but Raven had been rather pleased with the results.

She moved closer. "You look good enough to eat."

"Now, now, none of that, my lady." He couldn't very well escort her into the ball with a visible erection. The attraction between them was ever-green and ever present, that much was abundantly, *firmly*, clear.

He cleared his throat. "I don't think that gown's a monstrosity. It's more like a superbly designed weapon of seduction." She'd moved closer. He slid his finger along the edge of one of her sleeves. "This subtle pattern worked into the silk, like the bull's-eye of a target—it's meant to draw the gaze."

"I may be wearing a seductive silk gown but I'm still me." She hitched her hem to show him that underneath her long skirts she wore her trusty black leather boots. "I drew the line at French heels."

A vision of her as a young hoyden sprang to mind. Indy wearing scuffed boots, running after him, falling and scraping her knees and getting right back up.

No tears. No fuss.

Emotion knotted in his throat. He wasn't himself. He had to focus, regain his balance.

They had a job to do.

"I'll bet you have that sharp dagger hidden somewhere," he said.

"I might have," she said with an arch smile.

Probably tucked into her silk garter. The garter that was currently hugging her supple, shapely thigh. The thigh he wanted to wrap around his hips as he drove home inside her silken heat . . .

"Raven." Her eyebrows lifted. "Are we going down?"

"Er . . . of course. But before we do . . . I asked you for a truce back in London. I'd like to ask again. We're on a mission and we're going to win. It's an equal partnership, and I trust you completely to uphold your end."

"Agreed. We're a team. Shall we shake hands on it?"

Another lump of emotion in his throat as her gloved hand slipped into his and fit so perfectly.

He lifted her hand and brushed his lips over her knuckles.

"My lady." He offered his elbow and she placed her gloved hand on his arm.

"These diplomatic affairs are usually quite dull," he said as they walked down the corridor toward the grand staircase. "Every rule of protocol and precedence has to be followed with precision or someone will take offense."

"You don't have to lecture me on protocol. My mother was the queen of protocol. She drilled me on every nuance of French and German court life on the off chance that I might meet a foreign prince and become a princess." She laughed. "Poor Mama. She always wanted me to have our engagement formally dissolved. My spinsterhood is a terrible cross for her to bear."

She said the words so lightly but they settled like a heavy weight across his chest. "I don't think we'll have any princes tonight. Mostly ambassadors. A few consul generals. A smattering of first secretaries and French ministers. I hate these affairs, the stiffness and formality of these dreary occasions. Everyone is on their best behavior because of mutual mistrust. If you scratch beneath the polite veneer, though, the room will be a seething hotbed of intrigue and secrets."

"I've heard that many diplomats are actually spies. Is that true?"

"Possibly," he said carefully.

They paused in front of the doorway to the ballroom.

"I'm sure we'll have to field multiple questions about our wedding plans," said Indy.

"Maybe you'll start a craze for pineapple gowns."

"Or you could bring back the fashion for pink silk doublets. Which, incidentally, would not be a good look for you."

"I would make it work," he said.

Indy laughed. "Onward into the fray, my antiquated dandy."

"Antiquated? I'm only one year older than you. And I'm not a dandy, I'm a rogue."

"You're my rogue," she said, placing her hand on his arm.

His heart beat faster. "And you're my adventuress."

"Let's have an adventure, then."

Sir Charles had hired a string quartet and they were playing something shimmering and virtuoso by Mozart. Raven had the thought that there should be music playing in every room he and Indy entered together.

Once upon a time he'd imagined entering every room with Indy on his arm, the proudest man on earth, the envy of every fellow in the room.

THE ADMIRATION SHINING in Raven's copper eyes made Indy feel drunk.

He'd wanted to give her something, meaning he wanted to court her. When he'd said those words, her heart had hopped in her chest like a child with a skipping rope.

Only, there would be no courting tonight. They were on a serious mission for crown and country. He trusted her. She trusted him.

But only for one night and only to see their task to completion.

But it did feel good to let her anger go, if only for one night. Just let it go.

Shrug off the weight of all the mistrust and hurt and fear.

She felt powerful with Raven at her side. Her step lighter. Her gaze keen and discerning.

They entered the room together with confidence and swagger as though they owned the place.

"There's the Russian ambassador, Mr. Petrov," he murmured in her ear, showing her with his eyes.

She scanned the room. "I don't see Lady Catherine."

"Or Sir Charles."

"Did someone take my name in vain?" Sir Charles appeared behind them with his wife on his arm. "Lady India you are bewitching. Is that the famous Wish Diamond?"

"It is," she replied.

Lady Sterling touched the necklace. "Simply stunning. Charles, why don't you ever gift me with ancient treasures? Oh, that's right, you *are* an ancient treasure."

So much tension between those two. Indy'd noticed it right away.

"Where's Lucy?" Indy asked.

"I don't let her attend these affairs yet," said Lady Sterling. "She's still too young and so many of these gentlemen are so . . . jaded."

Everything she said was a barb meant to wound her philandering husband. Indy sympathized. It must be terrible to be betrayed by the man you love, especially after you'd exchanged vows of fidelity.

"Have a wonderful time, Lady India," said Lady Sterling. "I'm afraid I must be the hostess this evening, so you might not see much of me."

"Quite all right," said Indy.

"Come along, my dear. There's the Spanish ambassador." Lady Sterling steered her husband away.

"She's the perfect hostess," said Raven. "She'd make a better diplomat than Sir Charles, I do believe."

When he said things like that, Indy wanted to hug him.

"Shall I introduce you to Petrov now?" asked Raven. "He's a war hero who played a significant role at Waterloo. Wellington singled him out for praise. He's been staring at you since you entered the room."

"I noticed. He's probably trying to decide whether this is the real Wish Diamond."

"No, he's staring at you." Raven grinned and her knees nearly buckled, which wasn't very conducive to prowling like a *femme fatale* in search of her next victim.

"No, wait," she said. "There's Lady Catherine."

Lady Catherine walked across the room, a tall figure in a long cape of white with a white turban upon her head, and a necklace shaped like two snakes' heads intertwining around her throat.

"Lady Catherine, it's been too long." Indy clasped her friend's hands. She had grown frail since the last time Indy saw her.

"Too long, my dear."

"Lady Catherine, may I present the Duke of Ravenwood?"

"You may, although I can't promise to be civil," said Lady Catherine.

Same old Catherine. Never one to mince words.

"Lady Catherine." Raven bowed. He was so delectable in formal evening attire. The tailored coat made his shoulders even wider and his midsection so trim. Indy knew wicked things about his body. She'd had her thighs spread over his narrow hips. She'd counted the ridges of muscles on that abdomen.

She'd opened her mouth and fit his . . . blast! *Don't think about that.*

"What's this I hear about you planning a wedding?" Lady Catherine asked with a disapproving glare at Raven.

She was disapproving of men in general, and marriage in particular.

Indy would tell her the truth later but for now she had to go along with the charade.

"We finally decided to tie the knot."

Catherine frowned. "No, no." She shook her head from side to side. "No, this simply won't do at all. He has a goodly nose, but his brow is deficient. Far too low and flat."

*Oh dear.*

"I beg your pardon?" asked Raven.

"You won't make a suitable husband for my Indy," Lady Catherine said sternly. "Your brow is deficient. And your eyes are too cold. And you have a deadened heart."

Indy laughed uneasily. "I'm sure no one has told His Grace that he has a deficiency before."

"Certainly not," said Raven.

"Lady Catherine believes in something she calls the portents and omens of a face," explained Indy.

"And my face is insufficiently auspicious," said Raven.

"It augers ill," agreed Lady Catherine. "Low brows denote a brooding disposition. Also a dominating one. And Indy will never be dominated."

"So I've learned," said Raven.

A slight man with pale blonde hair wearing a white coat trimmed in gold approached.

"Oh there you are Dr. Lowe," said Lady Catherine. "I want to introduce you to my friend Lady India. My dear," she said to Indy, "this is the Dr. Lowe I wrote to you about. He hails from Vienna. And this is the Duke of Ravenwood."

Dr. Lowe bowed. He had a thin moustache and his hair was thinning on top.

"You are a doctor of medicine?" asked Indy.

"A mesmerist," replied Dr. Lowe. "As a young

boy, I studied by the side of the distinguished Dr. Franz Mesmer who, sadly, passed through the veil fifteen years past. I now continue his work in healing the gravely ill and giving hope to the hopeless."

"I've heard of Dr. Mesmer's theories," said Raven. "Some believe them to be quackery."

Dr. Lowe bristled. "Fools. Dr. Mesmer was a genius of the highest order. Soon the entire world will celebrate his teachings on the natural energetic transference known as animal magnetism. Lady Catherine has kindly agreed to be my patroness in the dissemination of the venerable doctor's theories."

There was something Indy didn't like about the sanctimonious and self-important Dr. Lowe, but if Lady Catherine was his patroness, she'd give him the benefit of the doubt.

"I hope you will come and visit me while you're here," said Lady Catherine.

"You purchased a chateau near Montrouge?" asked India.

"Dear Dr. Lowe advised me as to the purchase. My apartments in Paris were too close and unhealthful. He says I must take more fresh air to aid in my recovery."

"Are you ill?" Indy touched her friend's arm. She wanted to speak with her alone, without Dr. Lowe in hovering attendance.

Raven caught Indy's eye and she understood that he would remove Dr. Lowe for her.

"Have you visited the ambassador's residence before, Dr. Lowe?" Raven asked.

"I haven't."

"Allow me to give you a brief tour." Raven led Dr. Lowe away.

"You're not really going to wed that overbearing duke, are you?" asked Catherine.

Indy led Catherine to a line of potted ferns at the edge of the ballroom. "I'm not," she whispered.

"I knew it! Then why tell people you are?"

"That's a question with a complicated answer. We're here together on a mission." Raven had told her not to trust anyone, but Lady Catherine was one of her oldest friends.

"What type of mission?" asked Catherine.

"I wonder if perhaps you've heard of any British antiquities that might have been stolen and brought to Paris to be sold?"

Catherine considered that. "Something of great significance?"

"Yes. Enormous significance."

"I've heard no rumors. Speaking of antiquities, that's not the real Wish Diamond necklace, is it?"

"What do you think?"

Catherine bent closer. "It's the real one."

"Yes."

"He must trust you to allow you to wear his priceless treasure."

"I think he does trust me, in his own way."

"Just so you don't give him too much trust. Men like him can never be owned by one woman alone."

Indy had thought the same thing when she set out on this journey. Now she wasn't so sure.

"Ravenwood says these affairs are dull but for

me it's very interesting. I've never seen so many foreign dignitaries gathered together. The collective power in this room is astonishing. These are the men who wage wars, or embrace peace, uphold treaties or violate them. They hold the fates of so many lives in their hands."

"Politicians and diplomats are merely men, and power has a tendency to corrupt," said Catherine.

"True. I can't help thinking that fewer wars would be waged if there were more females in power."

"Hear, hear." Lady Catherine lifted an imaginary glass.

"Are you still feeling unwell, Catherine? You're awfully slender."

"I do suffer those debilitating vertigo spells from time to time. Dr. Lowe has me on a strict diet to quiet my animal spirits."

"How did you meet him?"

"He found me. He told me that I called to him across the ether and his spirit responded to mine."

"But what exactly does he do for you if he's not a medical doctor?"

Catherine laughed softly. "You wouldn't call it doing anything but the effects are so powerful. He makes gestures, and places his hand just here," she touched her solar plexus, just below her rib cage. "Sometimes he'll leave his hand there for hours. And then I have the most peculiar sensations and eventually I will have a convulsion, which is a crisis of sorts and brings about the cure."

Indy wondered if perhaps the man didn't put

his hand a little bit lower on Lady Catherine's person. She'd experienced a few convulsions herself lately.

She'd never ask her friend such a personal question, of course.

Before Indy could express more concern, Dr. Lowe joined them again.

"You're looking peaked, Lady Catherine. It's time for your treatment. We will leave now."

Indy watched in consternation as her normally irascible, opinionated friend was led away like an invalid.

"If that little man hails from Vienna I'll eat that diamond for breakfast. Liverpool more like," said Raven, appearing at her side.

"I was thinking the same thing. It's almost as if she's in thrall to him somehow. I don't like how much influence he seems to have over her. She said he treats her by passing his hand over her body and producing convulsions."

"It's all a bunch of charlatanism."

"I'll have to go and visit her when our search is concluded so that I may determine whether she's being taken advantage of in some way."

"Most likely he's after her fortune."

"Look sharp, Your Grace, the Russians are coming," Indy whispered.

"That's Petrov's aide, Mr. Sokolov, approaching," Raven replied.

"Your Grace." Mr. Sokolov bowed. "His Excellency Boris Petrov conveys his greetings."

Raven inclined his head. "Mr. Sokolov, allow me to present Lady India Rochester."

Sokolov bowed over her hand.

"Would you and your charming companion care to join His Excellency for a drink?"

"We would be delighted," said Indy.

They followed Sokolov across the room. Ambassador Petrov was a handsome, forceful-looking man with iron gray hair and thick black eyebrows, whom Indy judged to be in his early fifties.

Introductions were made, Ambassador Petrov speaking more to her bosom than her face.

"It's such an honor to meet you, Your Excellency," she said. Now she could practice her newfound feminine wiles. She fluttered her eyelashes. "His Grace told me about your bravery during the war."

Petrov puffed out his chest and the many gold and silver medals pinned to his black coat caught the light from the chandeliers.

"I've heard many stories about you as well, Lady India. About the unusual color of your eyes. Though I must say the stories were all false."

"Oh?" She pouted. "I don't live up to the stories?"

"On the contrary," said Petrov. "Your beauty far surpasses expectations. I never thought it possible, but your eyes outshine even the Wish Diamond."

"Do you take an interest in antiquities, Your Excellency?" asked Indy.

"I am a connoisseur of all things of rare and priceless beauty." His gaze slid across her bosom and Indy suppressed the urge to cover the tops of her breasts with her hands.

Raven cleared his throat. "I beg your pardon, but I must go and have a word with Sir Charles."

"Of course," said Petrov. When he'd left, the ambassador waved his hand and a servant appeared bearing a tray of small glasses filled with clear liquid. "Would you care to try some superior Russian vodka, Lady India?"

That's what she was here for. To use her feminine wiles, drink any man under the table, and find the Rosetta Stone. "But of course. I adore vodka."

"Have you visited Russia?" he asked.

She replied that she had. In Russian.

He smiled the first genuine smile she'd seen on his lips and switched to Russian, praising her accent, as well as her eyes.

Indy followed his lead and swallowed one vodka, and then another, waiting to turn the conversation back to antiquities.

SEVERAL HOURS LATER, Raven signaled to Indy that it was time to leave for their next engagement at Le Triton's gaming house.

He'd watched her work with so much pride.

She was a natural.

She knew instinctively how to work a room without appearing to have any aim. He had no doubt she had catalogued everything she saw and heard in the same way she collected artifacts and information on her archaeological expeditions.

She'd had Petrov eating out of her palm and plying her with the superior Russian vodka that

Sir Charles had made sure to have on hand for the ambassador.

Raven hadn't been worried about Indy holding her alcohol. Any other female of his acquaintance would have been falling over drunk after the amount of whisky she'd consumed on their carriage ride from London to Dover.

Even in Paris where people were freer with their emotions, she was like the diva in an Italian opera. All the world was her stage, and men only the bit players.

He wanted to be in her show. He wanted to be in the chorus, his voice the foundation for her soaring high notes.

"It's not the Russians," she whispered as he helped her into her velvet cloak.

"What makes you so sure?"

"It's only a strong feeling, but there was no gloating, no indication that Petrov had anything on his mind except the desire to peer down my bodice."

She tied purple silk bonnet ribbons into a bow under her chin. He had the strangest sensation that she should be donning a black beaver top hat instead. She had looked quite dashing under the curving brim of a top hat.

"Everything leads to Le Triton," she whispered.

"He won't know what hit him," said Raven.

He didn't bother to deny it. They were a team now and he was lucky to have her in his corner.

She took his arm as they waited for their carriage.

She was her own woman.

No man would ever own or tame her.

If Raven had her as his own he would know that it wasn't in his power to give her a long rein or to allow her to have her freedom. It wasn't a question of giving her freedom.

The only question would be whether he could keep up with her.

# Chapter 19

INDY PRESSED HER nose against the carriage window. Paris by way of superior Russian vodka looked different—fuzzier, friendlier, even more romantic.

The elation in her heart expanded to include every person they passed on the street. Everyone looked so beautiful. The moon was shining so brightly. Everyone had a smile on their lips.

Raven had trusted her to interrogate Petrov. He hadn't interfered or tried to direct the conversation.

"Do you think Sir Charles could be involved in the theft?" she asked Raven. He'd spent much of the evening in conversation with their host.

"I hate to think so, but it's possible. His mistress, Margot Delacroix, is one of Le Triton's close associates."

"She could have compromising information on Sir Charles. She could have blackmailed him into giving Le Triton the information about how to remove the stone from the Society of Antiquaries while it was there on loan from the museum."

"It seems the likeliest explanation at this stage. Miss Delacroix is bound to be at La Sirène this evening."

"There are ladies at the gaming tables?"

"I wouldn't call them ladies."

"They're just women earning a living, they've been left few options in this male-dominated world. I feel no enmity for them."

"You have revolutionary ideas."

"I've never taken my privileged birth for granted. I was born wealthy and titled. I didn't earn these privileges, I was born into them. I don't think they make me any better than anyone else. I'd live as a commoner if I didn't benefit so much from my brother's bottomless pockets. Which I intend to dip into this evening at the *rouge et noir* table."

"You're going to play?" asked Raven, clearly surprised.

"I'm not going to drape myself on your elbow and look decorative, if that's what you're suggesting."

"I didn't know you gambled. Do you know the rules of the games?"

"Of course. What do you think I do on those long sea voyages? The sailors and I have lively contests. I can best any man at cards."

"Of course you can." Raven laid his gloved hand close to hers on the carriage seat. "Society always judges a lady who chooses a different life. I've never told you this before, Indy, but I'm so very proud of your accomplishments."

"I wasn't doing it to make you proud."

"Whatever your motives, you've accomplished so much and your achievements should never be downplayed, or dismissed."

"I do believe you've had a bit too much tipple, Raven. You're losing your mocking edge."

His gaze intensified. "You're the bravest person I know."

This new side of Raven was making it difficult to remember why she used to hate him.

Of course, she was probably just looking at him through vodka-colored spectacles.

"Isn't Paris beautiful?" she asked. "I won't be able to live in London after we break off our engagement. I'll be a pariah. I think I'll move here. I've always been more at home in Paris than in London. There are too many restrictions in London." She stretched her arms wide, nearly touching the walls of the small carriage. "I want to give Paris a hug."

She wanted to give Raven a hug. Tell him that she loved being here with him. That she . . . loved him.

That was the vodka talking. It made her overly courageous. Of course she could never tell him that she loved him.

Not even on this magical night when she felt like they owned Paris.

Raven tucked the edges of her black velvet cloak together, his knuckles brushing her chin. "Easy there, my lady. How many glasses of vodka did you have?"

"Don't be a stick-in-the-mud." She prodded him with her finger.

Solid steel under that coat. She poked his arm again.

He had to be flexing his muscles. No one walked around with arms of steel like that.

"You were always accusing me of being too serious and studious when we were children and you have this reputation for being the life of any party. Where's the Rogue Duke tonight? That's what I want to know."

"Perhaps my reputation has been exaggerated."

"Apparently. And that's why I know there's more to you than you want the world to see. But don't worry, I won't go down that conversational dead end again."

He looked relieved by that. He really was hiding something. She was absolutely convinced of it.

"Can't you feel it?" She hugged her arms around her chest. "Just look at them all." She gestured out the window. The carriage had stopped at a crossroads and there were two lovers kissing in a doorway, lost to the world. "Paris is for lovers. See how happy they are? You were right, Raven. Life isn't all work and no play. Sometimes I feel as though life is passing me by. As though I have a protective coating over my senses and nothing feels sharp or clear. Everything's muted. Tonight I want to feel *everything*."

A drunkard stumbled past them and into the door of a café.

"Tomorrow there will be headaches and heart-aches," said Raven.

"There is no tomorrow," she declared. "Only this night. One life to live. We know where the stone is and now all we have to do is charm our way inside the dragon's lair."

"I don't want to rain on your optimism, but Le

Triton is a crafty and volatile man and if he suspects that I have an ulterior motive for seeking to enter his fortress he'll disappear faster than a gambler's inheritance."

"You've said that he's evil. I'll be very careful."

"You carry a dagger, but I've heard on good authority that Le Triton keeps razors about his person—in his boot, his hat band, and his cigar case. He's an expert with blades of all kinds. He only has three fingers on his right hand but he throws with his left, and can sink a blade into any target from forty paces."

"Why do you sound like an authority on knives suddenly?"

"I never said I didn't know anything about knives."

"Then what was that clumsy attack in the alleyway in London?"

"I was testing your reflexes."

"I was testing yours, and I found them sorely lacking."

And then, all of a sudden, she was sitting on his lap.

What had just happened? She'd been sitting over there on the seat next to him one second ago. He'd moved but she hadn't registered movement until she was . . .

*Sitting on his lap.*

"My reflexes are lightning quick," he said gruffly, stroking her hair away from her face.

"What if I did . . . *this*?" She had been going to jab him in the ribs but he easily caught her wrist before she could.

She tried to surprise him with a left-handed slash. He caught her left hand in his.

He lifted her hands by the wrists. She was well and truly trapped.

"If we weren't in a carriage I'd be able to break this hold," she huffed.

"You should be able to break it anywhere. You're skilled with your knife but you should have more lessons in hand-to-hand combat at close quarters. When you return to London I'll send you an instructor."

"Yes, but what if I did . . . this . . ." She brought her lips to his and kissed him.

He only stiffened for an instant, then he kissed her hungrily.

His hands still gripped her wrists. She loved knowing that all of that strength and muscle was at her command.

She took his face in her hands. "This is probably, no definitely, the vodka talking, but I think you're the most intriguing, handsome man in the world. If our lives were simpler, if we didn't have this bitter history, if you weren't the Rogue Duke and I wasn't an outlandish archaeologist . . . we could drink wine and kiss on the streets of Paris."

"Right now that sounds like heaven."

She nibbled on his lower lip. "Mmm. Vodka-kissing."

When his lips touched hers nothing else seemed to matter except the next kiss, the next sweep of his tongue. How his hands closed around her hips, guiding her over his stiffness.

What power to part her thighs and sink on top of him. His hands moved to her hips.

"We're nearly to the Palais Royal," he said.

She rocked against him. "Yes, nearly there."

His thumb sought her sex beneath her petticoats and skirts. Her drawers had an opening down the middle. He slipped inside. She moaned when he swiped his thumb over her sex.

She felt beautiful and powerful and she never wanted this night to end.

"I want to feast on you, devour you," growled Raven. "What I really want to do is lift your hips, unbutton my breeches and sink my cock deep inside you."

His words nearly made her climax. She rubbed her sensitive flesh against his cock.

"Take out your cock," she said.

He shook his head. "I can't do that."

"Just . . . for a minute." Her mind had gone wanton and wild. She wanted to feel his cock touching her intimate places. "We don't have to . . . do anything. I just want to feel it. I want to see it."

She lifted her hips, holding on to the solid wall of his shoulders. He undid the buttons of his breeches and his cock sprang free. He ringed it with his fist. "Is this what you want?"

She bit her lip, staring down at the glorious sight of Raven's arousal. "God, I want you, Raven."

He groaned. "I want you, Indy. More than anything in the entire world. But we're . . . in a carriage and we're about to arrive at the Palais Royal."

"Then we'll have to be quick about it."

She closed her thighs around his cock, rocking against him. He didn't go inside her. He would never do that until she granted him permission.

They didn't have time, and the urgency made it even more erotic. His thumb moved to the hood of her sex and as she rocked against him, he touched her, slow and soft at first and then hard and fast in a staccato beat in march time.

"Ah . . . ah . . . that feels so good." She fell forward against his shoulder as pleasure rippled through her body. She lay still, wrung out and limp.

Holding her limbs tight around his cock, he thrust upward between her thighs, never entering her. The full length of him sliding against her sensitive folds nearly made her climax again.

"Indy, Gods. Indy," he moaned. One last upward thrust and warmth trickled down her belly. He'd reached his pleasure as well.

He wiped her belly clean with his handkerchief.

She climbed off his lap and rearranged her skirts. He refastened his breeches.

"I've marked you," she said in a breathy, pleasure-laden voice that she almost didn't recognize as her own. "You're going to have a damp patch on your breeches."

"I don't give a damn." He smiled at her. "Let the world see. It's a badge of honor."

She wanted to kiss him again.

And again.

Their carriage entered the yard of the Palais Royal.

She wanted to ride him, in truth this time. Take him deep inside her body. Give herself to him. It would be so sweet. So hot.

She heard the distant sounds of gentlemen and ladies calling to one another. All of this merry-making, the rush and revelry of life, could be theirs as well.

"To be continued," she whispered in his ear as the carriage slowed to a stop.

# Chapter 20

"*Le jeu est prêt, Messieurs et Mesdames,*" announced the dealer, a slender man wearing a red-and-black-striped waistcoat that matched the alternating colors on the gaming table.

*The game was ready.* It certainly was, thought Indy. And not just the game of chance she'd staked her brother's money on tonight.

Raven was staring at Le Triton, Le Triton hadn't stopped staring at the necklace Indy wore, and Le Triton's stunningly lovely companion, Miss Delacroix, hadn't taken her eyes off Raven since the moment they entered.

Raven hadn't been exaggerating. Evil emanated from Le Triton in an almost visible aura. His gaze gave her a cold feeling in the pit of her stomach.

His face had flat planes, as if drawn on a cave wall by an ancient artist who hadn't learned the meaning of dimensionality. He could be considered handsome, though he had a slight overbite that brought his upper lip into prominence. His eyes were light blue and his hair red brown. His ears were set high, and had hardly any lobes, just a slight incline into his jawline.

The dealer flipped another card face upward. "*Noir.*" He would continue dealing until the cards turned exceeded thirty points in number. Then he'd do the same with the packet of red cards.

When she looked at Le Triton she heard sinister music playing in the background. Cellos scraping rhythmically, drums beating in an insistent rhythm, music to signal that something ominous was about to happen in this room.

This opulent, ostentatious room that looked like a giant ormolu clock, all creamy walls and gold coating every available surface. He wanted the world to know he was wealthy and powerful. The pettiest tyrants usually did.

There was nothing tasteful about the room. Everything was designed to overpower the senses with overstated luxury. He was a man obsessed with wealth who would do anything for gold. He'd trample anyone in his path.

Miss Delacroix was merely an expensive accessory, valued only for her pale golden beauty.

If Indy had to hazard a guess, she'd say that Raven and Miss Delacroix knew each other quite well. Funny, because Raven hadn't mentioned that he knew her, only that she was Sir Charles's current mistress.

She must be Raven's former amour. A rush of red-hot jealousy made Indy's fingers shake against the table. *None of that, now. You can't be possessive of something you don't own.*

Indy watched Monsieur Le Triton as the cards turned.

Her thoughts flew as quickly as the cards. She barely noticed when red was announced as the winner.

A break in play was announced and most of the punters dispersed. Miss Delacroix approached Raven and Le Triton joined Indy.

"Are you enjoying yourself, Lady India?"

"Immensely, monsieur."

"Or perhaps I should call you Lady Danger?" His pale eyes wrinkled around the edges but his lips didn't smile.

"I answer to both."

"How did you receive your nickname, may I ask?"

"Oh the scandal sheets love to give everyone nicknames. I'm a female in an unconventional occupation so I must love danger."

"You are an archaeologist, which is inherently dangerous, is it not? Tombs may collapse upon one's head. Sands may shift."

Was that a veiled threat? Indy wished Raven would stop talking to the gilded Miss Delacroix. Indy would even welcome the aggressive ownership he'd displayed at the Louvre. Talking to Monsieur Le Triton raised the hairs at the back of her neck.

"I've never been one to back down from danger," she said.

"I noticed the necklace you're wearing. Perhaps it's a replica?"

*Oh you did?* she thought sarcastically. She flashed him a confident smile with plenty of teeth. "Not at all. It's the real necklace."

He raised his brows. "Indeed. Then the duke has gifted it to you?"

"Only on loan for the evening. Too ostentatious

for my tastes. And far too weighty. I feel as though I'm wearing a manacle around my neck. I told him to sell the necklace. Why should he keep it? He has me now."

Le Triton bowed. "And you outshine any diamond."

"Thank you, monsieur."

"May I?" His hand hovered near her throat.

She swallowed back revulsion and gave him another brilliant smile. "Of course."

He caressed the diamond at the center of the necklace with the tip of his finger. "Flawless."

She was playing Le Triton like a violin, and Raven wasn't even watching. He and Miss Delacroix appeared to be having a heated argument.

Indy should be the only woman allowed to argue with him.

"Did you know that I was nearly the one to find the Wish Diamond?" asked Le Triton. "His Grace and I were racing and he beat me by only one day. I've always coveted it."

"I believe he does intend to sell. But only to the right purchaser and only a deal committed in person, at a place of his choosing."

"I do covet the necklace, but I'm not in the market for more antiquities at the moment. My collection is so vast that I'm focusing now on my other ventures, such as this gaming establishment."

*Bollocks.* That had been the whole plan. Entice him into an invitation for Raven to bring the jewels to his house. Now what was she supposed to do?

"Will you take some refreshment, Lady India?" asked Le Triton. "You must sample my excellent champagne. I hear that your wedding to the duke will feature a champagne fountain. You must allow me to supply the champagne. Gratis." He lifted two shallow, broad-bowled stemmed glasses from the tray of a passing waiter.

He held his glass up to the gilt chandelier and candlelight danced through the bubbles in the champagne. "Legend has it that the coupe glass was designed to mimic the shape of Madame de Pompadour's breast."

That's what she deserved for coming to a gaming house where she was the only true lady present.

Indy didn't bat an eyelash. She lifted her glass. "To Madame's perfect tits."

He smiled for the first time that evening and drank with her.

She'd made him smile, that was a good start.

"You surprise me, Lady India."

"Why is that, Monsieur? Because I speak of bawdy subjects?"

"Because I don't receive proper British ladies in my house very often. Never, actually. I wonder why you chose to come this evening?"

He followed her gaze across the room, where Raven and Miss Delacroix were still arguing. Did his head have to be so very close to her head?

"Ah." Le Triton laughed. "I understand now. You don't want to let him out of your sight. I don't blame you. But if I may give you a word of advice, my lady, I wouldn't try to keep too close a hold on that one."

Indy shrugged her shoulders. "I don't own him. He may do as he pleases." She sipped her champagne too quickly and the bubbles nearly made her sneeze.

"You're not a very good liar, Lady India," said Le Triton.

The undercurrent of coldness in his voice put her on notice.

"Ours will be a marriage of convenience. Two venerable houses aligned."

"An antiquities dynasty. The archaeologist and the fortune hunter."

"I hear you have a bust of Cleopatra in your collection," said Indy. "How do you know it is she?"

"I am quite the Cleopatra enthusiast. I have paintings, sculptures, coins with her likeness. I have one remarkable painting where she's holding the asp outstretched and its head is nearly touching the point of her breast. I do love a *femme fatale*."

He kept staring at her breasts. And his conversation was insufferably lewd and familiar.

The hairs on the back of her neck were now attempting to pluck themselves away from her skin. She didn't know how much longer she could pretend to be fascinated by this conversation when what she wanted to do was slap him.

"I'm sure the duke would find your collection most appealing," she managed to say.

"If it's true that you and he are not exclusive in your affections, I would be most honored to invite you to come and see my collection."

That wasn't the plan. She was supposed to entice Le Triton into inviting Raven to his home.

"Well," she said. "I suppose we must wait until after we're married to cast our glances elsewhere."

"Too bad. I was looking forward to showing you my antiquities."

What was she supposed to do now? The necklace was meant to have been Raven's entrée into Le Triton's fortress. But he'd just invited Indy to view his collection. Alone.

"I am so very curious," she said hastily. "But I'm not sure how the duke would feel about my going alone to a stranger's home."

"Does he appear concerned for your welfare?" he asked.

She glanced back toward where Raven and Miss Delacroix had been standing.

"Where have they gone?"

"I have several private chambers for the use of guests on the floor above us."

The man was goading her, poking at her to make her angry.

It was working.

She gripped her champagne glass. "Might I have more champagne?"

"Of course. Anything the lady desires. Anything at all."

She didn't have to feign her pique. "Perhaps I will accept your invitation, after all, monsieur."

He bowed over her hand. "I'd be happy to show you my collection tomorrow. Though you must promise to come alone."

"Don't worry, I will."

"Excuse me, Madame, this note just arrived for you." An attendant handed her a note. She broke the plain red wax seal and read the brief note. It was from Lady Catherine.

"Is something wrong?" Le Triton asked.

"I'm afraid I must leave. Please donate my winnings to a worthy charitable concern."

"Are you sure you must leave so suddenly? We were just beginning to become better acquainted."

"We can resume our conversation tomorrow."

Indy left hastily. She had to find Raven to tell him about Lady Catherine's note.

She walked swiftly to the door where she'd last seen Ravenwood. The hallway was empty save for a waiter with a cart piled with little plates of delicacies. "Have you seen the Duke of Ravenwood?" she asked.

"I haven't seen him, my lady." But he made a furtive little glance to the left, which told her all she needed to know.

She headed left. She didn't have far to go.

He was there, one arm braced against the wall beside Miss Delacroix's head. She was laughing at something he'd said.

He leant closer, bending to whisper something in her ear.

Indy's vision blurred. Her stomach roiled.

Suddenly she was seventeen again. Standing

on the edge of a ballroom waiting for an invitation that never came.

Cool air assaulting her face as she walked outside. The tinkling sound of laughter and Daniel's low voice as he whispered into the beautiful woman's ear, before kissing her.

Anger and humiliation flashed through her mind like lightning.

She couldn't do this. Not again.

Never again.

Seventeen-year-old Indy had cried hot streaks of humiliating tears. She'd cried because her dreams and trust had been destroyed forever.

Tonight there were no tears. She'd known better and she'd stuck her tongue on the wintry gate anyway.

You're a fool. Such a bloody fool.

Allowing him to rip your heart out yet again.

RAVEN HEARD A noise and turned around just in time to see Indy fleeing down the corridor in a swish of mulberry silk.

"Damn. *Damn!*" he said.

She'd seen him talking to Margot and by the looks of things she'd assumed the worst.

"What's wrong, Ravenwood?" Margot asked.

"I have to go. We'll talk later." He walked swiftly down the hallway. He caught a glimpse of deep purple silk around the corner and he nearly collided with a waiter carrying a heavy tray.

She wasn't going out the front door; where was she going? He chased her in earnest now, not wanting to lose sight of her. She fled down the servants' stairs and out the back door.

She hadn't even collected her cloak.

A carriage was waiting halfway down the street and she ran toward it.

"Indy, stop!" he yelled.

He didn't recognize the carriage. What was she doing?

He caught up with her just before she reached the carriage. He grabbed her by the shoulders. "Wait, please. Let me explain. It wasn't what it looked like."

She wrenched away from his grasp. Her eyes were cold. "I can't do this. I just can't. I can't trust you. I can't rely on you."

"I wasn't making love to her, I was questioning her."

Her shoulders shook. So much pain on her face. It twisted his gut with fury at himself that he'd hurt her again. "Please let me explain. She's Sir Charles's mistress and I think she may be involved in the theft."

"I don't care about her. It's not about her. It's about you. You will always hurt me. Always betray me. And it doesn't matter why you do it or what your intentions are. I won't give you any more power over me."

"Whose carriage is this? I'm not letting you go alone. You didn't even collect your cloak. You'll catch cold."

She pulled the clasp of the necklace loose. "I don't want your diamond."

She flung the necklace at him and he caught it before it hit the ground and tucked it inside his pocket.

"That's not what I was concerned about. You're angry. You have every right to be angry."

"Feeling things so deeply is a curse, Raven. I wish I had your ability to disconnect from your emotions, truly I do. But my highs have always been very high, and my lows very low. And my trust, twice betrayed, is lost forever."

"Please allow me to explain."

"I have to go. This is Lady Catherine's carriage." She pulled a note from her bodice and handed it to him. "Lady Catherine is ill and has something she wants to tell me urgently. I must go to her immediately."

"Are you sure that this is her handwriting?"

"I think I know one of my oldest friend's handwriting. I recognize the distinctive cramped lettering. She's in trouble and I must go to her. She means more to me than our quest."

"Indy, you asked me to trust you, and I did. Now I'm asking you to trust me. Allow me to come with you, please. I may be able to help Lady Catherine. It's late, and you're alone. Please accept the help of a friend."

"A friend?" she asked bitterly.

"Business associate, then. Allow me to accompany you, and you may send me on any errands Lady Catherine may require."

Indy shivered, her shoulders hunching in the cold air. "You may come as my associate. But only because Catherine might require your services."

They walked together to the carriage. "Are you Lady Catherine's groom?" Raven asked the young boy waiting by the carriage.

"Aye, sir. She said I was to bring the lady to her. She didn't say anything about a gentleman."

"This is the Duke of Ravenwood and he'll be accompanying me," said Indy.

"How long is the ride to Lady Catherine's estate?" Raven asked.

"No more than a half hour," said the groom.

They climbed into the carriage.

Raven removed his coat and set it around Indy's shoulders. She didn't push it away, so he took that as a hopeful sign.

They rode through the Paris streets in silence this time. Indy sat next to him but she was a world away.

If he tried to explain his interrogation of Margot, he'd open himself up to having to explain that other time, so long ago, in the garden.

She was furious, and her anger was an offering, a way out.

*The easy way out. The selfish way.*

He had to tell her. He had to confess his secret. She deserved an explanation for why he'd chosen his family, and service to his country, over her love.

He must find the words, must suppress the conditioning that screamed inside his head that an agent never confessed, never admitted to anything.

"She means nothing to me, Indy," he said softly.

"She used to be your lover."

"Yes, she did."

"Why didn't you tell me that?"

"I didn't think it was relevant to our quest. Tonight I wanted to speak with her alone about her amour with Sir Charles."

"You left me with Le Triton."

"I thought that was the plan. You wanted to speak with him."

"That was the plan, until I realized how right you were. The man is . . . unsettling to say the least. There's an almost palpable corruption in every word he says and every move he makes."

"I shouldn't have left you alone with him."

"I volunteered for the duty."

"I would have returned within the next five minutes. How did the conversation go?"

"Not as planned. Instead of inviting you to his house, he invited me. And he asked me to come alone. I think he was trying to seduce me." She shuddered. "It was horrible."

"Don't even think about it. I'm not sending you in there alone."

"I can do the reconnaissance just as well as you. I'll see how many guards he has, where they are situated, where the stone could be kept."

"I won't let you do it."

"Oh we're back to this, are we? He's not going to murder me, not when he knows you're waiting for me to come home."

"He might murder you."

"You said yourself that no one has been invited into his fortress. I just received an invitation into his lair. What was I supposed to do? You were off with Miss Delacroix and Le Triton wasn't inter-ested in purchasing the necklace."

"I'm not faulting you, I think you did a wonder-ful job."

"But you don't trust me to finish the job I started."

"I don't trust Le Triton. There's a very big dif-ference."

"I don't think there is."

Raven pressed his fingers to her lips. The carriage had taken a wrong turn.

"What is it?" she whispered.

"The carriage turned the wrong way."

"A shorter route?"

"There's only one way to reach Montrouge and this is not it. This isn't Lady Catherine's carriage. We've been misled. Prepare yourself," he said tersely. "The carriage is slowing."

"Prepare for what?"

"For a fight," he said grimly. "You have your hidden dagger at the ready?"

She nodded.

The carriage slowed and stopped.

The door opened.

"Out of the carriage, both of you," a rough voice said in French. "And hands where I can see them."

# Chapter 21

❧

$\mathcal{R}$AVEN COUNTED FIVE enemy combatants, though there could be more men in that nearby copse of trees. His mind went to that cold, efficient place it had been trained to go. Kill or be killed.

*Head down and plow through the enemy line.*

He'd protect Indy with his life. "What do you want?" he asked the enormous man who'd made them leave the carriage. He must be nearly seven foot tall.

"Don't play coy." The man raised his pistol and pointed it at Raven's head. "Surrender your weapon and hand over the diamond."

"Le Triton decided he didn't want to pay?" asked Raven.

"That's not your concern," said the giant with the pistol.

Indy caught Raven's eye. The moon was shining overhead. For a split second he marveled at how beautiful she was by moonlight, then he returned to the task at hand.

Four hulking men and the groom, who was no more than a boy and hovered near the carriage as if he wanted no part in the violence.

Raven reached behind his back but raised his

hands again when the man cocked his pistol and pointed it at Indy.

"No sudden movements," the man growled.

"I'm surrendering my weapon," said Raven.

The man jerked his head. "Do it, then."

Raven pulled the pistol from the back of his waistband and threw it across the ground toward the man.

The man gestured with his pistol at Indy. "Where's the purple diamond? Not around her pretty neck anymore. Tell me or she dies."

"I stuffed the necklace down my bodice," said Indy boldly. "Come and find it."

Raven's first reaction was to try to silence her, to physically place himself in front of her, shield her from their attackers.

Then he realized what she was doing.

*Men always underestimate me,* she'd told him.

He'd been underestimating her.

She was bringing them closer, within striking range. He caught her eye and gave her a swift nod of encouragement.

"Why don't you both have a search, my fine fellows?" she said in French. She shrugged out of his jacket and it dropped to the ground with the Wish Diamond in the pocket.

She wiggled her chest. "I have enough for both of you."

"Search her and be quick about it," said the gigantic man with the pistol who was obviously the leader.

"Don't mind if I do," said his associate with a nasty sneer that curdled Raven's blood.

Indy lifted her hem and posed her leg. She caught Raven's eye. The dagger must be tucked inside her garter.

"And search him for weapons," the giant said.

Two of his men approached warily while their leader covered them with his pistol.

"On my count," Raven whispered to Indy. "Back to back. Stay low. Roll to the ground."

She made no move, not even a twitch of her eye. She remained focused on distracting the men with her body.

The men drew near. The giant with the pistol moved closer to keep watch, and one man stayed back. Only the leader openly carried a pistol.

The groom remained near the carriage. Raven decided he wasn't a threat, too young. He could see from the way the groom held himself that he wanted no part of the fight. Probably a son or nephew of one of the men, not a hardened criminal yet.

"Don't try anything, or I'll drill you with a bullet," said the leader.

"She's a prime article, isn't she?" Raven asked the two men. "Better than you'll ever have."

"We'll have her *and* the diamond and we'll tie you up so you can watch."

*Like hell they would.*

"Now," Raven whispered.

He and Indy moved back to back. She drew her blade in a flash of silver and slashed at one of the men. Raven's fist crashed into a jawbone. There was the cracking sound of a pistol firing but Indy was low to the ground, slashing at the man's hamstrings, and Raven was shielded by the bulk of the man he'd knocked out.

He threw the man off and lunged for the leader. He knocked away the giant's pistol and turned to deliver a kick to the fourth man's head. The man fell easily.

The giant was another story. He roared a battle cry and threw himself at Raven.

The man was no thick wit. He'd been trained. Probably one of Le Triton's elite guard force. Raven wasn't able to see what was happening to Indy with her opponent because he had his hands full with the towering giant, whose fists were the size of Raven's head.

Raven kept landing blows and the giant just kept coming.

He locked his elbow around Raven's neck.

"Here you, move your arse and fight like a man," the giant called to the groom, who was watching with a stricken expression on his pale face.

Raven jabbed his elbow into the giant's kidneys and broke free. "Stay right there, boy, and I won't slit your throat," he croaked.

The boy wavered.

"I'll stick you myself for being a dog coward," said the giant, between blows to Raven's ears. "Go help Antoine with the fancy piece. She's got a knife and she knows how to use it."

"I won't attack a lady," said the boy.

The giant spat out a tooth. "You won't make it far in life, then."

Raven risked a swift glance at Indy. She had

the man down on the ground with her knife at his throat.

Raven and the giant exchanged another round of blows. Raven staggered. If he could find a way to use the pocket watch with the sleeping powder inside, he could fell this Goliath, but the man wasn't exactly giving Raven any room to breathe.

Out of the corner of his eye Raven caught a flash of purple silk.

His vision narrowed. Land a blow on the giant's nose and move in for the kill.

THIS WAS WHY she never wore tight bodices and puffed sleeves. She couldn't take full breaths in this infernal corset. At least she'd worn her boots, one of which was currently crushing her assailant's windpipe.

"Stop moving or I'll slit your throat," she said coldly. She pressed down harder with her boot.

The man whimpered. He wasn't going to stop fighting if she released him. So she did what she had to do.

She drove her knife into the heavy canvas of his trousers, grazing his thigh just deep enough to make him shriek with pain but not to permanently wound him. She shoved the dagger deep into the ground with her boot, trapping the man down.

She finished him off with a swift kick to the groin. The man yowled for a few seconds and then fell silent.

Raven had already felled two men and was

working on the final threat, the towering man who had ordered them out of the carriage.

The giant pummeled Raven with his huge fists.

Raven caught her eye. "Indy, run!" he shouted. He must be daft; she would never desert him.

Raven's pistol lay on the ground only a few feet away. She darted forward.

"Stop, or I'll shoot this pistol," she shouted.

Both men stopped swinging and turned to face her.

"Not if I kill you first," roared the giant and barreled toward her.

She fired. The bullet struck his knee. He fell to the ground, howling in pain and clutching at his knee.

Raven finished him off with a blow to his head. The giant finally lay silent.

She lowered the pistol. Her hands were shaking so badly she was afraid she might injure herself. Raven was at her side. He took the pistol.

There was blood all over the man's knee and on the ground.

She'd shot a man. But she hadn't killed him. He'd live if he received medical attention.

"Are you all right?" asked Raven.

She attempted to smile but her lips were frozen. "I think so." She glanced at the scene before them. Four men down. "Where's the lad?" she asked.

"I'm here!" The boy who had posed as the groom sat atop a carriage horse he'd unhitched. "And I've got the diamond." He waved the necklace like a flag. He flashed them a grin and set off at a gallop into the night.

"After him," shouted Indy, running for the horses.

"Stop." Raven caught her arm. "You could be injured."

"But he's escaping with the diamond."

"Let him go. What I want to know is whether you're injured."

"A few scratches and bruises. My attacker is far worse off." He was still stuck to the ground with her knife, and he'd fainted dead away.

"You were very brave."

"They don't call me Lady Danger for nothing." She lifted her hand to his face and her fingers came away soaked with blood. "You're the one who's injured."

"It's nothing. Come, we must leave before one of these fine fellows wakes up." He strode toward the horses and began unhitching one of them from the carriage.

Something tugged at Indy's mind. Raven shouting for her to run in that deep, gruff voice. The way he'd fought with lethal precision. The way those huge men had sailed through the air as if they'd sprouted wings.

Of course! Why hadn't she realized it before? He *was* a spy. It explained everything. And not only that . . . he was the man who'd rescued her in that alleyway in Whitechapel.

"Indy, watch out!"

She heard Raven shout but she didn't have time to react. The man who had been lying behind her must have recovered.

The blow caught her in the back of the head and knocked her to the ground.

*Bollocks*, she had time to think, before darkness descended.

RAVEN MADE SWIFT work of Indy's attacker, cracking him alongside the head with the pistol. He should shoot the man for wounding Indy, but he never killed unnecessarily.

Indy lay sprawled on the cold ground, her body twisted at an unnatural angle.

His worst nightmare come to life and it was his fault. He should have known this was a trap.

He should never have allowed her to come to Paris in the first place.

Raven dropped to his knees and took her pulse. It was weak but it was there. Not her blood, on his hands, thank God. Mostly his. He had a scratch where a bullet had grazed his shoulder, and several deep cuts and bruises from the giant's pummeling.

He must bring her to safety before any of the other men regained consciousness.

He lifted her gingerly into his arms. Her head flopped down and hit his arm.

Tears stung his eyes and mingled with the blood from the cuts on his forehead.

With a severe blow to the head, she needed to be kept warm and jostled as little as possible, but what choice did he have? He must convey her to safety and there was only one way to do that, since the lad had stolen one of the horses.

He hoisted her onto the horse and climbed up behind her. He'd ride for Lady Catherine's house. They were close, he'd kept track of where the carriage was going. It would be faster than returning to Paris.

He wouldn't allow himself to think about Indy suffering permanent harm.

She'd wake up soon and first she'd insult him, and call him a pain in her arse, and then she'd kiss him.

Everything would go back to the way it had been only a few hours ago.

Indy kissing him in the carriage. Whispering in his ear . . .

*To be continued.*

That's what he had to believe with all his heart.

That she had a future. That they could have a future.

Together.

# Chapter 22

❦

LADY CATHERINE'S BROODING gothic beast of a chateau crouched in darkness. Indy was still slumped
in front of him when Raven arrived at the house.
She hadn't stirred.

He lifted her off the horse, handed the reins to
a sleepy groom, and carried her up the walkway.
No one answered the knocker. He knocked again
more loudly.

Finally the door creaked open. "Do you know
what time it is?" asked the elderly manservant at
the door.

"I've no time for conversation. I'm the Duke of
Ravenwood. This is Lady India Rochester, a personal friend of Lady Catherine's. Lady India is
injured. I require a comfortable bedchamber, hot
water, and fresh towels."

"What's all this then?" asked Lady Catherine,
appearing behind her servant. "Your Grace, is
that you? What's happened to Indy?"

Raven carried Indy through the door. "She's
had a bad blow to the head. She needs rest."

Lady Catherine took one look at Indy and didn't
ask any more questions. "This way," she said. The
servant followed, holding a lantern aloft.

"Just to clarify something," Raven said. "You didn't send her a note this evening, did you?"

"No."

"I didn't think so. It was all a ruse. She received a note purportedly from you saying that you were ill and she should come right away. We climbed into a carriage and were set upon by thieves when we were nearly here. They stole the Wish Diamond."

"Heavens," said Lady Catherine as she led the way into a spacious bedchamber. "How dreadful."

Raven laid Indy down on the bed and began removing her clothing.

"Will she live?" asked Lady Catherine anxiously, wringing her hands over Indy's bedside.

"It was a forceful blow," said Raven. "The good news is that he hit the back of her head on the thickest part of her skull."

"Should I send for Dr. Lowe?" asked Lady Catherine. "Or another physician?"

"There's nothing any doctor can tell us. All we can do is wait now."

"There are cases where a person recovers but the memory does not," said Lady Catherine. "I had a friend once who developed amnesia after a blow to the head."

"Those cases are rare, I believe."

"I can't believe they used my name to lure her into a strange carriage," said Lady Catherine.

She was very pale and her lips had a bluish tinge to them. Perhaps it was the candlelight, but Raven knew Indy had been worried about her friend's health.

"Why don't you get some rest, Lady Catherine? I'll keep watch over her."

"I do feel a little tired. I don't know if Indy told you, or not, but I suffer from vertigo."

"Please have a good night's rest. I'm sure Indy will be back to herself by morning."

She took her leave and Raven closed the door behind her. His entire body ached from the punishment he'd received. When a servant brought hot water and towels, he washed the blood away from his face. The bruises would be there for a long time.

He bathed Indy's face with hot water. She stirred in her sleep. A good sign.

He removed his coat and boots and climbed into bed next to her.

"If you wake up, Indy, I swear I will never tell you another lie as long as I live."

There was no response. She slept, her chest rising and falling in a regular rhythm. Her profile was so heartbreakingly beautiful.

He never cried, so of course that wasn't a tear sliding down his cheek. Must be sweat.

"If you wake up, Indy," he whispered, "I'll lay my heart at your feet. I'll beg you for forgiveness."

He loved her. He'd always loved her. What a bloody fool he'd been to give her up, to make decisions on her behalf without giving her any choice in the matter.

He'd been too young to make that kind of decision.

"Please wake up," he said.

No answer.

He curled his body around hers, as if his warmth might communicate directly to her body, while her mind slept.

He wouldn't sleep. Not until he knew she was out of danger.

He rested his head on her shoulder.

"RAVEN?"

His eyes flew open. He must have fallen asleep.

"Indy. You're awake."

Hope filtered through his heart like sunlight through a diamond.

She tried to sit up and he placed gentle hands on her shoulders. "Don't try to move yet."

"Raven," she whispered. "It was you. In Whitechapel. You're the one who saved me."

He smiled. "Yes."

All of his secrets would be revealed now. He didn't care anymore about the consequences. He could no longer lie to her.

"You had a blow to the head," he explained. He left the bed and fetched a glass of water.

"Drink some water." He lifted her head and helped her take a sip.

"Where are we?" she asked.

"Lady Catherine's house. She was here by your side and then she went to bed." He held up three fingers in front of her face. "How many fingers am I holding up?"

"Three."

"What's your name?"

She rolled her eyes. "You don't have to interrogate me. I feel quite normal. I don't need to be coddled." She tried to rise again and he held her down.

"Stop restraining me," she said indignantly. "There's a throbbing pain in my head but you're becoming a worse sort of pain in my arse."

He laughed. "You don't know how good it is to hear you insult me. Seriously, Indy, please lie still awhile longer. You were hit in the back of the head."

"I remember," she said ruefully. She rubbed her skull. "Ouch. That smarts."

"Do you want something to eat? I'll ring for a servant."

"I'm all right. Stop fussing. I don't like being the damsel in distress. I want to leave this bed."

She was so tough and brave, his Indy. "Everyone is still sleeping."

"Then climb into bed with me," she said. "It's the only way you'll make me behave."

That he could do.

She watched him from the bed, the light from the bedside candelabra shifting across her face and over her long, unbound hair.

His heart hurt to look at her. "Indy, you're so beautiful. Have I told you that?"

"Not in so many words. But you did say I was a formidable weapon."

"You are that. You know that you saved me from being beaten to a bloody mess? You charged right up with my pistol. That giant didn't think you'd fire but I knew better."

She laughed. "Blasted him right in the knee-cap."

"He won't underestimate you or any other woman again." He climbed back into bed. "And neither will I."

"Now that Le Triton has the necklace, you've lost your bargaining chip," she said.

"Sir Malcolm has a team in place to storm Le Triton's stronghold."

"Sir Malcolm? A team?"

He was getting ahead of himself. He slid beneath the covers and fit his body around hers. She felt so right in his arms. He wanted to sleep curled around her for the rest of his life. "Indy, you might not want me in this bed with you after I explain myself."

"Here's what I know already. You were the one who saved me in Whitechapel. And you definitely don't need lessons in how to defend yourself. And you probably run around saving the world, and such, because you're a secret agent for the crown."

"And you're too clever by half."

"I should have realized it earlier. You stopped responding to my letters because you embarked on another life. One that didn't include me."

"I'm so sorry. I went about it all wrong, I see that now." He filled his lungs and exhaled slowly. "My father was a spy as well as a diplomat. Before he died, he wrote in his journal that he wanted me to become a spy. He had planned to induct me into the knowledge of my heritage in espionage when I turned fifteen. Sir Malcolm gave me the journal. He knew it would make me want to become a spy."

She turned her head. "Sir Malcolm is . . . also an agent?"

He nodded. "You talk about me being detached from my emotions and that's because I was trained in the art of detachment. The school I attended in Scotland was no ordinary school. I can't divulge details, I can't go that far, but I can tell you that it shaped me in profound ways. Brutal ways."

She laid her hand on top of his arm where it curved around her waist.

"I was searching for some meaning to it all. My father had been accused of treason. I thought that if I became what he had been I would be able to prove his innocence. I did it for my family, Indy. So that Colin would have something to inherit. So that my mother wouldn't have to live with the taint of being a traitor's widow."

"I'm beginning to understand now."

"My father's death hurt so much, it was this cataclysmic event that shaped me and I became defined by it. The espionage business thrives on boys with wounded hearts and voids to fill. You were right when you accused me of living selfishly. I was trying to make sense of why I was left fatherless and alone, and I hurt you and that makes me hate myself."

"You were so young when your father died. You had to become the duke. I understand what a burden that must have been. And then to discover he'd been a spy, and wanted you to become one as well. That's why you stopped writing to me."

"After I graduated from the secret training program, Sir Malcolm gave me a talk. He told me the truth about his wife and daughter's death. They hadn't died in a carriage accident, as was the official story. They'd been poisoned by his enemies. The poison had been meant for Sir Malcolm."

"How awful. Those poor innocents."

"He told me never to marry. Told me that my profession could only bring suffering to those I loved."

"And so you shut yourself off from me, and from your family. You pushed us away." She turned in his arms so that she faced him. "And that night at my coming-out ball . . ."

"I planned the whole thing, Indy. I planned to have you discover me there in the garden, kissing Mrs. Cavinder. I hated myself for hurting you. Gods, how I hated myself."

"How I hated you."

"I've never forgotten the sight of your ashen face . . . your eyes hazing like lavender fields viewed through a mist of rain. Betrayal settling like a veil over your face. The memory has haunted me forever."

"Why did you do it? Why didn't you just make up some story about another woman and ask me to end our engagement?"

"I thought if I made you angry, you would jilt me. You could be the injured party and maintain your reputation. If I jilted you, there would have been whispers about your virtue. I fully expected you to formally end our engagement. I expected you to marry another."

"I told myself that I never brought suit to break our marriage contract because I never would marry and so what was the point? But I think the truth is that I wanted to keep the connection to you. The attachment."

He stroked her cheek. "I felt the same way, though I wouldn't admit it to myself."

"I told you I would uncover your secrets eventually," she said with a tremulous laugh.

"Actually . . ." He touched her face. "I had already resolved to tell you. I was going to confess everything in the carriage on the way here. I couldn't live one more day without telling you the truth, even if it meant breaking my code of silence. I'm a brick wall, a blunt instrument. I do my duty. The trajectory of my life was predetermined by the choices I made when I was young."

She squeezed his bicep. "You are a brick wall, aren't you?"

"You don't have to make a joke. I know the pain I caused you. I'm the biggest numbskull known to man."

"That's my line."

"Then say it. Say something. Tell me that you hate me, or that you can forgive me, or that you . . ." He paused. The words wouldn't come. The words he wanted to say. Had to say.

He'd lived so much of his life denying that those words even existed.

He only spoke those three words in his dreams. When she sat next to him by a fireplace.

And there were two children playing with alphabet blocks. The girl forming a word with her blocks that started with *L* and ended with *E*.

He knew when and why he'd driven away the possibility of everything those four letters contained.

What he didn't know was how he could find his way back, and whether Indy could ever forgive him for pushing her way.

"Can you forgive me, Indy?" he asked.

"First, I heartily approve of your clandestine activities. All that single-minded pursuit of justice and that unerring sense of duty is actually quite attractive. And I've always wondered why a man who is supposed to lead such an indolent, intemperate existence has a body that is sculpted from marble."

That certainly wasn't the response he'd been expecting. But then Indy always surprised him.

"Espionage isn't a glamorous profession, Indy. Violence begets violence. War begets war. I've seen terrible things. I've seen men treat each other like animals. Men thinking of other men as less than human, as other. But we all bleed, Indy. We all bleed the same red blood. Inside we're all the same. I'm not trying to excuse the way I treated you. I know it was wrong for me to push you away, to make you hate me. I only thought . . . I thought I was doing it for your protection."

"Second," she continued. "I had a realization today. I thought it might be the result of looking at you through vodka-colored spectacles, but now I know what I felt was true. Everyone wants to be loved, Raven. I want to be loved. I don't want to be hurt. But I can't have one without the possibility of the other. I'm strong enough to admit that I love you with no requirement that you say the words back to me."

"Indy." He clasped her against his chest. "Why?"

"Why do I love you? Because you trust me. Because we make a good team. You make me laugh. You love your family and made sacrifices so that they could have a better life. I love you because you rescued me from that madman with a knife."

She lifted her head and stared into his eyes. "I love you because you laugh at my jokes, but you never laugh at my ambitions. And I love you because . . . I always have. And I always will. Now kiss me, you big dolt of a duke. And don't worry about my head, I have a thick skull. Must have, if I love you."

He was hers to command.

His heart overflowing, he kissed her tenderly, memorizing the shape of her lips, the sweetness of her words.

She loved him.

And he loved her. He just had to find a way to say the words, and to make her believe them.

A PART OF HER wanted, needed, him to say he loved her. It had been sheer theatricality, saying she didn't need to hear the words.

But for now it was enough to kiss, to be kissed. To be adored by his body, his tongue, his hands.

Her emotions had been ungloved. She opened her heart, giving herself permission to be fully

present with him for the first time. Maybe she'd
be hurt again.

But right now she was going to revel in this
closeness, this warmth and tenderness between
them. Her body alive with pleasure from the
crown of her head to her toes.

She wore only her chemise. He must have un-
dressed her earlier. Eager to feel his skin, she
fumbled with the buttons on his breeches.

He drew his shirt over his head.

The map of his scars. Each one a story. A mission.

She trusted that he had lived his life by a strict
code of ethics. As strict as the one she lived hers
by. He'd thought he was being noble when he
pushed her away.

He hadn't been idly watching life go by. Col-
lecting stolen antiquities was his cover.

He wasn't a mercenary, but he'd stolen her
heart when she thought she had no heart to give.

His hands found the hem of her chemise beneath the coverlet and lifted it slowly up her
body. She lifted her arms to help him remove the
garment.

Nothing left between them. Skin to skin. Heart
to heart.

She sighed when his lips claimed the peak of
her breast. Lovers throughout history had made
these secret sounds.

He ran his hands along her waist and over her
hips.

He was sculpted from marble, from his biceps
to his bum.

And his cock. That part of him was hard as

stone yet warm and soft to her touch. She guided him between her thighs. She needed to feel him inside her.

"I want to make you come first," he said, halting her progress with his hand.

"You already did, remember? The carriage?"

"Again." He slid down her body, parting her thighs with his hands and burying his tongue between her legs.

She wasn't going to argue with the sentiment. What he was doing with his tongue felt too exquisite.

She didn't have to be the perfect seductress.

She didn't have to be perfect at all.

It was such a relief. So freeing. He admired her strength and wasn't deterred by her many flaws, her pride and defensiveness, her drive to control every situation.

She never let her maid or her friends care for her; she kept everyone at a distance because she had to be so strong all the time.

But this was almost like being born over again, a chance to experience a different way of being, where allowing someone to do something so nice for her didn't diminish her independence, it increased it.

This wasn't about control or surrender. No one had to win.

This was simpler than a game, more elemental. Two lovers entwined in an ageless act of devotion.

She guided his head with her hands, helping him locate the perfect place. A few more strokes of his tongue. Just . . . there.

"Raven," she cried as her muscles clenched and released and pleasure burst in her mind and pulsed through her body.

She reached for his shoulders and pulled him up her body. She kissed him, tasting herself on his tongue. "I want you inside me now."

He curled his fist around his cock and parted the folds of her sex with his other hand. She wasn't going to close her eyes. She wanted to witness this moment.

Record and remember the first time their bodies joined. It gave her a primal thrill, even as it pinched and stretched her body, to watch him bury his cock, inch by inch, inside her.

He moved slowly, pausing often to allow her body to adjust to this invasion. "How does that feel?" he asked.

"It stings a little."

"I can stop at any time. If there is any discomfort, if your head aches too much."

"I don't want you to stop. I want more of you. I'm not going to break. I'm strong enough."

He eased more of his cock inside her.

"Sex should always feel good, Indy. If it doesn't, someone's doing something wrong. Some women counterfeit their pleasure, focusing solely on pleasing a man. I know you won't do that. You'd better not. I'll know if you're pretending," he said sternly.

She couldn't help laughing a little bit. "I swear I won't pretend."

"My guide and my aim is your pleasure." He buried more of his cock inside her. "Your pleasure is the key to my own release."

"Harder," she gasped. "I can take it all."

He grasped her hips, angled her body upward, and thrust his entire cock into her in one smooth stroke.

"Raven," she moaned. "Yes. All of it."

He thrust again, harder this time. His chest brushed against her nipples as he moved above her. Angular jaw set in a near-grimace, copper-brown eyes open and filled with awe.

"My Indy," he said. "Move with me."

She matched his movements, rising to meet him, opening wider for him.

She stopped watching and surrendered to sensation. She reveled in the sound of his harsh, quick breathing. She loved that he called her his Indy.

His pace increased and she threaded her arms around his neck, drawing him against her breast. They moved together, shaking the bedframe, startling the ghosts in this drafty old castle.

He reached his hand between them and touched her, stroking the inside of her sex with his cock, and the outside with his thumb. The dual sensation built to a nearly unbearable height.

"I think . . ." she said breathily. "I think I'm about to have a very real, very not-fake . . . release."

"Excellent," he panted. "Because I won't be able to hold back much longer."

A few more delicious strokes and she dissolved into pleasure, digging her fingernails into his back as he rode her to his own shuddering bliss.

She would always remember the way his eyes opened and his gaze held hers, afterward, as they lay entwined.

He was her charming, carefree Daniel, the one with the devilish grin.

And he was Raven, the spy who loved her but hadn't found a way to tell her yet.

# Chapter 23

❧

THEY MUST HAVE dozed off. The next thing Raven knew, Indy was shaking him by the shoulders.

"Do you hear that, Raven?" she asked.

"What, what is it? What time is it?" he replied, disoriented by the unfamiliar surroundings and the light stealing in from behind the curtains.

"I heard a woman scream. There it is again." This time Raven heard it as well. A high-pitched wailing.

"Let's investigate," said Indy, leaping out of bed.

Good lord. Would she always leap out of bed in that sprightly manner at such an ungodly hour? Though when she leapt about quite naked it was a hell of a way to wake up.

She was so beautiful with those long limbs and full breasts and her hair wild about her shoulders.

He stretched and yawned.

"Raven. Wake up. I think Lady Catherine is in trouble. I have this terrible feeling that something is very wrong here."

Half awake, he fumbled into his clothing. What was wrong was cutting short the first night of peaceful sleep he'd had in ages. He'd slept like a baby, dreamless and deep. Sated and satisfied by the best sex he'd ever had in his life.

He'd always known it would be the best with Indy. She was good at everything she put her mind to.

He needed some coffee.

"The noise is faint but it was almost as if it were emanating from the walls," she said. She walked the perimeter of the room, leaning her ear to the wall at intervals. She stopped by a large relief of a lion carved into the stone walls. "Here. It's coming from below."

The hairline crack around the lion's head would have been easy to miss unless one was looking for it. He pushed on the lion's head and a doorway opened in the wall.

"A secret passageway! We have to follow it," cried Indy.

The high-pitched moaning sounded again. Now the eerie noise was accompanied by a thumping drumbeat.

"Something's happening below the castle, in the dungeons, perhaps. My dagger is lost. Do you have your pistol?"

"No." He'd been too concerned about taking Indy to safety to retrieve his pistol. "I do have this, though." He held up the timepiece.

"A pocket watch?"

"Not just any pocket watch. It contains a powder that I've been assured will send even a very large man into a sound slumber for several hours."

"Well, it's better than nothing. Hopefully we won't require weapons. Perhaps it's only a friendly ghost haunting the castle."

She grabbed a lamp and disappeared into a narrow stone passageway sloping downward.

Slithering sound of insects scurrying out of their path. The moaning and the drumbeat grew louder as they descended into the bowels of the castle.

The passageway descended more steeply now. They emerged onto a balcony overlooking a cavernous space fitted with rusted iron hoops embedded in the walls. "The old dungeons," Raven whispered.

"Look," whispered Indy, her eyes widening.

Standing by a fire pit in the center of the room, Dr. Lowe raised his hands and began to chant what sounded like gibberish to Raven.

"He's speaking Coptic," said Indy.

Lady Catherine sat in a chair near the fire. A chair that had blue painted legs shaped like lion's paws.

"It's the chair from the Louvre," Indy whispered urgently. "And is that . . . it can't be. It is! It's the Rosetta Stone!"

# Chapter 24

❧

$I$NDY STARED IN astonishment. Lady Catherine had stolen the Rosetta Stone?

It made no sense.

"What on earth?" Raven muttered.

"There's a whole collection of stolen antiquities in that room—I can't understand it. Why would Lady Catherine be involved in such nefarious goings on? She's wealthy in her own right."

They watched, hidden behind the railing, as Dr. Lowe lowered his arms and approached Lady Catherine. He placed his hands upon her midsection and began chanting again.

Lady Catherine moaned, her eyes fluttering back in her head.

Raven's eyes widened. "Lowe must be behind all of this, not Lady Catherine. He's controlling her somehow, using her fortune and connections to steal antiquities."

"He's manipulating her mind. We must rescue her from further harm."

Raven nodded. "And recover the stone. On my count," he said. "You take the right stairs and I'll take the left. We'll surprise them. I don't see any guards. Should be a simple matter to overpower—"

He stopped talking because someone had grabbed him by the nape of the neck. Someone even larger than the giant of a man Indy'd shot last night.

Raven dangled from the giant's hands, kicking his heels at the air ineffectually.

"Look what I found, Dr. Lowe," shouted the enormous man. "Intruders."

Dr. Lowe glanced up. "Bring them to me, Baptiste," he said, without lifting his hand from Lady Catherine's abdomen.

Indy attempted to escape but Baptiste set Raven down and clamped one hand around Raven's neck, and one huge hand around the back of her neck, effectively immobilizing both of them.

The huge guard marched both of them down the staircase. Raven's twisting and kicking hadn't hurt the hulking beast at all.

Raven glanced down at his pocket watch and gave her a significant look. She remembered what he'd told her about the sleeping powder. It might be their only hope. The man appeared to be impervious to pain.

"Well, Lady India, I see you've recovered," said Lowe. "And Your Grace, how humiliating that my guard can lift you so easily, as if you were a featherweight."

"Lady Catherine," Indy cried, reaching for her friend, but Baptiste tightened his grip on her neck and she couldn't escape.

"She's in a trance, she won't be cognizant for hours," said Lowe.

"What have you done to her?" Indy asked.

"Mesmerism, my dear lady. I control her mind now. I tell her what to do."

"You've been using her wealth and influence to steal antiquities, I see," said Raven.

"One might see it that way," said Lowe. "Or one could call it by its rightful name. I am the reincarnation of the god Osiris. And therefore, all of these possessions belong to me."

The man was obviously a lunatic.

"And now you belong to me, as well," Lowe said coldly. "What should I do with them, Baptiste?"

Indy caught Raven's eye to let him know she would provide a distraction.

She made her body go limp.

"Fainted dead away, has she?" asked Lowe. "Leave her. Bind the gentleman."

Baptiste let go of her and she slumped to the floor. Through slitted eyes she watched as Raven calmly held up his pocket watch and pretended to consult the time. "You may bind me, but Sir Malcolm Penny and several men are on their way to this house as we speak. He'll have you arrested."

"What's that?" asked Lowe, alarm raising his voice. "You're bluffing."

Baptiste glanced uncertainly at Raven.

Raven must be bluffing. He'd said that Sir Malcolm had a team of agents in Paris, but how would he know where to find them?

"Bind him, I said," shouted Lowe.

Indy chose her moment carefully.

Before the giant had bound Raven's hands fully, she drove her foot into his knee with all her might. The guard stumbled, loosening his hold on Raven.

"Cover your nose and mouth," Raven yelled at Indy, as he launched the contents of the watch into the giant's face.

Indy threw her voluminous sleeve over her nose and mouth.

Baptiste rubbed his eyes wildly, cursing and stumbling across the floor.

Raven lunged for Lowe, pinning him easily, and Indy ran to Lady Catherine.

She cradled Lady Catherine's head in her lap, slapping her cheeks lightly. "Wake up, wake up Catherine."

Catherine's eyelids fluttered open. "Indy?"

Baptiste crashed to the floor in a heap.

"Hurry," Indy said. "Her pulse is very weak."

Raven finished tying Dr. Lowe's wrists and led him to the Louvre chair. "Your throne awaits," he said, tying Dr. Lowe's bindings to the legs of the chair.

"You may laugh all you want, but the vengeance of Osiris shall be wreaked upon you," declared Lowe in an imperious voice.

"You can tell yourself that, if you like. But I rather think the French police will wreak their vengeance upon you, Osiris," said Raven.

He lifted Lady Catherine into his arms. "Let's take her above."

They followed a wider staircase this time and emerged in the main entrance hall. "She needs fresh air," said Indy. "She's barely breathing."

Raven carried Lady Catherine across the hall

and out the front entranceway with Indy following. As they exited the house, Indy saw a carriage in the distance.

"Look," she said to Raven. "Someone's coming."

Raven set Lady Catherine down on the front steps and sat next to her, chafing her hands in his. "Are you feeling better, Lady Catherine?" he asked.

Her eyes fluttered open. "Indy," she said. "What happened? Where am I?"

Indy kissed her friend's withered cheek. "You're safe now. That odious man will never harm you again."

The carriage arrived in the yard and a groom emerged from the carriage house. A tall man with gray hair alighted from the carriage.

"Sir Malcolm," said Raven.

"You weren't lying when you said he was coming?" Indy asked.

"Actually, I was. I've no idea how he knew we were here. He's a very resourceful man. Why don't I take Lady Catherine to her chamber, and you can escort Sir Malcolm inside."

Indy nodded and Raven supported Lady Catherine around the shoulders and led her back inside the house where her manservant was waiting with a perplexed expression on his face.

"Sir Malcolm," Indy said, meeting him halfway to the house.

"Lady India." He bowed. "We meet again. I had hoped it might be under happier circumstances, though. I know everything. I understand you sustained a blow to your head. How are you feeling?"

"Quite happy, actually." She grinned. "You must not know everything. I told you I'd return the stone to you within the fortnight."

Sir Malcolm's gaze sharpened. "You know where it is?"

"I do indeed. Why don't you come inside with me? I have something to show you."

"HOW REMARKABLE." SIR MALCOLM stood in front of the stone, tracing the lettering with his finger. Raven had left Lady Catherine in her chamber with servants to attend her. He'd found Sir Malcolm and Indy in the dungeons, examining the stone.

Dr. Lowe had been removed to a locked chamber which he shared with the still-groggy Baptiste. Miss Mina's invention had worked like a charm.

"It's the real stone," said Malcolm.

"I know," replied Indy. "If we hadn't come here after my injury, we never would have guessed where it was hiding."

"I was convinced Le Triton had taken it," Raven said.

They'd found the stone. The search was over in the most unexpected of ways. The only thing missing was the Wish Diamond, but he didn't care about that. Indy was safe and they'd found the stone, that was all that mattered.

"How did you know where to find us, Sir Malcolm?" asked Indy.

"Sir Charles made a confession to me when you

never returned from Le Triton's gaming house. He told me that he was in league with Miss Delacroix and Le Triton to steal the Wish Diamond. He was to receive a cut of the profits. He only confessed to his part in the matter because he feared that you might have been harmed. I located one of your assailants, who told me a very colorful tale."

Raven took Indy's hand. "If you're ever outnumbered in a fight, Sir Malcolm, you'll definitely want Lady India by your side."

"Since you hadn't returned to London, I figured that you would be here at Lady Catherine's house. I had no idea the stone would be here as well."

"Neither did we," said Indy.

"Such a bad business," said Raven. "I knew Dr. Lowe was a charlatan, but to dupe an elderly lady in such a heinous way, the man deserves a harsh penalty."

"He'll pay his dues," Sir Malcolm assured them. "His name's not Dr. Lowe, by the way. He's Mr. Hackett, a two-bit actor from Liverpool."

"Did you recover the diamond necklace?" Indy asked.

"Unfortunately, no. Disappeared into Le Triton's fortress, and now he knows we're on to him. He's probably fled Paris already."

"My lady," said a servant, entering the room. "Lady Catherine is asking for you."

Indy nodded. "I'll be right there." She squeezed Raven's hand. "You know where to find me."

He kissed her cheek. He didn't care that Malcolm saw him do it. He'd kiss Indy as many times as he could for the rest of his life.

When she'd left, he turned to Malcolm. "We need to talk."

"I know. Shall we at least find some brandy first?"

"I need coffee more."

They climbed the stairs and found a sitting room on the main floor that had a lit fire. Raven ordered coffee and brandy from a servant.

They sat by the fire. How to begin? He had so many things to get off his chest.

"You love her, I can tell," said Sir Malcolm.

Raven closed his eyes. "I do. But I haven't been able to speak the words. You made me this way, Malcolm." He opened his eyes. "You made me this thing that can't express love. You stole my emotions. You bastard."

Malcolm didn't attempt to defend himself. He met Raven's gaze squarely. "I thought I was doing the right thing. Your father wanted you to follow in his footsteps."

"But that didn't give you the right to shape my life in such profound ways. I was too young to make such a momentous decision."

Their drinks arrived and they fell silent. Malcolm sipped his brandy and Raven took a grateful gulp of fortifying coffee.

"I needed a father, not a harsh taskmaster who sent me off to that brutal training ground to make a killer of me."

"And I needed a child. I had just lost mine."

"We were both lost souls. Both grieving," said Raven.

"Having guardianship of Mina has shown me that I was wrong to control your life in the way I did, even though I believed I was doing it for your own good. If there's some way that I can make amends, please tell me. I will go and talk to Lady India, tell her it was my fault."

Malcolm was apologizing? Raven had never expected to hear those words. "Not necessary. I made the choice. You never coerced me. You told me what I would be giving up and you asked me to choose."

"And now you can choose a new life," said Malcolm.

"It's not that easy, and you know it," said Raven bitterly. "I don't know if I can love her the way she loves me. She loves the boy I was, not the man I am now. I can't go back to being that child. I can't undo the things these hands have done."

"If you love her you'll find a way to be together. It seems to me she has a very clear picture of who you are. And she loves you anyway. I hereby accept your resignation."

"What resignation?"

"The one you're about to give me."

"I'm not ungrateful, Malcolm. The values you instilled in me have served me well. I've had a good career. I'm proud of the lives I've saved. I've been proud to work toward exonerating my father."

"And you will exonerate him fully someday. You've always had an innate goodness in you, Raven. You avoid bloodshed when possible. Many agents turn to violence as sport, you always stayed true to yourself, and your ethics."

"I have to find a way to make her trust me."

"You've always been resourceful. Even as a young lad you could make something out of nothing. Make a coin appear from the air. You've grown into a man I'm proud to call my associate and one I would be honored to call my son. Your father would be so proud of you. Sometimes we take a longer route to arrive at where we need to be. Just remember, the destination is what matters."

"She's what matters."

"Go and find that troublesome female. If she won't agree to wed you, then she's a fool. Because you're a good man."

Raven swiped the back of his hand across his eyes. He rose from his chair and walked to Malcolm. "Thank you," he said, leaning down to give Malcolm a brief hug.

Malcolm nodded, blinking his eyes. "Off with you now," he said gruffly, clapping Raven on the back.

# Chapter 25

ɞ

RAVEN FINALLY FOUND Indy sitting in front of the Rosetta Stone on a low velvet divan.

"There you are," he said, sitting beside her. "Well? Did you find the answer you were searching for?"

She sighed. "I've checked and rechecked but I keep coming up with the same problem. The temple indicated on my map isn't dedicated to either Isis or Osiris, and therefore, if my theory is correct, it's not Cleopatra and Antony's burial site. All of this turmoil and strife to come up empty-handed, it's beyond disappointing."

"I'm sorry to hear that."

"Back to the search, I suppose."

He hated seeing her distraught about anything. How had he kept her hating him all these years? All he wanted was for her to be happy.

"You'll find another clue," he said. "Or you'll embark on a different quest. Uncover another powerful female's story. I do have a very interesting Greek urn in my collection that depicts a warrior woman riding a horse and wielding a lasso. Do you think these warrior women really existed? Wouldn't it be wonderful if you could prove it to the world?"

She smiled at him and his heart lifted. "Now that's precisely what's up my alley."

"I thought as much. The urn is yours."

*My heart is yours. Just say it. Raven, say it.*

"Are you telling me to journey to Greece? What will you do? Will you go back to your . . . work?"

"Actually, I just submitted my resignation."

"You what?" Her eyes clouded over. "You can't do that. I mean, I hope you're not doing it for me. I would hate to be the cause of you giving up your career, and the job that gives you satisfaction and purpose."

"I was already losing my edge. There was an incident in Athens. You noticed the bruise on my cheek at Somerset House. I was careless. I was too blind to see that my fellow agent had become a traitor. He was murdered by Le Triton's hired assassins. I nearly died."

"Raven, you never told me that."

"It's been on my mind this entire time."

"Is that how you came by the bullet wound near your heart?"

"I was so close to death. I lay in a church, bleeding my life away and looked up at the stained-glass window and I saw . . . you. I saw you, Indy. I saw the life I could have had with you. And it shook my conviction. It made me question everything."

"Oh Raven." She held his hand. "Tell me what you saw."

"I saw us grown older. We were sitting by a fireplace. You had faint laugh wrinkles around your eyes. Your hair had one or two streaks of silver. I saw . . . two children playing at our feet."

A tear fell down her cheeks. "Children? I don't know why you saw that. I haven't a motherly bone in my body."

"Then perhaps we adopted, because there were two children there. A girl of about four or five, and a younger boy. The girl was playing with blocks, forming words, and the boy kept trying to put the blocks in his mouth, much to his sister's annoyance."

She wiped her eye with her sleeve. "Sitting by a fireplace with children at our feet. It's all so very domestic and conventional. What of my expeditions? What of my work?"

"I don't know where the fireplace was. It could have been in Greece. It could have been anywhere."

"Raven. I don't want you to give up everything for me. You'd never be happy being idle. Strange that I should say that when I believed you were idle for so long."

"Not idle. Don't you need an archaeological assistant? Can't I carry your shovels, or your provisions?"

"Be serious, please."

"I'm deadly serious."

"You just said that I dull your edge. You would resent me if you followed me around the world instead of following your own path."

"That's not what I said."

He was cocking this up. *Tell her you love her. Tell her you'll die without her.*

"When you're on an archaeological expedition, and you uncover a vessel with a crack down the side, does that make the bowl worthless?" he asked her.

"Of course not. It means that the vessel was useful. I think the flaw makes it more beautiful."

"I'm a cracked bowl, Indy. I have this flaw running through me. I can't express my emotions because I was devastated by my father's death and then I was trained to hide my feelings. But I've been useful, and I want to find new ways of being useful. We both chose solitary roads but I believe that we're stronger together."

INDY'S BREATH CAUGHT in her throat. *Stronger together.*

He was saying all the right things . . . except for the one thing she needed him to say the most.

"We do make a good team," she said, tentatively. "We've fought our way out of some highly unusual and perilous predicaments."

He cupped her cheek with his hand. "I'd rather we avoided the perilous part."

"I'm not sure that's possible. There will be snakes. And madmen. There are always madmen. And probably there will be fraying rope bridges across steep ravines. There may even be more gigantic opponents to subdue."

"Are you saying you'll accept me as your partner?"

"I might be."

He snapped his fingers near her ear and a coin rolled into his palm.

"Where did that come from?" she asked, startled.

"Had it up my sleeve," he said with a devilish grin.

He handed her the coin.

There were two clasped hands on the face of the coin. "Is this . . . is this the coin I chose for you, Raven? You kept it?"

"You're not the only one who kept a talisman. I've carried this coin with me every day of my life. I hollowed out a chamber for it in my boot heel. It's my good luck charm. I believe it's what kept me alive that dark day in Athens. Some part of me must have known that I needed to live, in order to give it back to you."

"I can't believe you still have our coin."

"Whatever happened to the rest of the coins?"

"I donated them to the British Museum. They're in a drawer somewhere gathering dust."

"Not this one." He closed his fingers over the coin. "This one is yours."

He drew her into his arms. "I'm yours, Indy. I've always been yours. And I swear to you that I will love you faithfully until the day I die."

His eyes were the same color as the coin she held and just as polished with hope and promise.

The most beautiful sight she'd ever seen.

"Do you remember the day you gave this to me?" he asked.

"Like it was yesterday."

"We lay down together, with our heads touching, and we talked about our dreams."

"It was such a perfect day, until it all went straight to hell."

He kissed her, or perhaps she kissed him. All she knew was that their lips met somewhere in the middle.

She stretched out on the velvet divan and he covered her with his body.

Her heart beat against his chest. He was so solid and rooted and strong.

This exchange of strength was such a gift. To give and receive. To open her heart. To allow herself to trust. And to know she never had to carry her burdens alone again.

"I love you," she whispered in his ear as he kissed the sensitive hollow at the base of her throat.

"I love you," he responded. "I want to help make all your dreams come true."

# Epilogue

❧

*A few weeks later . . .*

"GENTLEMEN, PLEASE COME to order," called Sir Malcolm.

The assembled antiquarians took their seats and quieted.

"Our esteemed Fellow, the Duke of Raven-wood, has been given permission to take the floor. Your Grace."

Raven walked to the front of the room and stood next to Sir Malcolm's desk. "Gentlemen, I am mounting an archaeological expedition this month in search of a priceless treasure, the nature of which I am not at liberty to divulge at the moment. I move that the society fully support this venture and agree to publish any findings. My partner in this venture will be Mr. Pomeroy."

Indy swaggered across the room wearing those figure-hugging breeches and that ridiculous moustache. It was all Raven could do not to ravish her on the central table.

"Hear hear!" shouted the members.

Indy stopped in the front of the room and threw her hand into the air. "There's only one small problem with this scenario, gentlemen. Mr. Pomeroy is a female."

She ripped off her moustache.

Raven grinned. He'd guessed she was going to do that. Gods, how he wanted to kiss her right now. She was so beautiful in those tight breeches, it made his heart ache.

The gentlemen rioted. Literally leapt from their chairs and started pounding the floor with their canes and shouting bloody murder.

"Order, order," shouted Sir Malcolm. "What is the meaning of this, Ravenwood?"

Raven had to yell to be heard over the hubbub. "I would further move to allow the inclusion of females into the Society of Antiquaries. My fiancée, Lady India Rochester, who stands before you in male garb, has made more important discoveries than most of you in this room put together."

If the gentlemen rioted and began to attack them, that wouldn't be a problem. He caught Indy's eye. They'd defend themselves handily.

"The duke has so moved," shouted Sir Malcolm. "All in favor say aye."

Raven said a loud *aye* over a deafening chorus of nays and indignant protests. He'd heard only one other *aye*. He caught his friend Westbury's eye and winked.

"I'm disappointed in you, gentlemen," declared Indy, her voice cutting through the clamor.

"Gentlemen, I hereby resign from the Society of Antiquaries. Please accept my letter of resignation, Sir Malcolm."

"Resignation accepted."

"Furthermore," shouted Raven. "Directly after our marriage, which will be a small, private affair,

I will be accompanying Lady India on her next archaeological expedition as her assistant."

The room fell silent for one ominous moment, and then erupted again.

"A duke as a lady's assistant!"

"It's anarchy."

"What's the world coming to?"

"It's an outrage.

Indy grinned at him. "I think we should leave," she mouthed.

The jeers and shouting followed them out of the room but Raven and Indy didn't care. They clasped hands and ran out the front door, giggling like schoolchildren.

They tumbled into the street and started running.

Raven tugged her to a stop in order to back her up against a wall and kiss her.

Passersby stared in shock. He didn't care what it looked like. He'd kiss Indy wherever and whenever he pleased, male clothing be damned!

"I'll have you know that was a treasure hunting-kiss," Raven growled.

"The world's not ready for us yet, Raven," said Indy, breathless and flushed.

Gods, how he loved making her breathless.

"But someday, someone will read our story," she said, her eyes sparkling like diamonds. "And we won't seem so very wild and wicked."

"We won't?"

"Don't be disappointed. You'll always be wicked to me." She kissed the corner of his mouth. "My wicked rogue. The one who stole my heart and never returned it to me."

# Acknowledgments

THANK YOU TO my agent, Alexandra Machinist, for believing in me, and to my editor, Carrie Feron, whose expert guidance illuminates my path. I'm so grateful to the entire team at Avon Books, especially Pam Jaffee, Carolyn Coons, and Jes Lyons. I'm blessed with the best beta readers a girl could ever have—Neile and Rachel, thanks for having my back.

A lovely reader recently wrote to tell me that she felt like I had given her "a hug in book form." This is why I'm writing romance novels. And so, to you: readers, bloggers, reviewers, librarians, and booksellers . . . all my thanks and a big, bookish hug!

# Author's Note

&

To this day, the lost tomb of Cleopatra, one of the greatest prizes in archaeology, has never been discovered. I found the inspiration for Indy's quest when I read an article about unorthodox Dominican archaeologist Kathleen Martinez. Her search to uncover Cleopatra's burial place continues today. Best of luck, Ms. Martinez!

Do you love historical fiction?

Want the chance to hear news about your favourite
authors (and the chance to win free books)?

Mary Balogh
Lenora Bell
Charlotte Betts
Jessica Blair
Frances Brody
Grace Burrowes
Gaelen Foley
Pamela Hart
Elizabeth Hoyt
Eloisa James
Lisa Kleypas
Stephanie Laurens
Sarah MacLean
Amanda Quick
Julia Quinn

Then visit the Piatkus website
www.piatkusentice.co.uk

And follow us on Facebook and Twitter
www.facebook.com/piatkusfiction | @piatkusentice

piatkus